NO FIXED GROUND

NO FIXED GROUND

John Roman Baker

WILKINSON HOUSE

For Rod

First published by Wilkinson House in April 2011

This second edition published by
Wilkinson House Ltd
July 2011

ISBN 978-1-899713-10-3

Wilkinson House Ltd.,
145-157 St John Street,
London, EC1V 4PW
United Kingdom

www.wilkinsonhouse.com
info@wilkinsonhouse.com

Cover photo: © Gautier Willaume/iStockphoto.com
Cover design: R. Evan

British Library Cataloguing-in-Publication Data
A catalogue record for this book is available from the British Library.

"And sometimes ... it almost seemed to him, that he ought to be happy."

Heinrich von Kleist

PART ONE

MICHAEL

I suppose I knew Nicholas better than anyone. I certainly put up with more from him than from anyone else. I was there, after all, when everything failed. But did I fail him? Now that it's over I sometimes ask myself that question. I don't think I did, but there is no way of telling. I did try and make myself available when the others turned away. I was there.

It's a year since he's been gone, and things, people and events can become terribly distorted. Let me say first of all that I was never really his lover. Maybe that fact was a saving one as far as our relationship was concerned. I could look upon him in an uninvolved, unemotional way. I could see him more clearly than, say, Peter, whose judgement was naturally distorted by passion. I was a friend, where most of the others were lovers. I personally believe he had very few friends, but then his character and manners were largely to blame for that. He wasn't easy, and God knows in our world today most people want ease - especially in relationships.

I have tried often to describe him physically, but each time there is an element that eludes me. I don't believe in the spiritual, otherwise I would say it was that spiritual something that defied description. Of course I can say he had black, curly hair and dark eyes, and that his skin was slightly disfigured, but that's not describing him. To make it that bit easier for myself I could say the indefinable something was in his eyes - in the expression of the eyes, that was both beautiful and terrible. Someone once said to me that he had eyes like guns, and I know what guns they were, fierce, burning, explosive in their attack, having more than once suffered their effect. So where am I? I am trying to describe the almost indescribable. He had magic I suppose, and that ambiguous word saves me from any further attempt at description. I must, of course, describe him by his actions. Because it was in his actions that Nicholas became real.

I said I was never really his lover. But it was in that way that I met him to begin with. I remember the night more clearly than I can remember many other things. It was in a park. The statutory park they have in most towns and cities where gays meet. It was in summer and I was on holiday from my teaching job. He was sitting on a bench, and it was getting dark, and he looked sad and lonely. I went up to him and offered him a cigarette. He smiled and shook his head, then turned away. I took this as a rejection and started to move off. After all, if he was that sad, then perhaps he didn't want to meet anyone. But then again nobody came to this park to be alone.

"Hey..."

He called me, and I turned round. He had stood up and came towards me.

"What's your name?"

He asked this, smiling at me. I sensed immediately that the smile was defensive.

"Michael."

"I'm Nicholas."

He shook my hand. I laughed at this. I don't usually shake people's hands when I pick them up. I don't have such good manners.

"Are you as sad as you look?" Remembering that question, I can't honestly say that I asked it seriously. As he had looked sad, it was one way of opening a conversation. But I was to get a serious reply.

"Yes, I am. I'm very sad. I'm in love."

The smile again. I thought - "Oh, Christ," dreading a heavy, self-pitying discourse on how sad it is to be young, (youngish?) gay and in love. Anyway I didn't believe in love. It wasn't even remotely in my possibility of things, so he had come to the wrong person. But instead of the discourse I got silence. We walked in silence to the end of the park, and then just as we got near the last fringe of bushes and trees, he reached out and groped me. This was funny because from him it seemed so unexpected. It was about as incongruous as the Queen farting at a civic reception. It just wasn't polite.

"You don't have to do that," I said. He looked at me, without looking at me, simply blindly reaching out, then kissed me on the mouth. I noticed his breath was a bit stale, unpleasant, but I let it pass.

"Do you want to go somewhere other than the park?" I asked.

He nodded his head, and we went to where I had parked my car.

"What work do you do?" I asked him when we were in the car and driving to my place.

"I write plays."

"Had any performed?"

"No."

"How do you manage financially?"

He looked at me, giving me his smile, which seemed more than ever to be a personal disappearing act. God knows where he was behind it, but at the time I didn't care much.

"Do we have to talk about it?"

"We don't have to talk at all," I replied.

And that was the last we said until we had gone back to my flat and had sex. How can I describe the sex? Shall I bother? It wasn't anything special for me. To be honest he wasn't very good in bed, or perhaps it was me not making him very good. He appeared to have a lot of inhibitions - the type that has to be handled with 'gentleness.' I don't care for this type. It bores me. I like to go with somebody who knows every aspect of the technique he is going to adopt with me. Nicholas had no technique. He seemed totally passive in bed, and yet I suspected that it wasn't entirely in his nature to be so. After sex we resumed our conversation. Now it was my turn not to want to talk, but he did, and literally bombarded me with questions. What did I do in my free time? Was I happy? (Yes, that.) He wanted to know if I had had lasting relationships, and I said that I hadn't, which made him go on endlessly about how important he thought they were.

Nicholas, you are a bore.

I didn't say it, but I did want him to go. At one in the morning I didn't give a sailor's fly buttons for personal relationships. All I wanted to do was sleep.

"Do you want to stay the night?"

This was one way of ending it. I yawned as I asked him. The charming, negative smile came back, and he got up off the bed.

"No, I'll go home," he said.

"Can I run you home?"

"I don't live far from here."

I wondered at that point why I hadn't seen him around before. Everybody got to see everybody else soon enough in this town. He appeared to sense my unspoken question, and said quietly,

"I've only just moved here."

"Then we must see some more of each other." I don't know why I said this, as it was almost the very opposite of what I was thinking. I had no urgent desire to further our acquaintance.

"Yes," he said, "we must."

That in essence was the sum total of my first meeting with Nicholas, and after it I hardly gave him another thought. The summer holidays drew to their close, and soon enough it was time to think about the return to a job that I imagined I hated. I suppose in this early part of the story I had better mention a few things about myself. I don't find myself particularly interesting, so I'll keep what I have to say as brief as possible.

I was younger than Nicholas. Although that fact may seem on the surface irrelevant, I sensed in many unspoken ways that he resented it. For despite his never actually mentioning it, I felt and saw by many subtle actions and gestures, that he dreaded growing old. To be exact Nicholas was three years older than me, although it was I who looked and felt the oldest. I am one of those people who have never looked young. At University I grew a beard, which hid the little amount of boyish good looks that I had. When I left University, and with it the 'passing for straight' role that I had adopted there, I still kept my beard. It was some sort of butch assurance that God knows why, I felt that I needed. Now that I have used the word 'butch' I can come onto the subject of role-playing, and of my relationship to and with the new gay society that was in the long and erratic process of forming around me. Needless to say I had decided with the rest of my gay sisters and brothers that defined roles were no longer possible. 'Butch' and 'passive' had to go into the purifying fire along with the rest of our homosexual ancestors' camp junk. I was the 'New' homosexual. I 'came out' in the year that marches rather timidly got off to their start in England. I went on them, and clutched a banner, and shouted slogans. We were free. Free from the club and pub ghetto atmosphere that most of us had been conditioned to use and draw sustenance from. Free too of love in the singular (or should I say singular for two?) and liberated with love in the plural. There were words like 'polymorphous perverse,' and cries of greater revolution to come when all of our sisters and brothers would join us. We were on the side of the blacks and their oppression. We were on the side of women in their struggle, and of the poor bloody workers who were less eloquent in giving voice to their protest than us. Yes, we were for the oppressed, but never once were we for those downtrodden gays still left romantically awaiting the arrival of a knight in white armour in their clubs and bars. (We never thought of gay women in this way. In fact we seldom gave them a thought, except when they were actually at meetings or beside us on marches.) Sometimes we paid lip service to the memory of those stranded in the bars and parks, sighing over the fact of how difficult it was to get across to them. We never tried anything as dangerous as communication. We simply shrugged our shoulders, murmuring that if they felt alienated, then perhaps alienation was not a bad thing. Instead of turning to them we renounced the 'commercial' scene, and set up our communes where we would talk far into the night about how everything should be, but rarely about how everything was. In the abstract we embraced all those women who never came to our meetings, and all those blacks and workers who had never even heard of us. We were proud of our (some of us) working class families, and hid our University backgrounds and educations. Those, I guess, were the good years. We were very, very young, and by mutual consent both the world and us passed each other by. Then bit by bit the whole thing broke up. Ideological divisions within our ranks split us apart. I still don't fully understand what it was exactly that dissipated the euphoria, but I hazard a guess that it was life, in the guise of everyday, banal reality breaking in. The abstract arguments had begun to grow stale. We had read and digested our various bibles and somewhere, somehow had found them wanting. A few of us got married, and by so doing, putting our 'we are all bisexual really' theory into a very socially accepted practice. Others in our midst joined less radical organizations, and some (but few, I will admit, as the general sexual climate was moving away from this) settled down to more or less permanent homosexual love affairs. The honeymoon of revolution was over, and the outside world, in all its lack and poverty of ideological glory, had to be lived. I went out into the world hiding behind my beard.

I came here. Here by the sea, which seemed as good a place as anywhere. I came with a few friends (now departed) leaving the big metropolis, and the husk of a former life behind me. I even decided to take advantage of the education I had had to get myself a job. I would be a teacher, and within the mechanism of a system that I hated, I would seize every opportunity that offered itself to inspire children to grow up to become the revolutionary that I had failed to be. But instead I found myself wiping infants' bottoms, and teaching them the rudiments of arithmetic and the ABC. Yet I still kept numerous gay manifestos on the bookshelf, and during Saturday nights, when others would be thinking about enjoying themselves, I would get them off the shelf and read chunks of redundant theory. At least it kept me out of the clubs and bars, for after all, I wasn't that sort of homosexual, was I? Occasionally, in the company of a few of my nostalgia driven friends, a decision would be taken that action was needed, and then we would go out into the streets (in broad daylight) with our 'Glad to be Gay' badges on. A few times I even managed it on my own. As I said before I am not religious, but the puritan ethic of my tradition is still buried there in me. Basically I don't approve of the word 'gay', being haunted by the pocket Oxford dictionary interpretation; showy, brilliant, dissolute. It was the last definition I couldn't take. Dissolute. When had I ever been dissolute? When, within the narrow confines of my liberation, had I ever allowed myself to be so? I didn't like the word, but it was there, and would be there, for a long time to come. I didn't like it because I was afraid of it, but I had to live with it. And in not liking those three words I went about transforming them. After a lot of perfectly useless analysis I reached the simplistic conclusion that gay was solely another word for happiness. Yes, that was it, our right to and striving for happiness. There, within that definition, it was at last possible to accept the word. I even had a pat argument to any straight's objections to it.

"Why must you go around calling yourself Gay?"

The letter G was spelt out large. And I would answer: "Why do you object to it so much?"

There would be the usual uncertain hesitation before the fairly stereotyped reply: "But isn't it a bit - you know - frivolous?"

(Frivolity being the terminal heterosexual sin and disease, to be avoided at all cost for the well-being of body and soul. I know. I once 'passed' for heterosexual. I was there.)

"Not at all," I would say, "but I can tell you why you object to it."

"Tell me."

"Because it means being happy. Gay is another word for 'happy'. Straights don't want us to be that. They want us to feel the guilt and the inadequacy that we are expected to feel. To drown in a pool of despond and gloom. But we are gay now. We are happy. Even you, my brother (or sister) unconsciously want our unhappiness. You may not realise it, but it's true. Our happiness is a threat."

I would finish on the personal note, leaving the threat bit a little vague, hoping that it would make them feel like hell. It usually did. Most of them were liberal in their feelings as well as attitudes, and my slight on their unconscious motivations was painful.

I suppose in this early part of the story I might as well say a few things about myself. That's how I started on this track. And I continued by saying that I don't find myself particularly interesting. I don't. I think I have said more about myself in the

15

belated lifestyle that I tried to lead, than in any welter of personal description. But personalities make the story, and I had better get back to telling it. I left London and came to this town. I took on my job as teacher, and loved and hated it alternately. In the wee small hours of insomnia I would be heard to murmur that it was a vocation. But then we all have our moments of vision and madness, don't we? Mine usually came when I couldn't get to sleep.

I said I never went to bars. That's true, and then again it's not true. I tried the bars, but somehow I neither fitted in with the atmosphere nor met anyone there. (Lie. I did, but meeting was all it was.) The mental barrier that I had put up in my Liberation days had done its work. It was still 'us' and 'them', and I was very much the 'us' stranded like a poor bloody Dodo on a bereft evolutionary shore. No one as far as I was concerned could have possibly read my bibles, and still go to places like bars. I despised myself for thinking it, but they were different from me, and I, in my quietly liberated way, was that much better. Now and then a man would approach me. (I resented the boys and avoided them. Liberation in the mind has nothing to do with liberation from envy.) Once met I would bore the man to death with 'coming out' and 'are you glad to be gay' etc. I hate bores, and to avoid totally becoming one, I left off going to the bars. Instead I took to the beach and parks where pleasure was instant and without the handicap of words. Most of the time even in that situation a semblance of ritual was gone through, as in the case of Nicholas, but it was a semblance, and mercifully hollow. I, who had cried out against sex objects, gloried in the fact that I simply was that. I had neither the place nor the time in my life for a one-to-one relationship, and in going to the parks I was pretty sure of meeting the type of person who would not demand it of me. Parks, in my experience, encourage those who want to avoid the commitment of love. Love. I haven't mentioned much of it, except once to say that it was out of my range of possibilities, but then it's also because there is so much of it to come. My story is haloed by love. Nicholas's love. But that will be told in its own time.

I said at one point that I believed I hated my job as teacher. Then I said that I hated 'and loved it. Contradiction is the essence of a healthy, confused mind. Whatever I really thought about work, I poured myself into it. Which brings me to this last part of personal story telling. Most of my 'gay bibles' avoided one subject in any depth, and that was the loss of having children. It seemed to be tacitly understood that wanting a child was a leftover reaction from the straight world that could be chucked out with the rest. Wanting children was wanting the nuclear family, and heaven preserve us enlightened gays from that. Sex could be discussed. Love could be discussed. Even death (with less enthusiasm) could be discussed. But the one taboo subject was children. Fuck the little buggers yes, but certainly not have, or want, any of your own. For after all that would mean a wife, and a wife, let's face it, isn't very gay. But I wanted children. I said I can't fall in love, but you put a curly haired little monster in my care, and I will be reduced to a quivering jelly of emotion. I will moan about wiping bottoms, and reciting the alphabet, but I would not miss a moment of those joys. End of sentimental wallow, and the personal me, and on with the story.

Nicholas, old as he was, was my child. He was the kid bawling in the long, dark night. Perhaps that is one of the reasons why, in the end, I was the only person to remain by him, to care. I had given him my telephone number, but all the same I was surprised one day to hear from him.

"It's Nicholas. Do you remember me?"

"Of course I remember."

A rather long, almost embarrassed silence.

"Well?"

I was the first to speak.

"I'd like to talk," he said.

"Go ahead."

"No, I mean it..."

"I mean it too. Go ahead."

"Can I come round?"

"I've got work I must get through. School reports."

"What about later - later on tonight? I don't care how late "

There was panic in his voice, urgency. He was obviously in need, but why ring me? He had only met me once, and I hardly considered myself worthy by that encounter to be elevated to the status of friend. I thought, "He must know others," but little did I know then that in fact he had no one to seek help from.

"I'll be free at about nine. Is that alright? I'm sorry, but I can't make it before. School reports have to be done."

"That's fine." A pause. "Would you prefer meeting me at a bar?"

"No, Nicholas. I'm pressed for time, and anyway I don't like bars."

"I see."

I wondered if he did, but it didn't matter.

"Are you alright?"

I was surprised at the note of genuine concern in my voice. After a couple of months without giving him a thought, I realised that this comparative stranger mattered. It's a good thing I have long since resigned myself to living with my contradictions.

"You know how to get here?"

"Yes."

I put down the receiver without saying goodbye, and spent the next couple of hours waiting for him to come. I scratched away at the school reports, but kept leaving off, going to make myself cups of coffee, and restlessly listening for the door bell to ring. In a very confused way there was something about Nicholas that was worrying me, nagging at my conscience. I think, if I try to formulate it, the main point was - "What does he want from me?" and even more acutely, "How am I going to give to him what he does want?" For after all I had a dread of anyone older than a child being in need. At nine o'clock the telephone rang again.

"Nicholas?"

"Yes."

"Where are you?"

"I've had too much to drink. I feel terrible. I take pills. I shouldn't drink."

"Don't talk now. Get a taxi."

"Are you sure? I mean, I don't want to be any trouble."

"Nicholas, shut up. Just come over."

I couldn't tell him that he had already been a trouble; that I had spent the past hours waiting for him to come, when I had precisely said to him not to come before nine. Anyway once again I put down the receiver. My hands were trembling. What, after all, was I afraid of? He was hardly a prehistoric monster about to invade the privacy of my home. Or was he? One thing I was sure of, I was not trembling with sexual anticipation. The threat of hang-ups loomed too large to encourage that, and then the first encounter with him had not exactly over-whetted my appetite. The door bell rang. What appeared to be a very gaunt faced boy stood there in the doorway. I felt that I was seeing and looking at him for the first time. It was raining outside, and he was soaked.

"You look terrible," I said.

He laughed at this, and I stepped to one side to let him into the flat.

"At least that's an honest reaction. I walked, you see."

"I said to get a taxi."

"I didn't like to do that."

"Why? If you hadn't the money, I would've paid."

He smiled, patting my face with a wet hand.

"That's kind, Michael. Very kind. I think I need to use your bathroom."

I showed him the way, than went to the kitchen to make coffee. I was not going to give him a drink. He did look terrible, and having seen the combination of drugs and drink in the commune where I had lived, I was certainly not going to encourage him to pass out on me. At the same time I had to laugh. He definitely had a way of making me feel protective. I took a wry look at myself in the kitchen mirror, and touched the place where he had put his hand. "Michael, this is trouble," I said, "and it's over ten years old." When I went back into the living room there was no sign of Nicholas. The front door was wide open, and on the centre table, I saw a hastily written message scrawled over my evening newspaper. "I'm going to be ill. I shouldn't be ill here"

"I angrily screwed up the newspaper, and threw it into the waste bin. Damn him. I crossed the room, out into the hall, but as I was about to shut the front door, I heard the sound of sobbing coming from down the corridor. I followed the sound to the curve of stairs leading to the ground floor. Nicholas was leaning up against the wall, and there were tears streaming down his face.

"I can't walk."

He spluttered the words between sobs, and I noticed with a barely concealed shudder of disgust a dribble of saliva running down from his mouth to his neck.

"Here, hold on to me."

I grabbed him hard, and pulled him to me. My first instinct was to hit him to stop the sobbing, but instead I half-carried, half-dragged him back to the flat. If this ludicrous performance was to gain my sympathy, then he certainly was not succeeding. I pushed him onto the bed as brutally as I could, then switched on all the lights. For some obscure reason I thought that this gesture would put an edge on my unkindness, and at the same time humiliate him.

"You should see yourself." I went into the bathroom and returned with a wet flannel. I wiped his face as roughly as I could with it. All he could mutter after I had finished was "Thank you." This absurdly polite statement made me even more angry.

"Don't thank me, just tell me - why all this behaviour?"

I sat on the edge of the bed, and he shielded his eyes from the glare of the light with his arm. This gesture reminded me of a small boy I had seen at school, trying pathetically to protect himself from a bigger boy's blows. I got up and turned off the main light.

"Nicholas, take your arm away at once and look at me."

(God, wasn't that just the teacher talking?)

He did what I said.

"That's better. Now, please, why all this?"

"I shouldn't have been drinking. I had no one else to ring but you."

"Don't you know anyone else?"

"Just people."

"Of course people. Don't you know any of them? What I mean to say is - why me?"

"Why not you?"

The voice was quiet and clear. He was smiling. For the first time this approached being a real smile, and suddenly I felt softer and gentler towards him.

"I want to understand," I said.

"He's left me."

"Who has left you?"

"Peter."

"Who is Peter?"

He got up off the bed, visibly unsteady on his feet and pointed into the living room. "Can I go in there?"

"I think you should lie down for a bit longer. Try and sleep for a while. We can talk later, if you want to stay."

"I'd prefer to go in there. I'm feeling better. Really."

The small, thin voice of the child, pleading to have its way. I touched at his clothes that were still wet on his body.

"Alright, but first take off those and put on a dressing gown."

I helped him off with his clothes, and handed him a dressing gown.

"Are you sure you don't want to stay in here? After how you were - "

"Please - "

The urgent tone returned to his voice. Then the totally unexpected happened, and he grabbed me by the shoulders, and pushed me down onto the bed. I tried to laugh the action off, but he was pulling at my clothes, clumsily trying to undress me as well. My mouth brushed against his, and I felt his tongue trying to forcibly open my lips. His breath stank of drink, and for a moment I experienced a feeling of overwhelming revulsion towards him. As savagely as I could I pushed him from me. Inside me the anger was returning.

"Nicholas, don't."

"I want to - "

"You don't want to at all. Anyway I don't want to."

"It was a way of forgetting," he said.

I replied to that in as acid a tone as possible.

"I've never been a way of forgetting for anyone, and I'm not starting now. Look, Nicholas, I'm sorry, you are in a state - but what happened just now must not happen again. I don't want it. You don't want it. Is that understood?"

I got up off the bed, then brushed the creases out of my clothes. He laughed at this, and I walked away from him into the living room. He followed me.

"It's a relief," he said, "that we've got that sorted out. It means we can be friends."

"If this is friendship," I replied, "then perhaps I would be better off being your lover."

Feeling rather battered, angry, and not a little tired, I went to pour myself a drink. I looked at him over my shoulder as I did so.

"And you are not having one."

"Not even a small one?"

"Not the smallest."

He sat down on the sofa, where I joined him. For a while we were both silent, then he said, "Michael, what do you live for?"

I groaned inwardly. If this was the prospect of things to come, then I would give him great quantities of drink, and all the available amounts of pills I had in the flat too. Just a minute ago I had felt battered and angry, now I felt plain bored.

"Nicholas," I said, "the last and first time we met, you asked me if I was happy. You asked me if I had been in love. In fact you asked me lots of questions that I felt I wasn't capable of answering. Why do you want to know so much about me?"

"I want to, that's good enough reason."

"Shall I tell you what I think? I think your questions about me are said to throw a smoke screen about yourself."

"No, it's not that."

"Around yourself - you know, concealment."

"Perhaps it's just the opposite. Perhaps I am asking you questions so you will ask me some."

He had out manoeuvred me there. I honestly hadn't thought of that.

"Fine, Nicholas, I get the point. Let's begin with an easy

question. How old are you?"

"Twenty-five."

"You're older than that. You don't look it, but you're older. You're older than me, and I'm twenty-five."

"Twenty-eight."

"That's nearer. And you've come down from London?"

"Yes."

"What did you do in London?"

"I wrote plays."

"None of which were performed. That's what you told me."

"One was once. At an art school festival. It wasn't a success. In fact it was rather bad. The best of my work I never seem to show to anyone. I sometimes write short stories too. I tried a novel, but I couldn't sustain it."

"Then what did you live on? Money must've come from somewhere. Did you live on the dole?"

He looked at me with his dark eyes, but said nothing. I sensed immediately that he didn't want to answer that question, so I asked him another. It could have been interpreted as being cruel, the next question, but I didn't intend it that way, and I don't think he took it that way.

"Has your face always been marked?"

"Not always, but for most of the time. Does it revolt you?"

"Nothing revolts me."

"But it doesn't exactly turn you on?"

"I thought we had already gone over the sexual ground."

He got unsteadily to his feet and stood over me. Despite myself I felt a twinge of desire as the dressing gown fell open. He was definitely quite beautiful in his way.

"If you have a spare bed, or some cushions on the floor, I would like to stay the night. I'm not sure I can trust myself to get home."

"I've already said that you can stay. There's my bed if you want."

I meant it to be an invitation, but he shook his head. No doubt he was remembering the words, "I don't want it. You don't want it." It was a fair enough reaction on his behalf to refuse me now. I decided not to pursue that unwise, contradictory course any longer.

"I'll get what you need," I said.

I got up, gathered the largest cushions from the sofa and chairs, than went to get some bedding. He was looking through an old book of Sandro Penna's poems when I came back into the room.

"I like this," he said. " 'Insomnia of swallows. The calmness of the friend who waits at the station.' It's a wonderful poem."

It didn't mean much to me. The thought of swallows with insomnia seemed to me faintly pretentious. But one man's image was very often another's anathema.

"It's a simple poem," I replied.

"No, it's not. Never to sleep. Do you realise the joy, the longing of that? Never to close your eyes, or at least never until you get to the station - until you arrive. And when you do arrive, he is waiting there. He has always been waiting there."

"You mean Peter," I asked?

"I mean - him." he said.

There were whole areas, spaces both open and confined, around his words that I did not, could not enter. He was beginning to deeply disturb me, and I threw down the bedding onto the floor. Then, suddenly, he was back to the attack.

"Michael, for whom do you live?"

I felt like a fish caught on a line. I wanted to escape. To hell with all his bloody stupid questions.

"That sounds to me like a permutation of, 'Michael, what do you live for?' "

"No - for whom?"

"For stray cats and dogs in the night who come to pester the shit out of me. Now make this bed, and get into it."

"I disturb you, don't I?"

"Frankly, yes. You are what we old fashioned liberationists call heavy."

"And some," he added.

I laughed. For a brief moment the tension was gone.

"And some," I replied.

There were no more questions that night. It was very late when I at last turned out the light in the bedroom, but I could see under my door that he had left the main one in the living room on. I turned my face to the wall, away from the light, and closed my eyes. No sooner, it seemed, had I gone to sleep, than I was awakened by violent screams. I jumped out of bed and ran into the living room. Nicholas was sitting naked amid a mess of bedding and cushions, his face covered by his hands. Through the clutching, wide apertures of his fingers I heard him groaning and crying. I saw one despairing eye, staring, wild. I pulled the hands away.

"No, no, no," was all he said.

"No, no, no."

The one word was said, than repeated, then repeated again, as if another voice were giving reply. It was a monotonous, terrible dialogue, consisting of one single sound. I cradled him in my arms, but after a short while he savagely pushed me aside, beating at my face and body with his hands. I struggled with him, trying not to hit him back, and eventually he quietened down.

"Pills," he mumbled, "I want my pills."

"Where are they?"

He was unable to answer, and I searched his clothes. I found some Valium in his inside coat pocket. I forced a couple into his mouth, and he swallowed them without water. I was too shocked to even think of going to get him some. For a while I sat beside him, but he wouldn't lie down, or close his eyes. Every now and then he would clutch at my arm and squeeze it tightly. Not knowing what else to do or say, I kept on repeating, "It's alright. I am here. Michael is here." Around five in the morning he started to doze off, and thinking that it was at last safe to leave him, I went back to bed. I tumbled into sleep as one would tumble over a precipice. Not for a very long time had I had such a frightening experience. In my dreams I still saw his figure, rocking backwards and forwards, head clasped agonizingly in his hands.

"No, no, no."

It was I who awoke, crying the single, repetitive word. My first thought was for him, and I ran again into the living room.

The cushions had been put back into place on the sofa, and the bed-clothes were neatly folded in a pile on a chair. There was no sign of Nicholas, and no note. Putting on my clothes I went out into the corridor, half expecting to see him huddled on the floor or in a state of collapse on the stairs. But he was nowhere to be seen. Shaken by the night's events I went back into the flat and made myself some strong coffee. God knows, at the time, I had no idea what had hit me. A few hours later, after the first impact of the night's shock had worn off, I began cursing him. 'You little bugger,' I said, 'I won't ever see you again.' Then there was the counter thought, 'But that's absurd, he needs you. He needs someone in all this mess. You must see him again.' The contradictions sped round and round, and the nightmare continued.

At nine-thirty I rang one of my colleagues and said I wouldn't be able to come into school. Immediately after that call I rang a friend, and told him the whole story. I questioned him about Nicholas.

"Have you seen him around," I asked?

My friend 'did' the clubs.

"I may have done," he replied. "The description doesn't mean much, but then he would hardly be my type."

I rang off feeling guilty. Talking about him like that was a betrayal. But a betrayal of what? We were hardly lovers. We were barely friends. I felt as if I had been in a circus performance at the receiving end of a knife thrower.

A week later our paths crossed in the street, and he chose to ignore me. He wasn't alone, but with a boy much younger than himself. My first reaction was, that's Peter, then I wondered why precisely he had ignored me. I supposed it to be guilt, and then he had, after all, come to me full of drink. Perhaps he hadn't recognised me, yet as soon as I thought that I realised I was lying to myself. I felt sick of the whole business and tried to cast him out of my mind.

The next time we met was under altogether different circumstances. A local cinema was showing a double bill of gay films that a group of us found a distortion of homosexuality. We ran off a hundred or so leaflets expressing our point of view, and went along to the cinema to distribute them. I had my 'Glad to be Gay' badge on, and felt old hat and silly. It seemed little more to me than giving the cinema queue an extra show for its money. A few jeered, but mostly the leaflets were thrown down into the gutter. Just as I was about to join up with my friends to leave, I saw his by now familiar face at the end of the queue. This time he was not going to ignore me. I went up to him and thrust a leaflet into his hand.

"This is for you," I said. "I think you need it."

He smiled. There was a trace of mockery in his voice as he replied, "So you wear badges?"

"I've always worn badges."

"The first and only time I wore one it fell off," he said.

I replied dryly, "Perhaps you didn't try hard enough to keep it on."

He reached out then, and touched me on the shoulder.

"I'm sorry."

"Don't be sorry. Just don't do it again - to anyone."

"Are you very angry?"

"I was."

My friends had seen me talking to him, and thinking no doubt that I was chatting him up, had gone away. A heterosexual couple in front of us were all too obviously listening to our conversation. At one point the man put his hand on his hips and let out a mincing 'sweetie.' The girl giggled, pressing herself against his side.

"Come on," I said, "let's go and have a drink."

Nicholas followed me without a word. I took him to a quiet bar in a street nearby, and after having bought him a drink, sat down and confronted him.

"I want to know everything," I said. I was surprised at my own words. They were not what I meant, yet by some strange paradox they were exactly what I dared not think.

"Everything?"

There was still that note of mockery in his voice. He raised his glass, and in a light hearted way that I found embarrassing, toasted me.

"Here's to you, Michael. Here's to what you had to put up with."

"Please, I..."

"No, I mean it." He paused. "But I'm alright now. I'm happy."

The words rang false, but I let him go on.

"I'm happy, and happy and happy. Peter's come back - and he'll never go away again."

Those last words troubled me. They were too much like a threat, and despite the surface frivolity I felt a deep and gnawing misery within Nicholas. His words said one thing. The real him was permeated with something else. I felt as if I were in the middle of a radio-active field, and the vibrations that I was picking up had a sickening intimation of death. In one moment the whole world that I knew and was used to, seemed swept aside. The eyes brought death. The marked features brought death. I had to escape from him, from all that he represented, yet I stayed.

"Let's go," he said. "We are going to meet Peter."

We went. I met Peter. If I were to give an exact description of his looks it would be false, and it would be so because I had the bias of finding him overwhelmingly attractive. My reason, and my past experience both combined to warn me that he was well under the age I liked, but another part of my reason added that despite his youth he had a way, a bearing about him that was well beyond his years. But let me say at once that there was nothing even remotely sentimental in this attraction. I quite simply desired him, urgently and passionately. I also realised that any positive move in that direction would have meant a betrayal of Nicholas. (Move? I must be joking. There were no ethics involved in my resisting making the step; no thoughts of Nicholas whatsoever, if I am totally honest.) For that night, sitting in the room with him, with Nicholas, it was as if I didn't exist. He was polite, but no more. He made us tea, and he chatted about this and that, yet it was clear all the time that I hadn't even marginally entered his world. I was that abstract thing on two legs - 'a friend who had called round with Nicholas.'

I left them the first moment that I thought was appropriate, and went home. Desire griped at me like an intense stomach ache, and to get some relief, I masturbated. I conjured up the boy's image and stripped him slowly of his clothes. I mentally played with the slim body; ran my fingers through his fair hair and kissed the wide, boyish mouth. I lay on my stomach and had him enter me. It was good, and this final image made me come. All next day at school I thought about him, wondering if he was faithful to Nicholas. The word, the concept meant nothing to me, but I wasn't so stupid as not to realise that in all probability it meant something to Peter. He did have a slight air of sanctity about him - the 'touch me not' look that was both attractive and dislikeable. But whether or not it had anything to do with the notion of fidelity was another thing. So after a few days of his invisible presence, and putting up with it like a nagging, unrelievable pain, I thought of other things. I returned to park-land, and gave myself up to the pleasure of anonymous hands. I experienced a week of debauch, closing it with a dose of anal gonorrhoea.

Nicholas faded out of my life. I wondered if he would ring me, and Christmas came and went before I received another of his phone calls.

"Michael?"

"Hello, Nicholas."

"You recognise my voice."

"Of course. How are you?"

Before I had time to finish asking how he was, he said: "Can I come over?"

My reply was half serious.

"If it's to give me a heavy time, no."

"I'm alone," he said.

"Peter again?"

There was a moment of silence.

"I'm out of my mind, Michael."

"Alright, come for something to eat. At about eight, and don't drink before you come this time."

"I'm out of my mind..."

"Nicholas, don't exaggerate."

But I should have known by now that Nicholas in fact never exaggerated. He simply lived by the standards of his larger than life truth.

He arrived at half-seven while I was in the middle of preparing the meal. I felt guilty about the way I had reacted to his despair. When someone says that they are out of their mind, you shouldn't react by saying, 'Alright, come over for a meal.' I had treated his statement as if I hadn't heard it. But in all fairness to myself, I needed to distance my response to Nicholas's pain. So when he turned up on the door-step, looking better than the last time he had come to the flat, I was relieved.

"You look good, Nicholas."

"The last welcome I got here was how terrible I looked."

"You did. You don't now."

I put the bottle of wine he had brought into the fridge. Then I took him into the living room, and told him to entertain himself while I finished the cooking. He went immediately to my bookshelf, took down a book, and that was the last I heard or saw of him until I served the meal.

"You're very quiet," I said.

He poured himself a glass of wine and smiled at me. I stared at him, and as I stared, a simple fact forced itself into my mind, reminding me with its insistence that we were utter and total strangers to one another. The words were, 'We are worlds apart. We have nothing to talk about, nothing to relate.' They didn't make me particularly sad, but they did make me wish that the time would pass quickly, so that I could be alone once more with myself.

As if reading my thoughts; as if rebelling against any reality that they could have, he said:

"Michael, I want to commit suicide."

"Explain," I replied.

He got up and paced the room. He passed a hand through his hair, and there was weariness in his voice as he said, "I had arranged to go and stay with him - with him, and with some of his friends. We had left it that he would contact me to arrange the final date. But he'd been gone ten days and I had heard nothing from him. I was demented with worry. I couldn't understand his silence. I had believed him. I had wanted to believe him."

His body began to shake, and he sat down heavily in the chair opposite me.

"Look, don't go on..."

"It's the pills. I took more than I should've before I came out. I know it's wrong, but I have to get through somehow."

These last words struck me as being pathetic. He was playing again for my sympathy. Now, with the passing of time, I realise that he depended too deeply on other people for his emotional and spiritual fulfilment, and that that was his mistake. No one - however patient they were with him - could rise highly enough to meet his demands. Everyone had to fail with Nicholas, simply because they were human.

He continued by saying, "I couldn't understand his silence. So at last I rang him, but there was no reply. After that I wrote to him, expecting a letter by return of post, but there was none. Then - it was the morning of my birthday - I ran down the stairs to the hall, sure that there would be some word from him. A card. But once more, nothing. I felt terrible. I crawled back to bed, and there I - "

He paused here for a long while. I thought of the experienced actor weighing his pauses.

" - I prayed. I asked God to stop the cruelty. Just that."

He laughed.

"Cruel? What have I known of it compared to others?"

(Well you might ask, I thought.)

"Have I been beaten, starved, tortured? Yet all the same I asked God to stop the cruelty. And as I drifted into sleep, a hand appeared from the darkness, holding a white cup, and a voice cried - Abba."

Nicholas started to shake again at this point.

"You don't have to - "

"Go on?"

He stared at me, and the question as answer seemed more true, and in its truth, more terrible than anything he had ever said to me before. I realised with dreadful certainty that all he could do was to go on.

"I had a vivid dream. I dreamt that it was Christmas, and that I was ringing him. He answered the phone, and his voice was distorted - not at all the voice I was used to hearing. I had to ask twice if it was him, and he appeared to pass me on to speak to someone else, but all the time it was him. I told him how I had been suffering. I said, 'If you didn't want me to come, you should have told me.' I said to him, 'I waited.' "

Nicholas's face was wet with tears.

"There was a long silence at the other end of the line. He didn't say a word. I replaced the receiver. I felt as if there was nothing left but cruelty, and it was unendurable. I rang him again, and he replied. The voice sounded strange and cold, almost evil. I just asked him, 'Why,' and he shouted down the phone, 'I don't want anyone here. Do you hear me? I don't want anyone here.' In the background I could tell that there were other people. Someone laughing. A baby crying. It was Christmas in my dream, and the dream was not finished. I went out into the street, and from there I went to the park. It was daylight, and I saw a lover whom I had ignored for years. He smiled at me. I returned the smile, feeling unutterably alone. It was when I smiled that I woke up. I cried out when I realised that it had all been a dream. My first thought was - it didn't happen. Terrible though the experience had been, it didn't happen. But that cry of hope was still filled with anguish. It was no better really to wake up."

He reached out for my glass of wine, and drank it down in one long gulp.

"Please, I must..." he said. The gesture, despite its simplicity, was almost melodramatic.

"So do you know what I did then? I decided to make calling him real. I rang his number. It was someone else who answered the phone. I asked if Peter was there, and the voice said, 'No.' I asked when he would be there, and the voice told me that he was due back on Sunday. It was a full four days to Sunday. I couldn't ask any more questions, for I knew that the voice, that the man on the other end of the line, hated me. I've met him, you see, and I know that he is in love with Peter."

Nicholas paused.

"So it was no better outside the dream after all," he said.

I looked at him. His voice broke into a sob as he murmured, "Father, take this cup from me."

I got up from the table, and went across to where he was sitting. I placed a hand on his shoulder.

"Do you believe?" I asked. "Do you believe in God? Is that why you call on Him?"

"No," he said, "but sometimes the distance and the impossibility of Him is all that I have."

My thoughts turned to Peter. What appeared to be cruelty on his side seemed to me to be mere thoughtlessness. Who knows, perhaps he was just quite simply relieved to escape from Nicholas for a while. Then a double, deceiving thought entered my mind as I asked, "Would you like me to go to London and see him? I would if it would help. Maybe I could talk to him."

His face cleared at once.

"Would you?"

"It's Friday tomorrow," I said. "I'll go at the weekend."

"I'll give you the address and telephone number. You will be able to talk to him. I'm sure of it."

I felt ashamed of his child-like confidence in me. I smiled at him as I asked: "Now do you still want to commit suicide?"

The question was a joke, but I should have learnt my lesson never to joke with Nicholas. Immediately his face became serious.

"Not alone," he replied. "I don't want to die alone."

The answer was ominous and disquieting. I steered the conversation into less dangerous waters, and the evening from that point on passed uneventfully. Just before he left he wrote down Peter's full name and the London address, and I folded the paper neatly into four and put it away.

"I'll do what I can," I said.

He hit me with playful gentleness on the arm, and then, what I had asked for earlier on in the evening happened - I was alone. But then, in my moment of asking for solitude, I had not realised that it would be shared with the ghost of Peter. I wanted to see him, and I allowed my imagination to run riot with erotic possibilities. 'Of course none of them will happen,' I told myself, 'but then - '. The 'but' was the strongest incentive to actually go. And yet there was Nicholas. The very real Nicholas who had talked of suicide and despair; the distraught and tortured man to whom I had offered my help. We were so dissimilar. Yet why then did I put up with him? His life was dark and full of drama, but wasn't my own life painfully void of dramatic conflict? He brought me nothing except his troubles, and in a perverse way I almost welcomed them. No one else would put up with it, I told myself, so that must make me his only dependable friend. Friend. The word laughed back at me. I was sure that I was nothing to Nicholas. Nothing save a human receptacle in which to put his despair. Father indeed let the cup pass from me. I was the cup, and I was full of his mess.

The first thing I did that Saturday when I arrived in London was to go on a sentimental tour of the past. How far away those days seemed when we used to meet, in numbers up to four or five hundred, in that large, rambling church hall. Then the fire of Pentecost had truly been upon us - or so I had then liked to believe. Anybody could get up and talk, and there was so much to say and so little time to say it in. We were learning our bibles, and it was a voyage of unlimited discovery. Now the texts had been learnt, and the sad truth was - what could be done with them? The word we had received was of no practical use in the world. But we had come. Over a period of about a year, thousands of us had come to that hall to hear and to talk. Where were they now? Where were the illusions and the cries of revolt? Absorbed, I supposed, in the vast network of streets in the city. Yet to comfort myself I imagined that one or two of those thousands still made the occasional pilgrimage.

I tried the church door and it opened. I went inside and found my way to the hall. My first impression was that they had given it a new coat of paint. Before it had been green and brown; now it was a muddy sort of cream. The change of colour disturbed me. It was yet another nail in the coffin of my past. An old woman was sweeping in a corner, and as I entered she raised her head and smiled. There was no need really to give an explanation why I was there, but all the same I said:

"I used to come here. I used to come here every week. Years ago now."

"The vicar still lets the hall. It's booked out most nights, it's so in demand. It's big, you see."

She smiled at me. I turned away from her without replying, and she went on quietly sweeping. I walked round the hall, wondering what Peter would have made of the meetings. There was no doubt in my mind that he had never come to any of them. It was at that moment that I realised with a sharp stab of bitterness that I was, now, of another generation. It was all past, everything, and as far as consciousness was concerned, far, far away. The memory of those evenings of confidence and deliciously sentimental idealism made me shudder. In my imagination the thousands appeared around me in the deserted hall. We were cramped together like sardines, or like Jews in a gas chamber, and each and every one of us had a beard.

"What are we?"

The chanting began.

"What are we?"

"Gay."

"What is Gay?"

"Proud."

"What are we?"

"School teachers."

"What are school teachers?"

"Alone."

I cried out then, and the thousands disappeared. The old woman had stopped sweeping and was staring at me.

"I'm sorry," I mumbled. "I'm sorry."

I rushed out of the church, and ran all the way to the nearest call box. I had to make contact. I had to make contact at once.

"Could I speak to Peter, please?"

"Who's calling?"

The voice sounded bored and a bit aggressive.

"Michael. He won't remember me."

"Hold on."

I held on. Then a soft, almost inaudible voice said: "Yes?"

"Peter?"

"Yes."

"This is Michael. Nicholas's friend. We met one evening at your place."

"Yes."

I felt angry and foolish. Wasn't there anything else he could say except that one word?

"I would like to see you. Nicholas gave me your number and the address."

There was a short pause before he asked: "Are you free to come over this afternoon?"

"Yes. I've just arrived."

"Can you come about four? You know where it is, don't you?"

"I think so," I replied.

"The twenty-four bus takes you almost to the door."

He hung up, and I stood there for a moment in the call box listening stupidly to the dead buzzing on the line. Then I slammed down the receiver, feeling a distinct and irrational hostility towards him. What did I do then until four? I walked aimlessly around London. I felt like a kid who is just about to take an exam. My stomach was churning, and a tiny, malicious voice inside me told me I was going to fail. At five minutes past four I was on the doorstep and ringing the bell. A dark haired young man answered and told me to come in.

"Peter's in the kitchen."

He pointed down a corridor, then turned away from me and went upstairs. I wandered down the corridor to the kitchen. Peter was seated at the end of a long wooden table reading a book. He looked up as I came in, put his book down, then stood up.

"It's been a long time," he said.

He smiled at me and pointed to a chair.

"Would you like a drink?"

"Thanks."

"Tea or coffee?"

36

"Tea."

He said nothing while he prepared the tea, and strangely enough I didn't find the silence in any way intimidating. On the contrary talk can very often be a distraction, and in this rather pleasant silence I found that I could observe him with more concentration. Was this the boy of my fantasies? Well, 'yes' and 'no.' For a start he wasn't as good-looking as I thought he had been. His face seemed pinched and ill. There were also the beginnings of a fair beard around his mouth and chin which wasn't becoming. Some people can have beards and some can't, and he fell very definitely into the latter category of those who can't. As if that wasn't enough he was wearing baggy old jeans and a voluminous sweater that did just about everything not to set his figure off to advantage. I smiled at that point. Wasn't I perhaps a little over-doing the criticisms precisely because I still did find him attractive? Often one can deliberately underrate those things and people that one most desires out of a fear of not obtaining them. The psychology of the 'put down' makes rejection easier to bear.

"Do you take sugar?"

I nodded. I decided then to open the conversation.

"Is this place a retreat?"

"Yes," he said.

"Do you know what I mean?" I asked.

"I think so. You are referring to Nicholas, aren't you?"

For a moment I was a bit taken aback by the directness of his reply.

"I suppose I meant Nicholas."

In fact I began to doubt if I had.

"I can always come here when life gets too much to bear," he said. "And just recently it has got pretty terrible."

He flicked through the pages of his book, then stared at me. I was afraid of that stare. Afraid of its nakedness.

"What do you mean?" I asked.

I had come to London to be involved - and here I was, involved.

"I don't think I will be going back to him," he replied.

He lowered his eyes and began to take small sips from his tea. My first instinctive feeling was one of pleasure. If this was true then I now had freedom to play the field.

"What made you come to that decision?"

"I don't like self-destruction. Nicholas is destructive. He said to me that you were a good friend of his, so you should know what I mean."

"I don't know him all that well," I replied.

This relative lie made me inwardly wince. Only boredom and a lack of drama in my own life had put me in this situation. I felt like a dog who steals from another dog's bowl.

"You must know about the suicide threat," he said.

I made a vague gesture with my hands that could have meant anything. At that moment the dark haired young man came in.

"I'll see you later, Peter," he said. "If there are any calls for me say that I'll be back about ten."

"Alright, Mark."

The figure went out, without so much as a look in my direction. Peter said: "I used to have an intense relationship with Mark. Except for the physical side the intensity remains. We try to protect each other from the outside world."

"That's not easy to do. To keep the world out. It has a way of coming at you when you least expect it."

My remarks were getting feebler and feebler. I hated to admit it, but I was beginning to find myself at a disadvantage in this situation. But I had come quite a distance to see the boy, and I wasn't going to leave without having achieved something out of it. I asked him for more tea, then took the plunge at what I thought was the deep end.

"I wondered if you had been the one who had hurt him, but he seems to have done a good job at hurting you."

I looked at him, then looked away. What I had said sounded false.

"Nicholas gives, but also expects a lot of pain in return," he replied.

He got up from the table and went to the window. He had his back to me. For a moment I was tempted to get up and go across to him. It would have taken the slightest of gestures to touch his body.

"You referred just now to keeping out the world," he said. "I don't intend to do that. But I do need a breathing space. After the pain has settled, and the pain will settle, and I feel more able to be constructive, then I will do something here with Mark."

He turned round and faced me.

"For a long time now Mark has wanted to open a centre where people can come and talk. There's room enough in this house. I think I will stay and help him."

"And Nicholas?"

"I can't do anything more for Nicholas."

"Do you love him?"

"I can't answer that. I thought I knew."

He smiled again, and I realised how much his smiles transformed his face. They made him very beautiful. I also realised how strong the feeling of quiet peace was that emanated from him. If he could only just let me remain, and be at peace with him. Immediately I dismissed the thought. There were to be no heavy pronouncements, or stupid declarations of love. And then, perhaps, the peace that I felt was not peace at all.

"Shall we change the subject?" he said.

He began clearing away the cups and saucers.

"I had better go," I replied.

It was the last thing I wanted to do, but I thought it was polite. He looked at me for a moment, then said casually, "If you have nowhere to go, then stay here. I'm presuming, of course, that you don't want to go back today."

"I hadn't planned, but..."

"Perhaps you have somewhere else to stay?"

"No."

"There's a spare room here, and Mark won't mind."

"Are you sure?"

I had hoped this would happen, but in a different way. I gave free rein to the fantasy of taking him out, of buying him drinks and a meal, then with single-minded insistence talking him into bed. But I knew that none of that would happen now. Even the fantasy appeared as a vulgarity that I should somehow be ashamed of.

"Peter - "

He looked at me sharply. Did he sense then that I was about to say something meant to disturb him?

"Peter, I came to go to bed with you."

(God, that was ludicrous.)

He turned away, ignoring what I had just said. I launched into an explanation, still floundering.

"I wanted to that first time; that first time we met - I know it's wrong, but - "

"It's not wrong, Michael."

His voice was brisk. Almost business like.

"It's not wrong, and I'm glad you told me, but I'm afraid that it's not possible. I may be free - and really I don't know what that word means anymore, but - " He paused. "Quite simply I have no desire to go to bed with anybody. And when I say anybody I do mean that."

"You're being kind."

I mumbled the words, knowing that he was lying, and hating myself for having made him lie.

"I'm trying to be honest," he said. Then he looked at me with an expression very near to tenderness.

"And now that that hurdle has been met, shall we try and get to know each other?"

I remembered Nicholas saying more or less the same words. But where he and I had mutually, if not explicitly agreed that we were not attracted to one another, I could not say the same thing in regard to Peter. Under these present circumstances there was very definitely a strong element of desire, however one-sided it may have been.

The evening passed pleasantly enough. We stayed in to eat, and Peter made me a good meal. For a few hours I allowed myself the luxury of imagining we were lovers, and that his looking after me was a permanent situation. So much for liberation and role-playing, I thought. We even had a couple of bottles of wine. During my fifth glass, and second bottle, I gathered up enough courage to say:

"Are you sure I can't seduce you?"

He laughed loudly. This was the first time I had heard him laugh, and it came as rather a shock. I was surprised to note that I didn't much like the sound of him laughing.

"Why do you want to seduce me?" he asked.

(Mother of Christ, I thought, it was easier in the old days.)

"Because - "

I trailed a frustrated hand in the air. Then I said, more out of desperation than anything else! "Does there have to be a reason other than attraction?"

"I suppose not," he replied.

"Do you find me attractive?"

He stared at me, his face becoming serious. I inwardly fought against the answer that was all too visibly written there. I tried to brush my question aside, commenting tritely about the beauty of some hideous, trailing plant that was stuck in a corner of the room. He respected the change of subject, and I felt with a pang of regret that any question of desire between us would, in all probability, never be opened again.

"I haven't had all that many lovers, except Mark and Nicholas," he said. "Partly because I want to be free - yes, even though I don't know what the hell freedom is. But it's also partly because I'm afraid of something. Something perhaps within myself. I feel so cold and detached. There's this feeling that no one will ever be the centre of my world. Only Nicholas came near, by the very force of obsession, to that centre."

This was the first time that Nicholas had been mentioned since the opening conversation.

"Shall I tell you about my first experience of falling in love?"

I finished my glass of wine. Suddenly all I wanted to do was to go to bed, sleep the whole abortive day off, and return in the morning to my town. Peter continued: "We were about the same age. He was perhaps a year younger. Anyway he was very uptight about being gay and wouldn't give me his address. We used to meet - always late at night, when he said his parents were asleep - in a local park. There we would exchange kisses. That was all.

This improbable situation lasted for a few weeks, and I was getting more and more deeply involved. Even the name he had given me I couldn't be sure was real. As for me I had told him practically everything about myself. Then, one night, he didn't turn up, and I waited several consecutive nights until I realised he wouldn't turn up again. Months passed by, and one morning, as I was leaving my house, a car drove up and someone waved to me. It took me a couple of minutes, and a few paces up the road, before I realised who it was. He got out of the car and called my name. I think I must have been shaking when I went up to him. He was handsome and smiling, and said he had just come back from a holiday. I asked him if he had come to see me. He looked surprised and said, 'No, I've got friends of my parents living a few doors away from you. I have to visit them. That's why I came.' What he said was enough for me. I walked away."

Peter paused for a moment.

"It was then I learnt my first and most important lesson. That only life could improvise such a corny, heart-breaking encounter. The next lesson was Nicholas. I learnt from that relationship that the heart, yes, the heart, must definitely break. It must break, to remain for ever cold."

He got up and came over to me. For a second he lingered by my chair, then went to the door.

"This isn't the right time to find you attractive. Not even if I allowed myself to."

The following morning early, I was at the station, waiting for a train to take me home. And during the journey back I kept thinking about what I could tell Nicholas. I felt more and more strongly that none of it was my business, yet I had obstinately made it my business. Out of my own boredom I had created a situation in which I was forced to act. So, two days after my return, I contacted him, and we arranged to meet. I had chosen of all places the park at the end of town. Somewhere in the confusion of my motives it appeared to be 'safe' and 'neutral'; an open place away from the morbid confinement of rooms. Yet all the same it was a bad choice. It had been raining, and the benches were wet. The park cafeteria was closed, so we had no alternative but to remain on our feet, walking up and down. I felt miserable and wanted to get the whole thing over with as soon as possible. I came to the point almost at once.

"I don't think Peter will be coming back," I said.

He looked at me and smiled. I expected a reply, but there was none. He rather irritatingly began to kick at an empty lemonade can.

"Did you hear what I said Nicholas?"

"I heard."

"Well?"

"I don't think he quite knew what he wanted when you saw him."

"But I only saw him a couple of days ago. I don't understand."

I didn't understand, until I stopped walking and looked at Nicholas's face more closely. I had been so concerned with my own ambiguous feelings that I had hardly bothered to consider what state he was in. I saw very clearly when I looked at him that the state was happiness.

"Two things have happened," he said. "And despite what you have just told me I think I have to thank you for one of them."

He pressed my arm, and we continued walking.

"First, good news number one. Peter rang me last night. He is returning. He wants us to try and make a go of it again."

"But - "

It was the only word I could say. I had to control a sudden desire to hit him across the face; hit him right there in the middle of his bloody smiling happiness. What was he playing at? What was Peter playing at? No, I didn't understand.

"God, give me children. At least their contradictions make some sense."

I said the words aloud, but Nicholas only laughed, and began to walk ahead. For a moment I was tempted not to follow him.

"Are you coming?"

He turned round and shouted at me.

"I'm not going to catch pneumonia in this place," he said. "I've got a bottle of wine at home. Let's go back there and celebrate."

I caught up with him.

"Shouldn't you save the bottle for Peter?"

I tried to put a note of spite in my voice, but realised that there was no way of getting at Nicholas. He had that armour of immunity called being happily in love.

"Alright," I said.

"Don't you want to know what the second piece of good news is?"

"Of course."

(Rather cynically I remembered there was another factor other than love to account for his joy.)

"I've had a play accepted. It's going on next month."

He began to walk more quickly, and I very nearly had to run to keep up with him.

"Is it really true?" I asked.

"Yes."

This news did abruptly widen the horizon as far as I was concerned. The narrow world of Nicholas's obsessions opened, and a new, confidant Nicholas, whom I had never seen before, was emerging.

"That's tremendous. I and Peter - "

I stopped. I wanted to say that both Peter and I would look forward to the opening performance, but his name caught in my throat. It was almost as if uttering it would bring about bad luck. Nicholas avoided what I had said, and I wondered for a moment if he had actually heard.

"Look, Nicholas, we'll go out for a meal."

He put a hand affectionately on my shoulder.

"It's my turn to give. Let me take you. Please. But first let's go and get drunk. I'll buy another bottle on the way home."

"One bottle is enough," I said. I had bad memories of Nicholas having too much to drink.

"Rubbish," he replied. "It takes two to be happy."

We bought the second bottle, and he took me back to his place. It mainly consisted of one room overlooking the sea. For some reason best known to him the walls were painted black. There was very little furniture, but there were plenty of books, stacked from floor to ceiling. On top of one pile I noticed a crystal vase, and in the vase a solitary, purple flower. It appeared to be made out of paper.

"Did you make it?" I asked. I pointed to the flower.

"It's real."

His voice sounded hurt. I should have stopped there, but I didn't.

"It doesn't look very real to me. Maybe I'm biased. I can't stand purple. Anything in purple always looks terrible."

"It's not a thing. It's alive. If you must know I use it for meditation."

"You would," I laughed. He began to shout at me. "Michael, stop trying so hard to fit everything neatly into a life-style that you can understand. For God's sake leave us poets some room for our poetry."

I had hurt him in the most wretchedly stupid of ways. But how was I to honestly know that he used the flower, false or otherwise, for meditation purposes?

"I'm sorry," I said lamely, "I don't respond much to that sort of thing: either meditation or flowers. And as for a life-style, well I don't consider that I have much of a life. Whatever life I do have is definitely not done with style."

"We came back for a drink."

His voice was edgy and nervous. I opened the first bottle while he got the glasses.

"When do you expect Peter back?"

I had meant to ask about the play. I had meant to avoid talking about or referring to Peter, but as I was doing just about everything wrong, my mind seemed to perversely return of its own accord to the subject of the boy.

"Tomorrow."

"Then let's drink a toast to that."

We drank and than remained silent. I wanted to talk, but felt intimidated by his silence, and by what I had said. The room was obviously a sanctuary to him, and so far I had inadvertently desecrated it. After what seemed a very long time I opened my mouth to speak.

"Look, if it's what I stupidly said about the flower, please forgive me. I am not the soul of tact, as you should know."

"It's not that. A few more glasses of wine and I'll be alright."

"Tell me about the play."

He looked at me with his dark eyes, and I felt them attacking me. What had I said now? There was another long silence, then I added: "You don't have to tell me if you don't want to. Perhaps there's too much poetry in it for me to follow."

(That was ridiculously defensive.)

He drank another glass of wine, then went across to a pile of books and literally threw a couple of them at me. One was a French edition on the life of Heinrich von Kleist. The second was a volume, translated into English, of one of Kleist's plays. The title: 'Penthesilea.'

"That man is my god," he said.

His voice was slurred, and I put the 'god' down without replying.

"Both his life and his work fascinate me. Especially that play. Penthesilea is Queen of the Amazons. She tears Achilles' body limb from limb. 'She tears the armour from his body, sinks her teeth and locks them in his milk-white breast, she and the dogs in savagery vying.' Kleist knew. He knew what we are capable of doing to one another. He understood, and the horror of it is still too much for most of us to bear."

He picked up the French biography, leafed through it for a moment, then read from it.

" 'The fact of the matter is that there was no help for me on this earth.' "

He closed the book and put it down. The black walls were oppressing me, and the atmosphere was growing heavier by the minute. What was I supposed to reply to that quotation? I said, "Are you talking about yourself?"

"I'm talking about Kleist."

He drank some more and I realised that he had had far too much.

"But you think it relates to you as well," I added?

He refrained from answering that question, and then did

46

something unexpected. He knelt down and put his arms around me.

"It's not everyday that I have two things to celebrate."

His voice sounded thick and drunk. I pushed him gently away from me and said: "I want to hear more about your play."

"I have a scene from another play. A play I've started to write. Do you want to hear about that scene? It has nothing to do with Kleist, but in a way it is a continuation of the play that I have had accepted. The same guilt. The same battle. The same atrocity. All themes from a life of Kleist, but different; chopped up and digested by my own wretched imagination."

He clung harder to me, his voice rambling a little as though delirious.

"The guilt is there. The guilt Kleist would have felt if he had seen what his country had become. If he had seen what the world, in all its relative horror, had become. But to return to the scene. I must return to the scene. The stage lightens. Standing there is the Pope. The living symbol of all our most absolute values. There he stands, less than God, more than man; infallible. He is alone on the stage, facing us, the eternal, questioning spectators. Yet we are in a theatre, and in a theatre the audience rarely asks questions."

He paused a moment and stroked my face.

"Go on, Nicholas," I said.

"But the question will be asked. Enter a Jewish child dressed in white holding a flower. She crosses the stage and gives the flower to the Pope. The Pope (the actor) accepts the flower and smiles. Then the child asks him quite simply, 'Why?' But we are in a theatre, remember, where questions are rarely asked. The actor as Pope could reply, but the whole meaning of life is to be found in that one question - found, but not comprehended. The Pope is less than God and more than man, and as such knows nothing. The scene changes. The actor as Pope is dressed as a Clown. The clown, with ecclesiastical cap, and balls that jingle on feet and arm. He is on his knees with arms opened wide. Standing over him is the child, spitting and kicking at his body. But the clown bears her anger, bears it with a jingle and an unquestioning smile."

"Nicholas," I asked, "is this really from the play?"

His face was gaunt, and his voice shaking, as he said: "You don't believe me, do you?"

I put my arms around him, and he laid his head upon my shoulder. For a moment I gave in to a sudden feeling of tenderness, and kissed his hair. I didn't understand what he was talking about, yet at the same time I was captivated by his words. In a way that was totally beyond my comprehension they burnt themselves upon my brain.

"I believe you," I said. "Finish your scene."

"The scene is finished. I never wrote that scene. I like to imagine Kleist could have written it. But he would have expressed it in such a way that it would have been original. There is nothing original in the way I have presented it."

"Why do you denigrate yourself so much?" I asked.

He pressed his face into my neck, and I felt tears on my skin. I stroked his hair mechanically for a few minutes, then I heard him mutter: "Let's go out to eat. We should eat."

"In a little while, Nicholas."

"Do you know something else - about Kleist? He was a nationalist. He would have probably supported the concentration camps and the gas chambers. He would have supported it all in the name of a purer cause. Yet he would have died a thousand deaths of guilt because of it. I understand the contradiction. I always have. In the end all atrocity is the same as love. And Kleist died for the need of love."

He took me to an expensive restaurant. We ate well. Once or twice I wondered if he would get through the evening, but Nicholas was stronger than I imagined. He drank some more and we talked neither of the plays nor of Peter. Afterwards he walked me back to my place. It was outside my door that the hammer blow fell. Looking back I am surprised that I had not even expected it to happen.

"Michael, did you fuck him?"

I laughed. I knew at once what he meant, but pretended I didn't.

"I asked you a question."

"I can't reply to it."

"I'm asking you, Michael."

"I don't know what you mean."

"You know bloody well what I mean. You see, when I've fucked him he's never really wanted it. But then I have never known how to do it so that it gives pleasure. There's only been pain between him and I..."

I was embarrassed. I fumbled with my door key and opened the door.

"I'm not concerned with what either of you do sexually."

"Come on, Michael, did you or didn't you fuck each other?"

I stared at him angrily. God, how possible it was in a single moment to hate this man.

"No, we did not. And you have no need to ask. No need at all."

I was shouting. We stood there, very near to violence. I felt his violence and I felt my own. Then I said: "You're drunk." Without another word I went into the house, slamming the door in his face. I stood in the corridor for a long ghastly nightmare of a time, then something happened that rarely happens - I burst into tears. I couldn't stop crying. I stood there, with my face pressed against the wall, and I cursed him as I cried.

The following day brought me back into the orbit of my 'normal' life. I worked hard and took it out in punishment on the children at school. I then went home and faced a bleak and lonely evening. To take my mind off all that had happened I set about doing a job that I had put aside for months. Quite some while back a gay magazine had asked me to compile a list of novels with a predominantly homosexual theme, and this miserable evening I began the task. During my long quest for liberation I had read most of those novels; even the ones that dealt with the subject in the most oblique of ways. Other than a few that I had found personally memorable, I had tended to reject them all outright.

Peter.

Yes, him. I was thinking of him. He was the boy of the future.

The boy that I had created in my mind, and that none of the books I had read, spoke of. Suddenly, overcome by a fit of anger and frustration I crumpled the list that I had made. I put on my coat and went out. I walked by the sea. After relegating all those books to the fires, I wondered what I was to do with myself. Shall I too commit suicide, and jump into the waves, I asked myself? Shall I make this my lands end and conform to the traditional, sad ending? Sad, sentimental - but never tragic. I imagined Peter walking down to meet the water, finishing it all in true romantic style, but the image could not fit. Then I thought of Nicholas. Yes, he had style. He had the romantic manners to fit the role.

Suicide.

The word hit at me. I ran to Nicholas's place. I rang his bell with terrible urgency. At last he came to the door, looking surprised.

I said: "I know you weren't expecting me, but after last night..." Then my voice trailed off dismally.

"I shouldn't have said what I said," he replied.

"Are you alright?"

(This was absurd. What was I doing at this time of night, here, asking him if he was alright?)

"Shouldn't I be?"

"I imagined - "

What did I imagine? Nicholas, hanging from a rope in his room? Nicholas, head in a gas oven or with wrists slashed in the bath? I stood there before him, unable to say a word.

"I can't ask you up."

I realised then that I hadn't even expected him not to be alone.

"You see, Peter has just come back," he said.

The name shivered through me like the beginning of a fever. He shouldn't have come back to you, I thought, but instead I said goodnight to him and walked away.

I saw very little of them after that week. Occasionally I would see them in the street, but it wasn't until the first performance of Nicholas's play that I came into direct contact with Peter again. He looked strained and painfully on his own, despite the presence of Nicholas, and the crowd around them.

"Are you nervous about all this?" I asked.

I touched him gently on the arm.

"I want it to be a success," he murmured.

In retrospect I can't help but feel that there was an unconscious threat implied in those words. (In fact the reality of this feeling was borne out once the play was over.) I think the impression came across in the way he said the words; the voice low, hard and determined. My immediate reaction to the statement was not centred on any implications concerning their relationship, but more on Nicholas and what the experience would mean to him. My first thought was, God help him if it isn't. I said nothing more to Peter and we went into the theatre.

Before I go on to the reviews, that I personally believe killed him, I had better say something about what I thought of the play. I don't know what a masterpiece is. I don't think I have ever read, seen or heard a masterpiece, but now and then a revelation in the arts has occurred and knocked me off my feet. This happened during Nicholas's play. In scene after gruelling scene I saw the whole naked reality of his pain, yet miraculously transcended. I allowed my eyes and ears to be receptive, and I heard the screams. I'm not saying that I completely understood what I saw and heard (most of the references to Kleist and his life escaped me), but what I did receive was a vision of agony that I will not forget. Above all else it was Nicholas's agony. In over twenty tersely written scenes he presented the audience with a stuttering, unlikeable figure, whose only joy was at the climax of self-induced orgasms; whose only hope was to present himself as himself on the stage, so that the world would understand. I thought of the Pope and the actor in the scene that Nicholas had described to me, but here, in this play, I was not at all conscious of the role between the actor and the part he was playing. For here the actor had totally identified with Nicholas (Kleist). The figure on the stage cried out for recognition, for understanding. Yet few, I think, did understand. The cries and the pleas went almost for nothing. The critics hated it. The people in the audience hated it. At the close of the performance the applause was sparse. One or two jeered, but not too loud. I noted with bitterness that more jeers would have at least been a confirmation of some effect. This play had had no effect upon them. And having had no effect they were hardly likely to make it a possible success by showing active disapproval. And the critics the following morning took their revenge. Most said nothing constructive about the play in any way, and reading the criticisms I began to wonder if they had really seen the same play that I had seen. I had the impression that they wanted to condemn it so thoroughly and totally that it would be as if it had never existed at all. The rest of the critics avoided reviewing it. What was wrong? I think, here again, that the problem was to do with ease. I have said before that Nicholas was not easy, well neither was his work. The heavy, humourless, yet at the same time lethal dialogue, hit out like a hacksaw. If I hadn't known him personally perhaps I wouldn't have responded to Nicholas's form of killing either, but at least I like to flatter myself that I would have noticed the birth of an original talent.

We went to Fleet Street, Peter and I, to get the first editions of the papers. We left Nicholas alone in a club, at his own request. He looked desperately tired and he made it perfectly obvious that there was nothing (except get the papers) that either of us could do for him. He was determined that the waiting should be done in a crowded solitude.

After we had read the handful of reviews, Peter turned to me.

"It's a massacre, isn't it?" I nodded.

We had found an all-night café, and were drinking from scalding, tasteless cups of tea.

"Are you very fond of him, Michael?"

The question surprised me, and I looked at Peter intently. What exactly was he trying to tell me?

"I suppose I am getting to know him. In this world that often passes for fondness."

"Then you will help him when he needs help?"

"Of course."

He looked down at the newspapers, as if trying to read there what he wanted to say.

"Because I can no longer help."

"When we met in the house where you were staying you said something very similar. Is it because of that house, of the centre you want to create there? Or is it because of Mark?"

I knew that it was none of these things really, but I wanted him to tell me what it was. He didn't, but continued staring at the newspapers.

"You realise, don't you, that if you leave him now it will just about finish him off?"

His voice hardly rose above a whisper as he said: "That play tonight terrified me."

"Didn't you think it was, if nothing else, accurate - and true to his vision?"

"I thought it was unbearable. As far as I'm concerned I'm going to try and forget that I ever saw it. Don't you see that it is Nicholas? I can't live with that."

"But he obviously needs you to love him - to live with him for what he is."

"I can't."

I didn't know what else to say. What with the play, and now having to deal with Peter, I felt exhausted. At last I managed to murmur: "What exactly is wrong between you?"

He looked at me sadly, then got to his feet.

"We had better go back to him. I haven't much courage, but what I have left I want to use in showing him these reviews."

I remained seated.

"Peter, why are you so evasive? Why is it neither of you ever seems to be there?"

I put all the force that I could into that last word. I meant a lot by it, but what I did mean I could not define.

"Being there is something people can't quite manage these days," he said. "Do you honestly want to know what I believe? I believe that we - you, I, everyone - must manage on our own. Nicholas's play was screaming against that. Just like a child in the dark. He can't manage it, but he must. We all must. Nicholas clings. He clings to life through other people, but in clinging to them he misses life completely. I have to let him go so that he can learn to be alone."

"But the character in the play truly was alone," I said.

"Yes, as Nicholas is, but in the wrong way. I mean aloneness with a sense of freedom."

Was it intuition that made me say: "But that sort of freedom will kill him."

He didn't look at me, but went towards the door. I went to the counter and paid the bill, then followed him outside. The night was dark, and I had to stop myself from reaching out and touching him. I felt suddenly afraid of the darkness of the streets, of the cold inner darkness that we all seemed to live in. I wanted to touch Peter for warmth, but knew even in the moment of that desire that there was no warmth there.

"Why does the night seem darker tonight," I asked?

He looked at me and laughed.

"It is no different from any other night," he said.

We rejoined Nicholas at about three in the morning. He read the reviews in silence, then turned to me and asked to be left alone with Peter. By four o'clock I was at the station waiting for the first train to take me home.

I said I was there with Nicholas when the others turned away. Peter did leave him, and I knew that this time it was for good. During the final stage he was almost completely alone, and like the dependent child that he was, he turned to me for love and protection.

I have missed out a lot, but I must describe in detail one of the last and most frightening evenings that I spent with him. It was in his black room, and he had as usual drunk far too much. I remember him clearly seated on the floor, and all around him, fanwise, the hostile press cuttings. He was swaying backwards and forwards, and his face looked pitifully haggard and old. I went up to him and put my arms around his shoulders. I did this more to quieten him down than to show any physical sign of affection.

"What's wrong," I asked?

"They're after me," he said. "They're going to get me. They've always been after me."

He was shivering, and I put my hand to his forehead. It was

burning hot.

"Put those bloody cuttings away." I decided that the best tactic was to be as firm with him as possible.

"There's nowhere left for me to go."

The way he said this made me shiver with fright. I too felt presences around me. I felt like he did. Trapped. The dark walls were closing in on us, and somehow I had to forcibly drag him from the nightmare. The nightmare of his situation; the nightmare of the room.

I pulled him to his feet and sat him down in a chair. He let me do this totally passively, and when I lifted him he felt unbelievably light. The sensation of lifting him was like lifting a doll. Then, slowly, the force of his terror seemed to return. He stared wildly at me, his hands reaching out, clutching at my hands; clutching so hard that he tore my skin and I began to bleed.

"This can't go on," I said.

I tried to put as much gentleness and understanding into my voice as I could, but deep inside I felt terribly afraid. Both of us were sliding into the darkest of pits, and at that precise moment I had the paralysing realisation that there was nothing I could do to prevent it. Then, suddenly, he started screaming. I cannot begin to describe the awfulness of those screams. It was as if he were being torn limb from limb. His whole being was a howl of agony. At first I cried out to him to be quiet. I raised my voice as loud as his own, imploring him to stop. Then I hit him. He slipped from the chair to the floor, and lay there on his back, the screams continuing. Phlegm was trickling from his mouth, and I was terrified that if the paroxysm continued he would choke.

"Have pity," I cried.

The words appeared to reach him. The howls, the cries changed to a deep, body racked sobbing. I stood helplessly over him and watched. It was as if the enormity of the sound of his despair had broken me. There was no part of me left that I felt capable of giving. I had to resist the inward wish that he would die.

"I can't help," I said.

He struggled to his feet. He crossed the room, and picking up the vase that contained the purple flower, hurled it against the wall. It smashed, and bits of glass flew in all directions. All I could stupidly think of when it happened was - how can a small vase like that break up into so many, many fragments?

"It wasn't real," he said. "Look, touch it for yourself. You knew all the time that it was made out of paper."

He laughed, and the laughter was more horrible than the screams and the crying. I took the flower, crumpled it in my hand, then threw it into a waste bin.

"That's where it belongs," I said. "That's where this whole mess belongs. Nicholas, you have to start again. Tear it all apart if you like, but start again."

"It's too late," he replied.

"Nothing ever is."

"You believe that?"

"Yes. I'm not trying to give you easy comfort, if that's what you're thinking."

He looked at me and for a moment he appeared to be calm.

"You find me ridiculous, don't you?" he said.

"I find your behaviour - avoidable."

I paused before using this last word. It was the only word that seemed at all adequate.

"Do you love life," he asked?

I made a helpless gesture with my hands.

"We've asked - we've said all this before."

He screamed at me then.

"Tell me. Do you love life?"

His eyes were large and black. I felt myself sucked, drawn into the vortex of his panic.

"No," I said.

"Then die with me."

As he uttered those words I felt the floor literally slipping away from under my feet. It was like being in a quicksand, and I had to make a frantic attempt to leave him in order to survive.

"Die with me," he repeated.

I turned my head away and rushed to the door. I felt like a

hounded animal determined on survival. For a while I thought that he would come after me. I ran. I suffocated as I ran. It wasn't until I was half way across town that I stopped for breath. Gasping, I caught on to a lamp-post and my body shivered with fear and the cold. I remember several people staring at me as they went past, with that suspicious stare that strangers give to drunks. I kept on repeating to myself, 'You have to survive. You have to live, even if he is willing your death.' Then I counted up to ten, then twenty, then on to a hundred, as if this ritual of number would release me from the spell. Eventually I let go of the lamp-post, and made my way to the nearest call box. I dialled the number that I had once used and that I would always remember. A quiet voice said: "Yes?"

"Peter?"

Absurdly, stupidly I thought that he would recognise the desperation in my voice. But I had mistaken the voice. This was not Peter.

"He's not in."

"Who am I speaking to?"

"Mark Bradley."

"It's urgent. Please - you've got to get him."

"I said, he's not in."

"When are you expecting him back?"

There was no reply to this. For a second I thought he was going to replace the receiver, but he held on.

"Look, I'm not joking," I said. "I have just left Nicholas. I have just come from his place. He needs Peter. He's in a terrible state. He'll do something - "

"I'll tell Peter."

The voice showed no emotion. I felt as if I had had cold water thrown over my face. The sobering effect was immediate. I replied to the indifferent voice as politely as I could.

"I'm sorry. It wasn't the right thing to have called."

I put down the receiver. A woman was staring in, waiting to use the call box, and I stepped outside. My legs felt firmer and the fear had subsided. I had revolved but for a short time on the periphery of the abyss. I was saved. How deluded I must have been to have believed that I had been broken. I thought with a sort of self-contempt that I would always be saved.

I walked slowly back. The door was still open, and I found him curled up, asleep on the floor. Of all the sounds that I find most ridiculous in the world it is snoring, and Nicholas was snoring. He lay on his side, with his knees curved upwards towards his chin, and the sight struck me as being pathetically sad. There is no tragedy here, I whispered to myself, only human disorder and mess. The flower had been made of paper, and I had known that all along. I closed the door and left him to himself.

I saw him a couple of days later, but only briefly and he hardly mentioned what had happened. I said that I had tried to contact Peter, but he shrugged his shoulders when I told him this.

"Would you have wanted him to come?"

He looked at me and there was great sadness in his eyes. He made no reply and I did not ask him again. A week after that meeting I read in the local newspaper about his death. He had committed suicide. He had thrown himself from a train as it was gathering up speed on leaving a London station. He had been killed instantly. The human mind is ridiculously strange. The one thought in my head when I read the article was a literary one - I thought of Anna Karenina.

There's nothing very much left to tell. I lied at the beginning of this story, but it has taken me all of this narrative to realise the fact. I lied when I said that I supposed I knew him better than anyone else. I really didn't know him at all, but I was involved. And yes, I almost loved him. Anyway all of our lives are a contradiction. That I do believe.

The town has closed around me like a shell. I lead a quiet life and no one comes to trouble my peace. But there are occasional evenings when I look up and long for that phone to ring.

PART TWO

NICHOLAS

1. The closed room.

The walls are black, but the bed is white. Upon the bed there are three people. The three people are my mother and two men. She lies there and they enter her in turn. Afterwards the two men reach out for each other. They kiss. My mother watches them. She raises herself up and watches them embrace. Then she lies back and shuts her eyes as the two men begin to fuck.

June 30

There are some nights that I fear I will never survive. I dreamt last night of a forest; a forest that appeared to have no beginning or end. I was in the middle of the forest. I had in my hands a round, golden ball and it was very precious to me. Yet the closer I held the ball to me the nearer I felt the invisible presence that would steal it away. I started to run. If I run, I thought, then the power will not catch me. After a while I reached a dark pond in the centre of a clearing. The golden ball fell from my hands, and before I could prevent it had rolled into the water. With feelings both of fear and despair I knelt by the pond, and put my hands as far as I could into the water. But there was no hope of reaching the bottom, or of recovering the ball.

"This is all I have," I cried, "and it is lost."

The cry echoed round the clearing. Then I knelt closer to the water and saw the reflection of a face. It was not my face, but the face of the other. I jumped back terrified, and as I did so two hands broke the surface of the waters; and held in the hands like a cup was my head, dripping blood. The vision was so awful that it choked me, making it impossible for me to scream. It was at that moment that I woke up, gasping for breath.

I turned on the light. I looked at the walls, still half-white, half-black; at the pot of black paint, and the brushes on the floor. I got out of bed and paced the room. I put my hands to my head, but it seemed that I no longer had a head. They had taken it from me. I was looking at the objects and things around me with other eyes. But what eyes? What eyes could I have had in an empty space where my head should have been? Shivering with fear I returned to bed. "There is no reason for this," I murmured, "no reason at all." My voice, my mouth seemed to come from the furthest part of the room.

"Who are you?"

I heard the voice. I was the voice, yet I was sure that it came from the other. The golden ball blinded the eyes that possessed me like a burning fire, and I turned off the light. Then slowly the strangeness and the panic passed. All I could think of now was that I had got through, that I had survived the worst. I began to feel once again that the head on my shoulders was truly my own. Suddenly I was filled with a tremendous hope.

"Will you let me come to you? Will you let me sit beside you?"

In the obscurity I saw him standing by the door.

I said to him: "Come."

He was tall and dressed in white. His face obstinately remained within shadow, and I could not make out his features. He sensed my longing to see him and whispered: "Leave the light off. I wish to speak to you in darkness."

I lay there and pushed aside the covering that concealed my body. I wanted him to touch me; to reach out and lie by my side. But instead he sat on the edge of the bed, and it was I who reached out and touched him; touched with the tips of my fingers. I had to make sure that he was real. I had to know that I was awake. I touched the soft material of his clothes, then drew my hand away, satisfied at last that this was not a continuation of my dream.

"I wanted to know that you are real," I said.

I felt intuitively that there was nothing I could possibly hide from him. He laughed, an echo of my own laughter, but there was no mockery in it, no hostility or question of doubt. It was nearer to the happy laughter of complicity. In it he was telling me that he was a part of me.

"Why do you dress in white," I asked?

As a child I had asked my mother a similar question. It had been one night when she had come, as usual, to read to me before I went to sleep.

"What would you have me wear," he replied?

For a moment the voice sounded higher than it had been, almost angry, and I was frightened that I had offended him.

"It is a question that I have asked before," I said.

"I know."

His voice was gentle.

"I know that you miss her. Now cover yourself. No, rather let me draw the covers close."

His hands with the softest of touch drew the covers over my body. With this one gesture he banished all sexual desire from me, and I felt deeply at peace.

"What did my dream mean," I asked?

He was silent for a long time, then he murmured: "I know too that the longing is great."

At first I was angry with him. Why had he refused to answer my question?

"I asked you about my dream. There are nights that I feel I will not survive. Explain to me. Tell me why I suffer."

"The longing is too great, Nicholas."

"I don't understand."

"The Prince is a monster at the bottom of the waters," he whispered. "The monster will only succeed in bringing you your own head. There is no escape this side of peace, but at least you must know this to be true. Do you know? Do you understand?"

I shook my head in the darkness. He was telling me nothing of what I wanted to hear. I began to feel the panic return that had overtaken me in the forest. Why did he keep his face averted from me? Was his the face I had seen reflected in the waters? I screamed out: "You are making me afraid."

He reached out with his hands, and with infinite tenderness, closed my mouth. I kissed the hands that touched me with yearning joy, but immediately afterwards my lips burnt as if they were on fire. I had desired pleasure from that embrace, but instead had received pain.

"How can you expect me to understand when you tell me, when you give me the very opposite of what I desire?"

I moved my burning lips with difficulty, and in my mouth I tasted blood.

"Am I the one who expects so much?"

He returned to me the question.

"I want to be able to understand," I said.

He stood up and in the half-darkness I saw him a little better. The light from the window glanced off the side of his face, and in that fleeting moment I saw that it was white as marble, as pure as cleaned bone. But in the moment of seeing he moved, and once more his face was hidden in shadow. My breathing became laboured and difficult, and the old fear of suffocation returned. I would die if he left me.

"It is true," I cried, "I will not survive."

"You will do what must be done," he said. "Always."

"Can you tell me if I am wrong to wait?"

At last my mouth said the words that I had desired most to ask. I saw him raise his hands upwards in a gesture that seemed both impatient and despairing. I lay very silent and still, and waited. I was completely bound within his power of mercy. After a long time I heard the words; the words that I had feared and known, and they sounded stifled and choked.

"Passion can only bring suffering. You know this, so why must I tell it to you again?"

"But you have never - "

I began to speak, but stopped. As I had begun the words, troubled memory reminded me that this was not the first time that he had come to me. "Oh, let me see your face," I whispered, "then I will know." But the words that I whispered in my heart were not the ones that I said aloud.

"If I believed you," I said, "then I would have to die."

"Yes," he replied.

Yes.

The echo reverberating through the darkened forest. The trees, thick and impenetrable. At the top of the tallest tree a bird with white plumage. I flew from the vision, afraid.

When once more I looked outwardly he had gone. I threw the covers from my body and aroused my sex with my hands. I fondled and caressed myself until the pain of death made me still. I lay in the darkness and wanted to call out his name, but it was a name that I could no longer remember.

The long night is over, and I am seated at my desk writing down these words. How many hours are there left before I have to face sleep again? I count the hours with both anticipation and fear. One night either he or the dream will take me away. It is terrible to realise that ultimately I will have to go.

July 2

My manuscript was returned today. Over and over again I kept on saying to myself - you have nothing to offer them. You have nothing to offer them that they will ever want to receive. I read the play and imagined that I was reading it with their eyes. I was so disgusted by the words and their lack of true power that I tore the manuscript to pieces. There is no rejection when you reject yourself. I fooled myself into believing this, and turning instead to less significant action, finished painting the walls.

Later in the day I went out into the streets, but the faces of the people around me seemed so very far away. Far away and flat, as if painted on to the back-cloth of a stage set. Only one person can be real, I thought, and he is to come. He is to come, and he will have the power and the truth that transforms.

After an hour of walking I retreated from the heat of the day into the coolness of a church. Responding to an old and familiar habit I genuflected in front of the altar, then walked up one of the side aisles. At the top of the aisle I stopped before a statue of Christ, who stood there with outspread arms. Before Him was a golden candlestick in the shape of a heart, and across the heart a tight belt of iron thorns.

"Will You bring him to me," I asked?

The face of Christ was radiant in the light of the candles. I lit a candle and placed it in the centre, between the belt of thorns.

"Will You tell me when it is time to end the waiting?"

I was crying and I could not stop the tears. I saw again the manuscript between my fingers being torn into many small pieces. I had destroyed, and in the act of destruction there was no bringing together. The statue smiled down at me with the permanent smile that holy statues have. Suddenly Christ was no longer there. I looked answering my own question as I stared. No, he will not come, I said. I looked and saw nothing but plaster. Christ had gone, leaving behind Him nothing but the smiling shadow of a hollow image.

"How is it that You can help some," I asked, "but not me?"

The candle that I had placed in the thorns flickered. I thought, if the candle goes out, then that in itself will be an affirmation of His loss of presence. But the flame did not go out. The light stayed. Without looking at the statue again I walked back down the aisle of the church, and out into the street.

Where can I go? What can I do?

For a moment I stood on the pavement overcome by nausea and vertigo. I put my hand out and leant against one of the outer walls of the church, until slowly I felt the sickening sensations pass. I must keep going. I repeated the same words over and over like an incantation. Then, feeling steadier, I crossed the road and into the busy shopping area. But the deeper I went into the crowd the further I felt from them.

Is there anything left? Anything at all?

I must have said this aloud because a man laughed at me as he went by. I saw the cruel lips part, then heard the mocking sound. I ran. I escaped into a side street where I was almost sure of being on my own. I cannot remember for how long, of either hour or distance, that I was out in those streets. All that I can recall clearly is that it was twilight when I returned to my room. Yet the second I entered the room I knew that someone had been there while I had been out. I felt the lingering of a presence like a perfume. But at the same time the ghost of the presence was both comforting and disquieting. I crossed the room, and as I did so I saw the purple flower. It had been placed in a vase that I had bought months before, and the vase stood on top of a pile of books stacked in front of the window. But who had placed it there? I remembered quite clearly having left the vase hidden in a cupboard.

"Did You answer me then," I asked? "Is this Your reply?"

I was not entirely sure what I meant by the words, but I spoke gently and firmly, addressing the flower and hoping by that action to awaken within it the living reality of the departed presence. I remained standing there until the room became completely dark, then I threw myself upon the bed and fell into a deep sleep, without dreams.

July 15

I have met him.

Him.

It is far into the night, and I cannot possibly sleep. I am too happy to close my day of happiness with the betrayal of sleep. I use that word because not to think about him even for a moment would seem to be a betrayal. I might forget his face, his voice, and there is no command of dreams to make me feel sure, that in sleeping, I will remember.

I have waited for so long that it hardly seems credible that it has at last happened. The longing was so great that it had to break free. Yet as I write these words another's shadow hovers ever me, reminding, recalling. But no, I will not listen. Passion brings joy, not suffering. It was, is, nothing but my own fear that brings back this shadow. The figure dressed in white does not exist. Only the boy that I have met is real. He has nothing of shadow. I held him in my arms. I touched his body. He is real. I must confirm this. I must write it down again so that I never forget.

We met only a few hours ago, yet there appears to be no 'before' that time. I went out for my habitual walk by the sea, and he was there on the promenade, standing before my house. The sun was going down after a hot day, and he was standing there, staring up at it.

"You will hurt your eyes," I said.

He smiled and shook his head, then looked at me.

"Can you look at the sun," he asked?

His words frightened me, but despite the fear, the reflection of the sun on his face had a calming effect. Yes, I could look at it through his eyes. I told him this quite simply, as if it was the most natural thing in the world to do. He turned away as I spoke, but I could tell that it was not a refusal, only shyness.

"Where do you come from," I asked?

I began to walk in step with him. We walked facing the east, and the oncoming darkness.

"London," he replied. "And you?"

I told him, then there seemed an endlessly tense time during which we said nothing.

"I feel embarrassed with you."

He looked at me quickly as he said this, then gently put his hand in mine. We had reached the outskirts of the town, and there before us was both downland and sea.

"You mustn't feel like that," I said.

The pressure of his hand tightened in mine. He stopped walking, then turned to face me. His eyes were closed and he was waiting for me to kiss him. I kissed him, but because I felt so much my body refused to be aroused. We walked on, and I became more and more frightened that he had found me cold.

"I wanted to do that too much," I said.

"What do you mean?"

"I don't want you to find me cold."

He smiled and put his arm around my waist. We were walking on the beach, down towards the shore, and it was almost completely dark. Inside me a voice kept on repeating that for this one night we must not make love.

"Let's sit down," he said.

We sat on the pebbles. We stared at the line, very light in the darkness, of the sea. I knew that he was waiting, but I was powerless to make a move. I knew that if I touched him in the same way that I had before, then the dream would be lost.

"Can we meet again?"

I said the words with difficulty.

"Of course."

"When?"

"Tomorrow? I'm free tomorrow."

I felt relieved and happy. I started to throw stones into the sea. It was alright. Everything was alright. The tension had gone. So until two in the morning, sitting there on the beach, we talked of many things, and I knew - I was sure; deeply sure that he was the single boy that I had been waiting for. The void of my life had been filled within the space of hours.

July 21

If he doesn't love me, no one will.

Who could love this face?

My face.

I feel it with my fingers. In the mirror I stare at it in horror. I am old and ugly, and without his love there is no future left and no possible life. I detest the body that I have offered him. I hate the skin that brushes against his skin. Yet if he said that he loved me I would be transformed.

Nonsense. Nothing - no, nothing can transform a lack of beauty into its opposite. I am myself and that self is enclosed within the walls of its crumbling flesh.

July 23

I have started drinking again. After a period where I thought I had managed to give it up, it has begun again. The pills and the drink. The fog and the euphoria that keeps the illusion alive. I have frightened him and he has gone.

Peter.

He has a reality and a name. The ideal face has a name, yet as soon as I learnt to call that name he ran away. I feel numb in both body and mind... I remember that time before - but no, I must not recall the past. I am here, now, and there is no past before Peter worth recalling. I look at this page that I have written and wonder at it. I read somewhere, a long time ago, that one should constantly keep the element of surprise alive. I am surprised at my own hollow romanticism. What makes me sure that it is he whom I have been waiting for? What audacity makes me dare to presume that it is so after so short a while?

I know little about him. He has told me that he comes from London, and although he hasn't exactly said it, I gather I am not the first. But then, who is the first for anyone these days? I asked him when we could meet, and he said, "Tomorrow." Tomorrow came, and then the next day. We went out for a drink and talked some more, but each time that I brought the subject round to the possibility of a single and lasting love between us, he evaded the subject. His eyes appear to have learnt the art of evasion extremely well. They see you without seeing you. They escape sideways, glancing always to the side, like a crab.

On the third day I brought him back to my place, but no sooner were we there than he began to kiss me and caress me. Physically he wanted me very much. Yes, there was that. But I didn't want it. The whole of me cried out against it - not so soon; please, not so soon. I sat at his feet on the floor and tried to keep the distance, talking all the while, sustaining a boring and trivial monologue, hoping desperately that the naturalness between us would return. But it didn't return. He kept up an obstinate silence, looking down at his thighs, where I could all too visibly see beneath his trousers an erection. He was ready for me, and I was not responding.

"Can we wait?"

I was the first to make a direct statement, to try to break the tension. He looked at me and smiled, but said nothing. At that moment I almost hated him.

"It's important for me," I added.

"Why," he asked?

"Because I believe I am falling in love with you."

He laughed, and the sound of his laughter made me go cold. I thought of ice congealing a river. I thought of ice eternally stopping the flow. Yet there were no words to say, nothing to express the horror of coldness I felt.

"Please..."

The only word I could say. He straightened up at the sound of it, and drew his legs in. The cold shivered between us.

"Don't you want to make love to me at all?"

His voice was abrupt, almost brisk, as he asked this.

I got up off the floor and took him in my arms. I felt nothing in my body that I could call desire, yet I knew that I had to touch him now or he would go away from me forever. I caressed him, undoing his shirt, then began to lick his chest and stomach with my tongue. At the same time that I did this I thought of myself alone, lying in bed, masturbating to his image. Eventually the thought aroused me and I had an erection. We went to bed and I think he wanted me to enter him, but there was nothing I could do. I brought him to his climax, and in a simulation of passion, swallowed his sperm. I said repeatedly in my mind, this is the boy I love. This is the boy I have been waiting for. Nothing more beautiful than these moments will ever come into my life again. I hugged him to me and started to cry. He must have noticed the tears, but he did nothing to comfort me.

"I have to go home," he said.

He got off the bed and started to dress.

"Will I see you again?"

My voice sounded edgy and frightened.

"Yes."

It was all the reply I got. He left the room and I listened to him go down the stairs. It was still light outside, and from my window I watched him cross the road to the sea. "Come back," I murmured, but it was no use, I knew that he would not return. Yet strangely enough once he was gone, I could talk to him more easily. I could explain in detail my desire to wait; my longing for the physical act to unite us, not divide. I was lyricism itself in my yearning for what should be - yet constantly, hammering at me I was conscious of what was.

The facts.

A list of facts.

I am approaching thirty. He is much younger. The youth that I have is old, and my looks, the little that I had of them, are going. The mirror tells me this every day and I would be a complete fool if I did not accept this as the truth. For years I have longed for a boy like him, and now he has come. But who is he? What is he?

How dare I say I love when I know nothing about him. Yet it is precisely because I know nothing of him that I love him. This fact shrieks at me louder than the others. No. No, it is not true. If it were true - then yes, I would be incapable of love.

As I write these words the horror and the panic returns. There are not enough drinks or drugs in the world to ease this dread, the terror of the single fact - that we are all strangers. A common fact in the market place of the world, yet the unique one that has the capacity for terrible imaginative renewal. I am a stranger to myself. An unreal stranger. When has my life ever been real? Forget about the word love. What about the meaning of other words? Words like cruelty and injustice? I write about them well enough. I fill pages with their significance. I burn with them, but I am not burnt by them. In my great solitude I am protected by an invisible wall of ignorance. I see the shadow of torture; I feel the flick of the torturer's whip, yet the madness of the world is only a map of disasters held within the covers of a book. I am spared. I am spared from it all, and the empty, hollow cry of all those who suffer without my knowledge damns me to the depths of hell. Because I cannot descend with them, I cannot ascend to greater heights. I am nothing but the appearance of myself. An ageing man lying on his bed, with the slime of his own sperm covering his hands.

July 27

I have tried to contact him, but I think he has left the town. His landlady keeps on saying that he is not in, but will give me no further information. To keep despair from utterly corroding me, I am working on a play. I am drawing on the life of a German writer. Themes from the life of Heinrich von Kleist. Not exactly about his life, but motifs, motifs and themes from the pattern of his existence translated into a contemporary setting. Then again I seek within his universe correlations with my own. It is the only means that I have of relieving the ache and the terror of loneliness.

July 28

The subject that I have been avoiding I must now write about.

I walked by the sea, along the promenade, to a place that I have been to before, but have mostly tried to keep away from. It is a park where men can meet and have sex. Within the winding circle of a path that swallows itself, like the snake that swallows its tail, they meet and make contact. Last night I went to watch, clutching at the pathetic thought that I would not be drawn into the circle. I believed until last night that one can stay on the periphery, but came away with the sure knowledge that there is no periphery. We are all exactly in the centre of whatever there is.

Imagination must mingle with fact from now on. I was there, in that centre, staring out, and I had like the ancient monster, many eyes with which to see.

Death.

Yes, it is. No other word, but the skeleton of desire clothed with rejection and loss. Death. He is my shadow and my stranger, and I walk with him around the circle of the path. On benches, against walls, the mingling and the parting takes place. The old, the ugly and the beautiful join in a dance where a contrived ecstasy mockingly calls the tune. We dance with them. We see the open clothes and the limbs, hung up like dark meat, and smell the putrefaction that draws the flies. We settle like the fly upon one piece of flesh, then pass on to another. We settle upon a penis or an anus and we drink. We drink our separate brew of anonymous passion, and fall back into communal death with ashes of disease in our mouths.

Is it hell? No, that would be too easy. Hell is an absolute state and many variations of that state. It is torture and pain, and here there is no torture or pain, just a simulated imitation of joy. Hell is for the real. It is for those crucified in the absolute, not adrift in the relative. It is a place of unique suffering, and there is nothing unique on this path. How can promiscuous flesh be unique? Where is the singleness of desire in a penis erect here, an anus gaping there? Where is there anything approaching an approximation of reality in a circular world of dehumanized flesh? No, this is not hell, but a factory producing love's counterfeit.

I must pause. The cold frenzy has paralysed my fingers. The tide of agony flows backwards, retreating into my body, for there is no way of it ever flowing out. I am drowning in my own incapacity to feel. I have forgotten Peter. Peter is the well of water into which my ideal has fallen. I follow the concentric path, and avoid the water. I drown in ice. I look to the shadows, but there are no faces to see. In the factory they are manufacturing desire, but they might just as well be weapons of murder. For I realise with the horror of certainty that these men could kill as easily as they love. The further we go into the night the easier promiscuous slaughter becomes. What deaths in our century have names? No, there are no human names to remember - only the names of places and vast deserts, very often even devoid of human bones. There are no names here either, in this forest of sexual possibility. Only indiscriminate flesh lying twisted on benches of wood. Only mouths and sexual organs without impetus or identity. The coming of the sperm is as easy as the shedding of blood. For when all bodies have a relative value, then murder becomes possible. Use a body and divorce its sexuality from the world of feeling, and you can easily dispose of it; equally use a body to kill in passionless frenzy, and you can easily dispose of it. The theorem of the anonymous. The circle and the constant dance.

"Boy, go away from here."

I see the innocent walk among us. He is the one that I have dreamt of above all others, and now he has descended into our world.

"Boy, go away before you touch the blood and sperm."

In the darkness I can only clearly see his eyes. They stare at me, and at all of us, but eyes within those who have denied the power of sight, cannot respond. We are blind in our essence, in the very murder of our world.

"Will you come away?"

He approaches my body and I hear his words. He selects me from the crowd. But at the moment of coming to me he turns from me. The man next to me acknowledges his question with a silent shake of the head. He goes on to the others, each in turn, and I know in my heart that we have all been selected. That within us all he is placing the gift of giving; the gift to renounce. But the ovens of the world have not burnt for nothing; the blood stained beneath the white of bombs has done its enduring work. We must all turn from him because our failure to believe in love has been seared and finally welded within a too burning fire. Children we are too, like him, but children of a tainted dimension; a legacy of a holocaust that he, in his unborn, un-manifested innocence, did not know. Slowly, and with a terrible finality, I realise, as my brothers have realised around me, that there is nothing exceptional, nothing angelic in this visitation. He is but one of us after all - in the guise of another.

July 29

The many men, so beautiful!

And they all dead did lie.

I read these words of Coleridge, and they take on a depth of meaning that they have never had before. My despair has burnt itself out. I return to the park.

I sat on a bench and I waited. Several men passed me, turned round, slowed down, lingered near my seat, but I ignored them. About an hour later, just as I had decided to go home, a man came up to me and offered me a cigarette. It was direct, and it was spontaneous, and this made it human. I shook my head. I didn't smoke. I wanted to speak to this man, but having grown used to silence, I found that I had nothing to say. Not surprisingly he began to walk on, thinking no doubt that I had rejected him. I called him back. I was surprised at my own need. I needed communication. I needed to relieve myself of the horrors of my imagination. I called with the one word, "Please." He came up to me.

"What is your name?"

It was all that I could think to ask. Please be human, I whispered to myself. Please deny all that I have seen and thought. Tell me that this world is not a charnel-house where any manner of atrocity is possible. Tell me that.

I shook his hand when he said, "Michael." Perhaps absurdly, the mannered forms of civilization seemed essential.

"I'm Nicholas."

Who am I? A name cannot have hands, feet and a face. A name is nothing. Who am I except a butcher's shop of limbs? I thought, if the miracle happens - if the naming becomes possible, then I will be Peter. I will be he and not the person who sees this world. It was from a great inner distance that I heard Michael's voice.

"Are you as sad as you look?"

Peter could change that. Peter could bring about rebirth within me, but first I have to have his name.

"Yes, I am," I replied. "I am very sad. I am in love."

I smiled at the thought. I know nothing about you, Peter, yet I dare to say that I love you. If only I could know you, possess you, so that I would lose my own wretched identity. That is the difference between the children of God and the children of the devil, I thought. The children of God are whole within their own names; those of Satan eternally desire to possess the name of another. I almost voiced these terrible thoughts aloud. This man next to me looked kind. I felt sympathy reaching out towards me, and I needed desperately to respond. But the working of my mind could not be translated into audible words. I was silent. I was silence itself within a darkness from which I could not ascend. Yet if I did, said nothing, he would go, and the prospect of that too great a solitude terrified me. We had almost reached the limits of the park and there was only one thing left to do. I reached out and felt for his body.

"You don't have to do that," he said.

But I do. I have to keep you with me. For an hour, for a couple of hours if I am lucky. I must not be alone.

The words ached in my mouth to be spoken. I kissed him without desire. We left the park and got into his car. All the time we were in the car I kept my hand on his thigh, as if clutching at a very intimacy that I dreaded. He asked me questions about myself, most of which I answered. How do I live? The usual, inevitable question that I shrink from. Why doesn't someone ever ask - why do I live? It is the 'why' not the 'how' for me.

"Do we have to talk about it," I said?

About the machine motions of living. That's what I meant to say, but I was powerless to express it, or just plain frightened of sounding pretentious or clumsy. Yet I longed to speak of important things, but first, I knew, something else must happen. We made love. The word in relation to what I did with him sickens me. He rubbed himself against my body and came, and afterwards I lay there, thinking, what a bloody farce this is. While he was on top of me I had kept my eyes shut, and had tried to recall Peter's image, but the image wasn't so easily captured. I could no longer visualize what he looked like or even how it had felt to be in bed with him. All I could feel was the body of this stranger, groaning towards the climax of his pleasure.

He lit a cigarette in the darkness, and I reached out and stroked his face. Now that the sex was over I wanted to be gentle. I wanted quite simply to be with another human being. I asked him questions about himself. My tongue at last felt free to talk.

"Why do you go there? Can't you see what it's like?"

He raised himself up and looked down at me.

"Why do you go there," he asked?

"I don't know."

"But you do go there?"

"Yes. I went - to look," I said.

He lay back on the bed and I asked him if he was happy. The question echoed within me with dreadful insistence. To my question it was I who replied; I who would always reply with the same words.

"There is no such thing as happiness in a world gone mad with pain."

"Then why ask?"

"But that place will kill all of us," I said. "I know it will. How can there ever be hopes of lasting relationships when we give ourselves to each other so casually, so easily?"

He moved restlessly, then after a few minutes got off the bed.

"Do you want to stay the night," he asked?

He came back to the bed and switched on a side light. I saw the flabby chest, and the penis and stomach still wet with sperm. I felt sick. I saw him, but I saw myself. I said the words, this is what I am, not what I could be. This is what I am for eternity. The nausea made me unsteady as I got to my feet. I had to have air. I had to leave this place. Outside somewhere there was Peter. I had to find him. The next minutes were the most difficult to get through. In the dark I would have been able to get dressed quickly, but with the white light glaring by the side of the bed my fingers became awkward and confused. At last, after a long void of time, I was standing by the door.

"We must see some more of each other."

My reply was automatic. Unreal.

"Yes," I said, "we must."

He scribbled down his telephone number and thrust it into my hands. I left the room quickly without a backwards glance. Once outside I felt better. It was like waking up after an unpleasant dream that hasn't quite been bad enough to call a nightmare.

I sat on a bench and I waited.

They are all dead, don't you see that? They are all dead.

I am writing these words for Peter, who alone in this world is alive.

July 30

A letter from him:

Dear Nicholas,

I'm sorry I haven't contacted you before, but I've had quite a bit to do in London. There is the possibility of a community centre for gay people in the area where I stay. It's a prospect that interests me a lot, although that's a side to me I don't believe we have ever discussed. Anyway I don't think it's the place to go into it here. I'll be back within a couple of days, and will contact you as soon as I return.

Yours sincerely,

Peter.

I screwed up the letter and threw it into the furthest corner of the room. Yours fucking sincerely. Not even 'best wishes' when you hope for love. What do I care about his centre for gays? The word 'gay' hit at me with all its absurdity. If this is all there is, then I never want to see him again. Yours sincerely. No explosion there, just a miserable whimper. Peter, for God's sake, we made love. Your sperm came in my mouth. That happened. It really did. It wasn't in my imagination. I licked your body. I pushed myself so hard against your flesh that I could have inflicted pain. I was that close, and all you can write me is a business letter.

I am calmer now. The anger has gone from me. I have even unscrewed the letter, and folded it, and put it neatly away. The time on the clock says three in the morning. I have sat here for hours without even daring to think. All I know is that despite the lukewarm letter he is returning, and with that small hope, I must be patient and wait.

August 5

"Nicholas, I have to be honest with you."

That was the first thing he said when we were alone together. I had gone round to him as soon as I knew that he had returned, but I did not find him by himself. There were two 'friends' there, who he said had brought him back from London. One was a dark haired boy whom I suspected of being in love with Peter. It was all that I could do to suppress the intense feeling of jealousy that I felt. I wanted to hit out and hurt.

"Nicholas, this is Mark and Andrew. They are both concerned about the centre that I mentioned in my letter."

I shook hands with them, and tried to catch Peter's eye, but he avoided looking at me. Then we all sat down, and they carried on talking among themselves, not once trying to introduce me into the conversation. Miserably I realised that I wanted to remain apart, yet resented them for leaving me outside their group. After a while I got up from the chair where I had been sitting, and began to look through Peter's books. Why was I there? There was no sense in being there. There is nothing I have to say to you, I thought, so I had better go. Just as I was about to move towards the door both Andrew and Mark got up and said they had better be getting back to London. They left the room, without saying as much as goodbye to me, and Peter followed them. Like a child that has been deservedly, yet cruelly rejected, I could no longer control the desire to cry out.

"Peter."

I called him. He opened the door the moment I cried out. I wanted to take him in my arms, and, as well as caressing him, I wanted to hurt him physically for having abandoned me. I did neither. We stood for a long while in silence, staring at each other.

"Nicholas, I have to be honest with you."

He was the first to break the silence. His look was hard. The tone of his voice frightened me, and I felt that there was nothing I could do to reach him in any way.

"I think it's only fair that I am honest."

"Yes."

I picked up one of his books at random, stupidly thinking that this would give me time. I needed time to gain strength. I had to have strength to endure any pain that was to come.

"Does that book really interest you?"

He was smiling now. He ran a hand through his hair. The gesture excited me. I wanted him. I loved him.

"No."

"Then put it down, and stop pretending that it does. Since you came in you have done nothing but look at those books. Looking and pretending. Now, let's have a drink, shall we? I've brought some wine back. Would you like some?"

I nodded my head.

"But I didn't use the word "pretending" for nothing."

He handed me a glass of wine as he said this.

"It's about that that I want us to be honest."

"I don't understand."

Inside a voice kept repeating, give me time. Give me time. I drank the wine far too quickly, and the useless thought entered my head that I had had nothing to eat all day.

"I think you do. It's about how you think you feel about me."

"I see."

My voice sounded icy. I felt cold.

"I wish I thought you did, Nicholas."

"Is Mark your lover?"

The question came before I could even begin to want to stop it. He stood there for a moment with a completely vacant look on his face, and this suddenly made me angry.

"Is he your lover? Yes or no? There's something between you. I felt it. I certainly felt his dislike."

"Mark and I were lovers once. Not any more. Does that satisfy you?"

His voice was as coldly angry as mine. We were moving into battle positions, and the nearer we moved towards fighting, the more acutely, the more painfully I felt the loss of love.

"But he did dislike me."

"I don't know. Perhaps he did. Does it really matter?"

"I'd better go."

I moved to the door, and he moved even more quickly to stop me.

"Please," he said, "at least listen to what I have to say."

"You want to hurt - "

I projected what I felt onto him.

"I want to be truthful."

We were standing very close to one another. His face was pale and drawn, and for the first time since I had entered the room, I felt a consciousness of him. This was the real Peter in front of me. Not the boy in my solitary fantasies, but flesh and blood. Unique for me, unique from me, and by being unique, a stranger.

"Talk to me," I murmured.

In my imagination I saw a man standing naked by a bed. I saw the man that I had had sex with while Peter had been in London. The man was bending over me, the cold sperm dripping from his body onto my flesh. I cried out. I put my hand to my face. The room was closing in on me; the imaginary body pressing down upon my body. I felt as if I was suffocating. Then the next thing I knew, he was helping me into a chair.

"I felt faint. I'm sorry. I shouldn't have had that wine. You see, I haven't eaten."

"There is nothing here I can give you. Some biscuits, perhaps?"

I looked at him and smiled.

"Any better," he asked?

"Yes."

"Rest for a bit."

He knelt beside me and took my hands within his.

"What do you want us to be truthful about," I said.

"Later."

"No, now. I'm better. I'm alright."

"I want us to be honest about how we feel. No pretence."

"You know how I feel."

"I know what you have talked yourself into believing."

"Peter, no - "

I broke my hands free from his grasp and touched his face with my fingers. The words came from a depth, that had been stifled for months, for years.

"Peter, I love you."

He moved away from me, and sat back on the floor. I clenched my hands into fists to fill the emptiness.

"Do you realise what you are saying?"

His voice was trembling with emotion. He seemed near to tears. Please let him cry, I thought. If he cries, then I have got him.

"Do you?"

His voice became angry. He got up, and began pacing the room.

"Don't ask me to analyse the word," I said. "I know what I feel."

"You know next to nothing about me."

"Then let me be with you so that I can get to know you."

He shook his head.

"It wouldn't work."

"Is it because of what happened the first time we had sex? I realise I wasn't that good."

As I said this I felt an intense desire for him. Perhaps the barrier of the situation we were in managed, in some perverse way, to increase the illusion that I could have sex with him successfully. Yet even as I felt the desire I was half-conscious of my basic impotence. The duality of these feelings made me shout at him: "For God's sake, Peter, give me a chance."

That seemed to break something. His voice was gentle as he replied: "I do feel for you. That's the truth, Nicholas. I've told myself repeatedly that it won't work, and I shall probably always have to run away from you because of it."

"Why?"

"You really don't know why, do you?"

I was no longer listening to him. He could say anything now, for it would not alter those last words, that he felt for me. He felt for me. Soon he would love me. I had him.

"Come and live at my place," I said. "It's small, but we could look for somewhere bigger."

I was drunk with my own increasing certainty. It was only after a few minutes of long silence that I saw he was actually in tears.

"Can't you begin to understand other people?"

He spat the words at me, and I saw that the anger was returning.

"That's why. Don't you see none of this is real? I would like it to be real, but it just isn't."

I put my arms round him, and we stood there in the middle of the room, without speaking, clinging together.

"Come to bed."

For a while there had to be an end to words. At that moment it was important that I prove to him that I could be good at sex.

"I want to show you," I said.

I kissed his eyes, then I put my tongue gently into his mouth. The image of the perfect boy broke to the surface of my mind. The image made me literally frantic with passion. I pulled at his clothes, and at my own, and there, standing in the middle of the room, I fucked him. As I came he buckled under me and we fell onto the carpet. The cries that I had imagined to be those of pleasure were in fact sobs. His face was wet with tears.

"Don't - " I said.

He got to his feet and arranged his clothes.

"But what about you," I asked? "You didn't come."

He looked down at me.

"It doesn't matter."

I am trying to record as accurately as possible what happened. I am alone in my room. We talked some more and I pleaded some more for him to give me a chance. I'm not going to write anything else down of that conversation, except a few words that he said just before I left. We had arranged to meet the following day (which is today) and he murmured quietly, almost as if he didn't want me to hear: "I don't know yet if I will be able to bear being in love."

I wanted to reply to this, but the intensity of his words forced me to silence. When I left him I felt a burning pain in my penis. It was both an ache and a fire.

August 12

Days of happiness. He is mine. There are few words spoken between us, yet in the essential I feel that there is little to say. Some nights he stays in my room; others I go to his. I would like him to live with me, but I cannot approach the subject again. I cannot help but recall his sobbing, and the tears on his face when I made love to him. There is a pain there that I dare not think of.

"The longing is too great, Nicholas."

When I do think of the pain those words return. No, no it is not true. I will not let the stranger haunt me. Peter is all that I need; all that I will ever desire. He is my future, and he will contain me utterly.

August 13

There is no escaping my dreams. Within the dream the house is dark and quiet, and the wide, circular staircase leads me upwards to the topmost room. Inside the room I hear the door being closed behind me, and when I go to open it, I find that it has been locked from the outside. At first I cry out, and hit at the door with my hands, but after a while I know that no one will come, and resign myself to my prison. There is no light except from the moon, which struggles feebly through thickly cobwebbed windows. I go to the wall directly facing me, and stand there for a long time, feeling its rough surface with my fingers.

"Do you ignore me still, Nicholas?"

The words are clear and precise. They seem to come from the wall, yet at the same time they echo all around me. I draw back in terror.

"Look at me."

The command makes me shudder. I run to the door, screaming to be let out, then slide to my knees, exhausted with fear.

"Look at me. Yes, here. Here."

The voice is close by. At my side, in a strangely mottled pool of light, I see what I imagine to be a large toad staring up at me. This is madness, Nicholas, wake up. I touch my skin and pinch myself, hoping desperately that I will awaken in my bed. But the dream persists, and the toad hops closer towards me. Its body is bloated and swollen, and I cannot conceive that the words I have heard could have come from that mouth.

"Is this the dream that you have been waiting for? Is this the Prince?"

The words come from the wall, and not from the toad. The creature hops nearer, then with one horrifying leap, hops upon my hand. I shout out my disgust, and try to shake my hand free, but there is no freedom from the slimy heaviness of the toad's body. I carry my hand backwards, and feel the flesh of a soft leg pressing against my palm. A moment later the hand is free, and I realise that I have thrown the monster from me. I cross the room to where I have thrown the toad. It lies there against the wall, with its head smashed open.

"Nicholas."

The scream awakens me. My hands are clutching at flesh, and in that instant I know that I have been trying to throttle Peter. He is struggling beneath me, and my fingers are tearing at the flesh on his shoulders, just below the neck.

"Nicholas, stop - "

I release the hold my fingers have had on him. He sits up, rubbing at the wounded skin.

"I was dreaming," I said.

There is no excuse. I bury my face in my hands. He reaches out and murmurs, "It's alright," but nothing is alright because I had wanted to murder him. I know this, and in the fact of that knowledge I am stripped bare of all illusions.

"Don't go. It's alright."

He is pulling at me to stop me getting out of bed, but there is no place for me in that bed next to him. I must get away at once from the proximity of his body.

"Don't you know what I tried to do?"

His voice comes from a long way away, and it doesn't sound like his voice at all. He is attempting to understand, and I am revolted by that understanding.

"It was a nightmare. I know, Nicholas, that it was only a nightmare."

I struggle against the words, but there is no holding them back. The force that impelled me to kill the toad is still working within me.

"I wanted to do it," I cry. "It was you in the dream that I had to destroy."

I put on my clothes. The torture of what I have done is pressing down on me. I can no longer stop either my words or my actions.

"We must never sleep together again," I say.

I am trembling, and he is by my side. I shrink away from him as he touches my skin. I know that if he touches me once more I will strike out, and it will be the end. I stare at him, and suddenly, brutally, the revelation of the dream returns. He is as ugly as the toad.

"Let me go."

He pauses a moment before answering.

"If that is what you want."

In the palm of my hand I can still feel the impress of the slimy leg. I make the gesture of throwing, and the involuntary scream that comes from my mouth pushes me with all its force of horror from the room.

I am out in the streets. I run towards the sea, and when I reach the shore I fall to my knees and splash sea water over my face.

"Nicholas, look at me."

The voice is behind me. I dare not turn round, for if do I know I will die.

"I will die," I say aloud.

The voice replies: "If you believe that, then have the courage to look upon the face of your death."

I turn my head towards the voice, and there in the moonlight I see the stranger dressed in white. I dare not look at his face. He whispers slowly, mockingly, "Didn't I tell you it all? Passion is suffering."

He comes to me, and reaches down to take me by the hand. I look up into the face that I have avoided, and see the crushed head of the toad. I push his body violently away and start to run. Gasping and crying, I struggle to reach the safety of my room. But as I run, I hear him following, laughing.

I am in my room. I am trying to suppress the panic so I can write this down. I desire sleep, yet am terrified to close my eyes in case I dream. There is a knocking on my door, and I know that it is Peter trying to make contact, wanting to come in.

"Are you better?"

His voice, like the voice in the nightmare room, is precise and clear. As he talks I stare at the marks on his shoulders and neck.

"I did that to you."

I say the words. As I utter them I realise how inadequate language is to express the shock of murder. There is no way that I can convey to Peter the complexity of my longing for his annihilation.

"I will have to go away."

He is talking to me.

"You understand that I need to go away."

I nod my head. He is speaking to me as if I were a child. He is talking to me, and it is baby talk. I want to reach out and rub at the red marks with my hands.

"I need to go so I can think. We both need space."

I cannot think. The process of thought is like a machine that has become finally clogged. I see myself before that machine, begging it to start. The image is nonsensical and I laugh. He sees me, hears me laughing, and I know that the laughter will drive him from me. I know this, but cannot stop. What is there to talk about or to say? The world has at last broken down.

"I want - "

I stutter the words. He gets up from the chair where he has been sitting, and crosses the room to the door. I feel like an invalid trapped in my chair, unable to move. In a moment he will be gone, and still the laughter forces itself out between the choked and stuttering words: "I want - "

"What?" he says turning to look at me.

In my mind I formulate the sentence - I want to kiss the marks. But it is too late. The door shuts, and I am powerless to call him back. Out of the corner of my eye, standing by the bed, I see the stranger. He looks exactly like Peter, yet I know it is not him.

"Did you really think that death comes so easily? Your belief is not yet strong enough, my friend."

He sits on the bed, and I remember a night when I had lain there naked before him.

"I don't know anything anymore," I say.

He smiles at me, then gently, lightly, smoothes out a crease on the cover of my bed.

"But now that Peter has gone you must not desire him back."

"That's not possible," I reply.

"Why not? He doesn't exist. You know he doesn't exist. If he did, would I look like him?"

He reaches up to his face, and with a quick, wrenching gesture, pulls at Peter's features. The face comes away like a mask, and there beneath I see my own marked skin and look into my own dark eyes.

"It's a trick," I say.

"No."

"It's a mask."

"I never wear masks."

His hands are empty. There is no mask there. He raises them up for me to see.

"I am simply destroying a resemblance," he says.

He shakes his head and starts laughing. The voice and the laughter are my own.

"Do you remember that night when you asked me why I wore a white suit? And I replied asking you what you would have me wear?"

I look at him, and the scarred and pitted face fascinates me despite myself. I get up from the chair, suddenly released from my bondage, and cross the space that separates us.

"Yes," I reply.

My voice is thick, and my breath is coming rapidly. I am beginning to feel desire.

"Well, what would you have me wear?"

He is taking off his suit, and although I know I will recognise the body, a tremor of excited anticipation runs through my flesh. I want him. I want him to know me, to feel me. I am delirious with the recognition of the division of my own self. And yet I need him and his sexuality precisely because he is other.

"Wear nothing," I say.

"But it is not only this white suit that can be thrown aside. Identity too. Identity must go. Nothing is the final resolve of all passion. Peter is nothing. Peter is dead. You killed him, and he walked away."

I turn off the light by the bed, and he reaches out and draws my body down to his own.

August 15

There is no one that I can turn to.

No one.

I lay in the darkness. Peter had gone, and the telephone was silent.

No one.

I realised that if I did not talk to someone then I would go mad. Someone. Someone, please.

My God, what to do with the pain? What to do with it?

Then at last I acted. I looked for the number that Michael had given me. I reached for the telephone, and dialled.

"It's Nicholas. Do you remember me?"

His voice replied: "Of course I remember."

"I'd like to talk."

There - it was said, and after that the rest came easily. He told me that he would be free at nine, and could see me then. I got up. There was something now to get up for. I had been lying in this bed of darkness for so long. And yet while I had lain there, there had been one moment; a moment of something else - outside I had heard a bird singing. I had remembered then a long, long time ago when I had been a child. A small boy staying with relatives on a farm. I recalled shutters at the windows, and outside the windows a bird, singing. The memory of that bird's song was filled with other memories. All the associations, smells and sounds of a spring dawn, and I had leapt eagerly out of bed, throwing open the shutters, longing for the day to really begin... But there was no leaping now. No shutters to reach up for, with a child's urgent fingers. Nothing of hope and no spring. My body felt heavy and old.

I dressed in my best clothes. I left the house at seven, and it being far too early to go to Michael, I went to one of the bars. I sat there on a bar stool and drank steadily. In order to not have to look at anything else around me I concentrated my attention on a bottle filled with a green liqueur. It looked like liquid drained off from a stagnant pond. Then suddenly I felt that I was going to vomit, and stumbled away from the bar. I went to the toilet, retched, but nothing came. After standing there for a long while with my mouth open over the bowl, uselessly gagging, I threw water over my face, then made my way to the nearest telephone. Feeling thoroughly ill, I rang Michael. He told me to get a taxi, which I presumed was to be at his expense. Outside the bar it was pouring with rain, and I walked instead.

The rest of the night passed like a slow-moving nightmare. I can't remember much, except his caring and fragments of my own abominable behaviour. At one point I had thought it better to leave, but had been unable to go. The combination of pills and drink had paralysed my legs, and I had realised then that I was moving slowly, but inexorably towards a state of hallucination. I was on the brink of the maelstrom, looking down.

Yet there was an experience there that brought me a few minimal expectations of what it would be like to exist in a state of order and sanity. As I write these words the recollection of those elusive expectations shines out in the gathering darkness. Michael had left me alone, and I had picked up a book. The first words that I read were two lines of poetry:

'Insomnia of swallows. The calmness of the friend who waits at the station.'

Two lines of words, and they glowed through me with the warmth and insistence of love. The slender thread; the thread of Ariadne, leading me out, leading me beyond a world of torment that I had created for myself. And there I was, safely out of the darkness, out of the labyrinth of my disillusion, standing in the bright centre of a hope that was good. The knowledge that I could hope for hope was the smallest, yet greatest of those expectations that the poem had inspired. The bigger waking dream was that I could actually love.

Michael had stood there, with a bundle of sheets and blankets in his arms.

"It's a beautiful poem," I said.

I knew perfectly well that he had not understood, yet I liked him. I could talk to him without the dangerous expression that a deeper hope desires. He was warm, and he was there, and the least I could do was try to transmit to him a little of what I felt.

"It's one of the most beautiful poems I have ever read. Never to sleep. Do you realise that? Never to close your eyes until you get to the station - until you arrive. And when you arrive he is waiting there, and he has always been waiting there."

He asked about Peter. Yes, I had told him about Peter, or had I? It was all so uncertain and confused. Yes, there was Peter. But more. Much more. I think I said the word, "Him," and in that word I saw the boy made of light. Perfect light without shadow, standing directly beneath the glare of the sun. Then the vision went, and I was there, alone in the room with Michael.

"For whom do you live?"

I wanted to know. I wanted to know if this man who had been so patient with me, felt even a little of what I felt. I had to know, because in that sharing, perhaps, after all, I could ease the solitude. But the light could only decrease, not increase. Then he left me to myself. Inside me the vision was dying, and worse, the black night was already laying itself heavily across my body.

"Michael."

I called his name once, frightened of the invading panic and the terror just about to explode. I stretched myself out and stared up at the ceiling. I thought of Peter, wondering where he was, and who he was with. Then the room started to slide away from beneath my body. The hallucination was beginning. I was lying in a black circle of darkness, and there, on the furthest rim of light, I could see Peter's face, and upon that face an expression of mocking disgust. I crawled on my hands and knees to get to him. I moved painfully over a sliding, plunging ground. The vertigo of touch was as sharp as knives.

"I will kill you."

I screamed the words. My hands reached out and I caught at his hair. The light at the edge of darkness had not been light at all, but the contained, white brightness of his hair. I entwined his hair savagely between my fingers. I wanted to darken the whiteness, blacken the contained illumination of his presence.

"I will kill you."

The words hissed at him like snakes. I heard his breathing and felt his fear. I was tortured by the realisation that I could release myself only in murder. My fingers tore out and extinguished the light of his hair, then they crossed the space of the face, covering the mouth. How wide his face was, like a universe to explore. And all the time, with dreadful slowness, I knew that I was approaching the throat. In a moment, in an hour; in a measure of time that would reach and go beyond the years, I would clasp at his slender neck and be the cause of his death.

"No, no, no." The cries saved him. At the moment of death I was letting him go. He ran from me, leaving me in total darkness. But there was someone else at my side. Inside the circular shell of death I was not alone, but held, and the invisible arms were lifting me up, and words were said to exorcise the desire to kill.

"I am here. It's alright. The stranger is here. Be calm, for this is not the death you need."

I sobbed and hugged him to me. In the very worst of myself I knew that I was known.

That was yesterday, and I can say with no great sense of assurance that it was mostly a dream. But Michael - he was there. Despite everything he is more real to me than the others. I move in a landscape that is becoming increasingly bereft of figures. I see the stranger, and I see Peter, yet they are nothing but shadows. I see Michael, and fragmentary though the vision is, he stands on solid ground. It is at this point that I must try to elucidate a contradiction within myself. With great difficulty I can recall trying to seduce him, even though I had no apparent desire for him. Why? Why should I have tried to seduce him? I cannot remember that heavy body without a sensation of nausea, yet I know perfectly well that I had wanted us to have sex. Then the quiet thought comes to me and eases the anguish - you had tried because he is real. Could it be that I had wanted to touch him simply because he is the only one who is made of flesh and blood? Could it be that he reminds me that the body exists in another form than my own? I don't know, yet I do know. The words will not express a need that fails to be defined.

Michael is there.

How simple it is when I just say those words and leave it at that.

August 29

For nearly two weeks I have avoided this diary. I have stayed, a self-imposed prisoner, in my room. The windows have been shut and the curtains drawn. The weather is suffocatingly hot, and because it is so hot it gives me an exterior reason not to think or move. I have tried to empty my body of all need for sensation, and my mind of all desire to dream and think. Once a day I turn on a lamp, and for a while, by the aid of artificial light stare at my purple flower. I know this helps me, but I cannot say in what way.

For nearly two weeks I have lived like this, and the present I live in must now become the past. My body and my mind have been moved to action again. The night of my room is over. Peter has returned.

I awoke that morning after a night of dreamless sleep to hear a knocking on my door. At first I thought it was Michael and made no reply. The knocking continued, and driven to anger because my solitude had been disturbed, I called out to whoever it was to go away.

"Nicholas, it's me - Peter."

On hearing his voice I felt such a strong impulse towards happiness that I could hardly reply. I called out to him, telling him that I was coming to open the door, but he could not have heard for the knocking continued.

"Nicholas, are you alright?"

I opened the door. The sudden glare of the sun reflected in the hall hurt my eyes. I was no longer used to intense light. I had only been out of the house twice since I had shut myself in my room, and on both occasions it had been for the sole purpose of obtaining food.

"This place smells awful."

He walked past me without any gesture towards touching me, and drawing back the curtains, opened the windows. Sunlight flooded in, and I saw for the first time what a terrible mess I had let the place become.

"What have you been doing?"

He turned, and stood with his back to the light. He was dressed almost entirely in white clothes, and looked more beautiful than any image I had made of him in my imagination. I wanted to hold him, but felt ashamed of my dirty clothes and unwashed body.

"Answer me," he said.

"Nothing," I replied. "I have been doing nothing."

"You look ill. Have you been eating?"

His concern made me feel loved.

"Not much. I couldn't."

"Well, you can now. We'll go out. We'll buy food."

He made just one move towards me, then stopped. The very brightness of him was dazzling in the sudden light of the room. I couldn't bear to look at him for too long. I picked up my watch to see what time it was, but then realised that of course it had not been working for days. And as I made this small gesture of doing, I ached for him. But before touching him I would have to make myself amputate the invisible limbs of my own incarceration; amputate the reality of my own stinking flesh that had turned rotten with waiting. I would cut away what I was, what I had been, with the icy knives of water. Everything, including the surroundings, would have to be worthy of him. At that moment I would have destroyed myself completely if it had been possible to make myself anew.

"I must do the room."

Hurriedly I made the bed, and tried to straighten out the room. He stood watching me, and there was an undertone of laughter in his voice as he singled out a dirty plate, and pointing to it said: "Which do you think I would prefer tidied up and clean? That or you?"

I caught his eye and laughed. The tone of his voice made it alright. I felt safe with him. I felt secure. He had come back. There was no longer any need for darkness; and all the phantoms, all the fears of the night were best forgotten.

"Go and have a bath," he said. "I'll clean up the room."

I wanted nothing more than to obey him. It was so good to hear him make decisions, to let him be in the position of control. In the bath I lay in the water for a long time, and as I lay there in the cold water that I had poured for myself, I imagined him giving himself to me. He was bending over and I was entering him. My cock was frozen cold in its power of erection, and there was intense pain as it encountered the heat of his body. It was as if I wanted to counter balance his dominance by my own icy physical assertion. In fantasy my clean-created flesh was new to any warmth. And yet it was he, in the first place who had ordered the re-creation of my body. Naked, I returned to the room.

"I want you."

Those were the last words I had said to him before he had left me. I remembered that moment quite clearly. Without waiting for his reply I took him in my arms. I kissed his neck and the place where the marks had been.

"Do you want me?"

With my tongue I licked the question into his ear.

"Yes."

"Are you sure?"

"Yes, I am sure."

"It was all a mistake, Peter. The night is over now."

"Don't talk."

He caressed me, biting and licking at my flesh. His touch gave me warmth, gave me life. Then he stood back and took off his clothes. In the full light of the day I made him spread himself naked on the bed. Slowly and with exquisite pleasure I studied every detail of his body. But at the moment when the possibility of fucking him was a reality I lost my erection. I made him come without coming myself. My penis, in my imagination still made of ice, denied me the power of inflicting pain within him.

"I thought I was going mad."

We lay side by side on the bed, and I felt the urgent necessity to tell him everything. Now that the ritual return of our sexual need was over he was willing to listen.

"What exactly happened while I was away?"

His voice was precise. Each word was pronounced slowly. I had an impression of great clarity. It was as if I could see through the actual sound of his voice, and through this glass vision of purest sound contemplate all the recent happenings. Once more I experienced the hope for hope inspired by the poem I had read in Michael's room. I told him about the poem. I told him how for once the world with all its torments had offered a glimpse of sanity and order; how in a moment there had been a sort of simplicity inspired by the most minimal expectations of what life could be like. He pressed my hand tightly within his as he replied: "Things can be uncomplicated. Easy to understand."

"No," I said. "Not that."

Suddenly his voice appeared to me no longer clear, but heavy and dull. Uncomplicated. Easy. No, I had not meant that at all. Simplicity was not a denial of complication. My very soul rebelled against the statement he had made. Intuitively I realised it was a statement that signified that he had understood nothing. Terrified of this alienating realisation, I stared hard at him. He had not understood precisely because he was not as I had imagined him to be. Yes, the dream of the perfect boy standing beneath the glare of the sun. Looking at him I saw that he came nowhere near the reality of that vision. Yet only a short while ago I had studied every line, every contour of his body and found it perfect. I had looked, it was true, but I had not seen. From a great distance I heard his words.

"I said the wrong thing, didn't I?"

He sighed and pressed against me.

"I know your pain," he said. "I know the cause of it."

What do you know? I couldn't say the words, but lay there in stunned silence, abruptly, brutally isolated from him. Uncomplicated and easy. By the choice of those words he had debased the moment that I had experienced and wanted to express into something trivial.

"I know we can never be totally one another," he said. "It is that you find hardest to accept."

The sound of his voice now possessed the power of inflicting pain. If the previous magic of that sound had been illusion, this was reality. The pain was almost unbearable. I heard what he had to say, and the words conveyed the truth of his separateness. In that truth was my torture. I had amputated the invisible body of my imperfection to unite myself wholly within his beauty. Now there was no beauty, only corruptible division. I kept my eyes shut. I could no longer bear to look. My hand in his was wet with perspiration. I took it away and wiped it down the side of my body.

"I know," I said.

What I knew was a divided truth that had the force of destruction. At last I opened my eyes. I had not felt him go, but there he was, standing in front of the window. As he had his back to me, his face was hidden. He could have had any face. The agony of my solitude forced me to reach out.

"Help me," I cried.

The light was fading in the room. The strength of the day was dying. Outside it was getting dark. The visionary boy of light was made of flesh, and it was this human, living boy that I was condemned to love until the day of my death. He returned to the bed, and lying down beside me said: "Will you promise never to shut yourself up again?"

"I had to do it. I believed that I could not live in the world without you."

My voice sounded weak. I was trembling after the shock of so much inner and outer contradiction.

"Closing yourself in is not ever going to bring me back."

"But it did bring you back."

"If I had known - "

He began the sentence, then stopped.

"Yes?"

"Do you want me to tell you about what I was doing? I would like you to be interested."

I nodded my head. I couldn't speak. The thought of using more words made me feel physically sick.

"Prospects for the community centre are good. It'll take time, of course, and then we do need more support than we have. Financial support mostly. Really, I would like you to be interested."

Not only was the dream destroyed, but he was trying to lead me into a world that could have no possible reality for me. If I had not felt so sick, I would have laughed. It seemed that the feet of my divine boy were made of communal clay after all.

"The area is poor, and there could well be hostility. A centre in North London had its windows broken last week. The words - no place for queers - were daubed on the walls and doors with paint."

"That's horrible."

I had used an unconvincing adjective. Atrocity was horrible, but not broken glass and smears of paint. I thought of how he had mentioned the word 'we', and the name of Mark came to mind. For a moment I suffered a stab of pure pain. I knew too that I could never be included in the 'we'. There was anger in my voice as I replied to what he had said.

"I feel no grief for smashed windows. Worse things happen. Have happened."

"Does that make it any the less bad?"

I wanted to mention my play and the endless, real slaughter in the world. I wanted to talk about the concentration camps and the Jewish child. I wanted to talk about the worst atrocity of all, the silence of orthodox Catholics when confronted with the truth. But there was no possible way of expressing these matters to him. I saw him as being immersed in a rock pool, while I was drowning in the sea.

"We don't feel strongly about the same things, and can't, it seems," I said.

"But each stone that they throw is a stone thrown at you."

I couldn't see it like that and said so. I felt no obligation to identify with a group of people that I considered myself only technically a part of. And the boy of my dreams - could he really be a part of it? I moved away from Peter and got dressed.

"Maybe we are fooling ourselves, but we do believe we can do something to help."

His voice sounded hurt, but there was no way now that I could convincingly reach out to him. 'Peter,' I thought, 'I am not in you and you are not in me.'

"When you say 'we' do you mean Mark and you?"

There, I had said it.

"Mark and I, and others. There are a lot of us who care."

"And a lot of us who don't."

If there was any guilt in that statement I had not meant it to be there. Rather I felt angry and sickened with him for wanting me to feel guilty.

"Don't let's quarrel about it," he said. "I won't mention the subject again."

There was a note in his voice that seemed to want to pacify me, and it was this that made me continue. Despite everything that warned against, I had to have my say.

"Other things I can understand. More terrible oppressions and torture, yes. The earth stinks of torture - and in comparison stones thrown at windows are nothing."

"It isn't as simple as that. You have to be on the receiving end to know."

"The entire universe has been on the receiving end since it was created. It's all a bloody abomination that we can do next to nothing about."

I was breathing hard. I hadn't wanted to speak, yet already I had said too much. I was suffocating under the nauseating burden of my own biased truth.

"Yet it's precisely that next to nothing that is important. The rest is just theory and abstraction. I was never in a gas chamber or a torture cell, and if it comes to that neither have you. You cannot imagine those things. But I have been inside a community centre for homosexuals that was threatened by hostility and ignorance. That was real."

Real. My hand wanted to lift itself and strike out at his body. I wanted to see and feel his reaction to an unreasoning, futile pain. The gathering tears scalded my eyes and I turned away. He was like a flame that would burn me with his wretched reality. I said as flatly as I could, "Shall we go out and eat?"

There was nothing else that I could say, but later that evening I felt close to him again. Once more the illusion came alive. I drank a lot, and under the influence of that drink he became again the boy I wanted him to be.

2. The closed room.

I do not know the day or the hour. He has left me for the night, and in my need for guidance I have just opened the Bible. The words that I read there speak for themselves:

'And the Lord hath given a commandment concerning thee, that no more of thy name be sown: out of the house of thy gods will I cut off the graven image: I will make thy grave; for thou art vile.'

I throw the book from me, but it will always be there. It is the one book that cannot be destroyed, and like lightning it has struck me down.

October 2

There is nowhere left for me to run, yet I go through the motion of running. Peter is with me most of the time, yet there are days when I have to escape from him. One afternoon while we were out together, I saw Michael on the opposite side of the street, but I was incapable of making the slightest sign of acknowledgement. Run. I have to run. Away from myself - and them.

Yesterday I caught a train to London. There was no other reason to catch that train than the thought of being on a vehicle that was moving fast and away. I sat in the train and watched the autumnal scene go past. The trees were covered in a white mist, and the whole of the countryside appeared as if behind a thin veil. And there I was in the compartment of the train, longing to tear the veil aside - but to get to what? I knew that there was nothing beyond that veil but my own death.

I reached London, avoiding the streets as much as I could, spending almost the whole of the day in a park. I thought of my play and the work I had to do; I filled myself with a sense of optimism that deep down I really did not feel. But the work must be done. It must be done. The work must be finished when you go. These words repeated themselves endlessly in my mind as I walked beneath the damp trees. Then suddenly I knew what I had to do; the false optimism opened up like a cloudy sky on a winter's day, and a fleeting light of real hope fell upon me.

"You will die."

The voice outside, inside, both a part of and yet totally detached from me.

"Yes, you must die, but you need not die alone. You can join with Peter in death and take him with you."

For a moment I thought I would have to scream. My body shook, and I could hardly stand. I pressed myself against the nearest tree, as if wanting to obliterate myself within the very bark. The pain was such intense happiness that I believed I would break and die under it. Yet the sustaining vision of a future death with Peter kept me alive, and somehow I managed to walk on. As I walked I tried to clear my mind of any remaining confusion and doubt. I was going to die, but not alone. I tried to make these thoughts as rational as possible. What followed then was an interrogation of my desires, and above all of my desire to kill.

"Why did you try to murder him?"

"It was the first revelation of my desire to join with him in death. I realise that now."

"But wasn't it also a revealing intuition of your capacity to kill - an anonymous, terrible passion to kill, without any sense of discrimination or desire?"

"No. No, it was not that."

"Are you sure?"

I wasn't sure. I was far from sure, but all the same I hurried on through the park, murmuring the reply to my own words.

"No, it wasn't like that."

For a while the voice was quiet, then the interrogation began again.

"Have you ever considered that perhaps you wanted to kill him because he was beginning to lose the magical, ideal form that you had endowed him with? That you wanted to end his life precisely because it was replaceable?"

"I could replace him without having to kill him?"

"But if he was alive he would be a constant reproach. He would always be reminding you that the ideal exists only within you."

"Don't speak like that, as if he were already dead. He is alive."

"Were you not afraid that he was becoming less than the ideal? That he was becoming ordinary? Ordinary and anonymous, like the other boys and men that you have met before? Or worse still, that the ideal would literally become the monster? The Prince become the toad."

"No, you are wrong. My desire for his death was the first proof of my desire for him to join me in dying."

"That's what you would like to think."

These last words were said quickly. The white mist covering the trees was dissolving into water. A thin fall of rain began to seep in between my clothes wetting my skin. I started to run towards a shelter in the park.

"There is nowhere left for you to run." The voice began again, and out of the corner of my eye I thought I saw the figure of the stranger running in the opposite direction to myself. I called out, but there was no name to call. The voice continued its questioning.

"Peter is losing what you thought was unique. You know that he is becoming like the rest."

"No."

"Replaceable."

"I could replace him without having to kill him?"

"Then why keep questioning that one statement? My dear Nicholas, you are asking me."

"No."

"The days you have to escape from him; the days like today. You leave him because you cannot bear seeing him for what he is. For who he is."

"I cannot bear being in the presence of the one boy I want to become a part of. I cannot bear the impossibility that a separate life together means."

"So you want his death."

"I want our death."

"His and yours?"

"Ours."

"But he is separate from you. He will always be separate from you."

"Death will unite us."

"There will be no meeting in death. There will be no more a meeting between you in death than there has been in life. Let him go."

"Life is separating us. Death will unite us. I am sure now that it is possible. And if he wants to die with me, then that alone is proof enough that he is the personification of the ideal."

"What if he wants to live?"

I reached the shelter. I stared out at the water falling from the sky. I could not reply to that question.

"You are a fraud, Nicholas. Man loves and kills with fatal anonymity. That is the truth. The only truth beyond this fallacy of illusion that you must create for yourself."

"I can't believe that."

"Love and death are both meaningless acts in a brutal world. What meaning they do have in the world is transitory and relative."

"No."

"Alright, believe in the lie, but remember that even if you convince him that he wants death, I know that he will prefer to live."

"Who are you?"

I turned round as if expecting to see the voice, as if expecting to see the words, but the words I did see were these, written on the walls of the shelter: 'fucking the arse off a pretty boy is lovely.' My stomach churned over with an even stronger desire to finish it all. With the end of a key I scratched out the words, and as I completed this action a cold sweat began to pour down both my face and my hands. A hideous sound of laughter seemed to echo round the walls of the shelter. The voice cried: "You can't do it without pain. You can't fuck without pain, and it makes you sick because others can."

I ran from the place. I caught the first train that I could back to my town. No sooner had I found a seat than a handsome youth sat down opposite me. My clothes were drenched, and I was painfully conscious of my own physical imperfection. The presence of this beautiful boy placed me in hell, but I could not move my limbs to escape from him. That is why I must die, I thought. I must die because compared to someone like him I am not perfect enough to live. From that thought it was but a step to a more terrible, yet pitifully logical realisation. There is no place in this world, I thought, for people less perfect than this boy. There can be no home for the ugly and the weak.

During the journey there was a breakdown on the line, and for what appeared like an eternity we remained in the same place, the rain pouring monotonously against the windows.

"Does this happen often?"

He smiled at me.

"I don't know."

Nothing in me was capable of smiling back. I looked out at the heavy wall of rain, but even there through the glass, I saw his reflection.

"I hope we get going soon. She's going to be furious, waiting for me at that station."

"Insomnia of swallows..."

I choked back the words. I closed my eyes, but there was no escaping the image of the poem, or the burning presence of the boy.

While I am writing Peter is seated in the room. He is reading a book, and has absolutely no knowledge of what is written here. I could look up and I could ask him, 'Will you die with me?', but the words remain on paper. For a moment before the interrogation began I had been sure, but now I no longer know. Yet what I do know is the impossibility of living with him and maintaining the level of ecstasy and happiness that I need. If only death could be that final and welding pull of desire. If only it was certain that in dying we could become one, but the doubt is, and always will, remain. I stare at him, and his beauty reminds me that it is corruptible and must fade. I look at the skin on his face, then look at his eyes, and realise that they are doomed to become nothing more than dust and water. I watch him as he puts the book down.

"I must get back to my place."

He smiles at me. Although I want to be on my own I dread him leaving for a reason that does not relate to myself.

"Is there anything that you have to do there? If there is, can't it wait?"

Will the jealousy never end?

"Mark has been raising money this week. He's organizing a dance to raise funds for the centre."

I tell myself that I don't want to know anything about it.

"Then you had better go home, hadn't you, if you are expecting to hear from him?"

There is a barely controlled note of anger in my voice. Jealousy torments me. There is no way as yet that I can tell him that I want him to die with me. I must be patient. And in the meantime I must put up with Mark, and the constant reminding that his very existence implies of a world that I long to leave. I look at Peter. I too smile. Getting up from my chair I cross the room and caress his face gently with my hands. I bend down and kiss his forehead. I must be patient, I tell myself, but to him I say: "I think I might see a film."

"Yes. Do that."

Once more that smile.

I then add that I will walk with him as far as his place before I leave him.

October 3

Last night I met Michael in the cinema queue. He was there with friends protesting about the films. I thought, this is Peter's world. He would understand this. When he came up to me he put a leaflet in my hand.

"So you wear badges?"

I reached out and touched the red words on a yellow background - 'Glad to be Gay.' The words were a mockery. For me there was no gladness, only an impossible happiness, but how could I begin to tell Michael that? But I could tell him how sorry I was for my behaviour the last time I had been with him, and did.

"Don't be sorry. Just don't do it again."

He took me for a drink. While we were talking I thought of Peter going to his place for news of Mark, and all the time I thought about it I had to fight back a feeling of savage resentment. He had friends. He had people to turn to, to care for him, but I had nobody. Nobody except Michael. Michael was my friend. I had this one person in the world who liked me, and I had to introduce him to Peter. I had to show Peter that someone cared.

"I'm happy."

In the same way that I had to let Peter know I had a friend, I had to show Michael that I had a lover. It was suddenly essential that they should both know that I was not alone.

"I'm happy, and happy and happy. Peter's come back - and

he'll never leave me again."

The repetition of the word 'happy' so many times was ludicrous, yet in a way it served as an incantation to ensure that I was. I trembled with the word. The impossible happiness was possible after all. I wanted to reach out and hug Michael to me. He cared. Peter cared. How rich I was with this word happiness. I felt buoyant with joy; dangerously so, for I was conscious all the time that this excess of light held its own terrible darkness. For in that world of night Peter was my victim and I his destroyer. However much I repeated the word happiness, it could only truly be that in conjunction with his death. But for the present there was to be a necessary rejection of darkness.

"Come on, I want you to meet Peter."

We walked to Peter's place in silence, and every now and then I touched Michael as if to make absurdly sure that he was still there. When we arrived it seemed an interminably long time before the sound of the ringing bell was answered. I heard it echo in the house; echo back to me a solitude and an emptiness that I dreaded. At last Peter appeared on the doorstep.

"I thought you had gone to the cinema?"

Then he turned to Michael with a questioning look, and I introduced them. I could sense at once that he was not pleased that we had come. For a moment I wondered if there was anyone there with him in his room. Was that why he had been so long in answering? But once inside I saw that there was no one there. When he said he would make some tea, I followed him into the kitchen, but in a sulky, almost angry voice he told me guarding his distance all the while, that I should re-join my 'friend.'

"You'll like Michael," I said.

"Will I?"

He smiled, but the smile was detached and cold, and it was all too obvious that he was thinking of other things. The image of Mark returned with renewed force. He was thinking of him and of that bloody centre. I wanted to lash out, to hurt, because it was clear that he was not thinking of me. Then the terrible words formed in my mind - has he ever thought of me? I caught at his arm and squeezed it tightly. I could see the look of pain on his face, but I did not release my hold.

"Let go, Nicholas."

"You don't want us here, do you?"

"Please, I'm tired. That's all. Aren't I allowed to be tired?"

I released him, and he carried on making the tea. His face did look tired, and he appeared frail and small. I stood against the door and stared at him. I looked at his flesh, at his white flesh, and thought - this is nothing more than meat. He could be cut up and eaten, and no one would know the difference. Meat is meat and he is a living animal like any other. The flesh of the god had truly fallen away, and in its place I saw only this. I opened my mouth to call him, to say the name Peter, for in naming him I had the instinct to save him. With a name I would redeem him from the flesh of the animal. But as I opened my mouth I tasted that meat; my teeth crunched against the bone of an arm, a leg. I was filled with his flesh: my throat suffocating with the fullness of his carcass body. I closed my eyes, and behind my eyes, a swirling interior vision of fire burnt his animal body away. My mouth was freed of the taste of him, and when I re-opened my eyes I saw instead of his body a living figure of bone. The skin had been stripped, flayed by flame. The meat had been devoured by the vast incinerator of my imagination.

"Nicholas, don't stare at me like that. You frighten me."

Suddenly I wanted to be as far away from him as possible. The prospect of his death no longer had meaning. He was already dead.

"Go back and join your friend."

I cried out then, the words coming in a rush of futile anger.

"Don't keep calling him that. His name's Michael, and he's not my friend. I hardly know him at all. I have no friends."

I opened the door and went down the hall to the toilet. For a moment I stood there dazed. Then, in a sort of quiet despair I undid my trousers and began to masturbate. I concentrated all my thoughts on Peter. I thought of what we had done together sexually. I recreated the feel of his skin, the meat of the corpse. But as the images succeeded one another a greater image took predominance. Peter, burnt of flesh, stood before me and I was reaching out to caress nothing more than blackened bone. "He is the fire." I cried the words aloud, and at that moment I came.

When I returned to the room they were sitting together in silence. I sat opposite them and sipped at lukewarm tea. I forced myself to talk. Words poured from my mouth. Empty, trivial words that somehow were meant to compensate for the failure of this meeting. Peter began to talk as well, but Michael remained silent. He looked uncomfortable and ill at ease, and I longed for him to go. I had brought strangers together, and there was nothing there. I too was a stranger, to both of them. No one cared.

"Nicholas won't let me see the play he is working on."

Peter had spoken. The statement hit at me. From meaningless chatter, suddenly words had meaning again.

"The first draft is always bad."

My reply sounded fumbled and unconvincing. Michael murmured something about the general state of the theatre, and abruptly the searching spotlight was switched off from me. But no sooner had he spoken than he got up and said he had to go.

"It's late. I have work to do tomorrow."

Peter stood up with him. I remained seated. They smiled at each other. Michael turned to me, raised his arm and opened his hand in a sign of farewell. I made no gesture and didn't reply, and he left the room. As soon as the door closed behind him, I said: "Why did you have to talk about my work?"

"It was something to say."

Peter's voice was defensive. I noticed a look of fear in his eyes. The look excited me and there was an abrupt stirring of my cock. Yet at the same time I realised that any physical manifestation of that desire was impossible. If I touched him I would kill. And his death would be nothing, nothing at all. I felt so sick of him that I had the delirious sensation of vomiting inwardly. Without looking at me he asked: "The way you feel about being gay - does it ever affect your writing?"

I hated the question. I hated him.

"Of course."

"I mean it. Does it affect what you write about? "

"The pain, yes..."

Now I too didn't look at him, but stared round at the room. The mediocrity of the worn and battered furniture appalled me. Directly facing me, on the wall, I saw a large brown stain. I thought absurdly that someone must have thrown tea there.

"What about the pride? The pride of gay love?"

I shrank from the word love in that context. I had a presentiment of what was coming, of what he wanted to say, but the sudden attack of his conversation only increased my nausea. I concentrated my attention upon him. The frail figure seemed glued to its environment, exactly like the brown mess on the wall. A piece of red meat in a mess of vomit.

"I am not writing about that."

"How can you not help but write about it?"

I wanted to run away; from the room and from every association that was connected with him. What he was saying did not matter because it mattered too deeply. I was contaminating his every hope and expectation of me by my presence. I hated him, and yet in those sickening depths it still had all the tender ferocity of love. I reached out for him, pulling him towards me, and pressed my mouth to his stomach and groin.

"I will one day."

He moved away. My mouth tasted bitter as if the brief contact with his body had poisoned me. It was not I who had killed him, but he who had killed me.

"What? What will you do one day?"

"Write about us." I paused. "After the play on Kleist."

A voice said within me that there would be no afterwards, but I smothered it at once.

"It's not so much us," he said, "but what we represent."

"What do we represent?" I asked. There was an intended tone of mockery in my voice.

"Something more than just a relationship. To write about us within the narrow confines of that is no longer possible. We have to be seen within the context of a new and positive life. Like the centre. Take that as an example."

"You know that's not how I feel it."

"Nicholas, there must be a new way. I want to show you what

that way can mean for a lot of us. I would like to bring you that hope. The hope that all of us can share."

"I am not us. I am me, Nicholas. The only us I recognise is you and I."

Then I added, as bitterly as I could: "You should have talked to Michael about this. He's the one to understand. Didn't you see the badge?"

I am not us. I am not us. The words echoed and repeated themselves. He and I together for eternity; that's what mattered, wasn't it? He and I never to be separated. The dream returned, and with it the only hope that I could ever acknowledge. Then I said: "There's only one hope you can fulfil."

He stared at me, and quite suddenly he looked frightened. It was as though he could smell that I was impatient for the kill. I thought of a young deer trapped by hunters in a forest. I was one of the hunters, but although I would bring about his death it would mean fulfilment for both of us.

"I don't want to carry on, Peter. I want to die."

He made a vague gesture with his hands.

"You say that."

"I mean it."

Quietly he said: "Do you want us to get a place together? I would if it would help."

"No. It would not help."

"Then, what? I don't see what I can do."

"You can die with me. You know that's what I have wanted."

I fixed my attention on the dark stain and waited. I heard the door shut, and when I looked away from the mark on the wall, I saw that he had gone.

December 16

"I don't want to talk about my work."

The stranger haunts me day and night. While I write my play he sits in a corner of the room, dressed in his white suit, with his hands folded in his lap. His hands are hidden by gloves the colour of flesh.

"But you must talk about it."

He is insistent. I put my fingers in my ears, but nothing can stop the sound of his voice.

"You must send him your play."

"I can't. He is famous. He will reject me."

I say the three short sentences with great difficulty. I feel that I am fighting for my breath. He replies by laughing at me. I whisper that his presence is unbearable, but he will not go away.

"Despite the fear of rejection, you must do it."

"Why do you torment me? What do I owe you?"

I wheel round in my chair and the manuscript papers on my table scatter to the floor. He comes to me, bends down, picks up the papers and replaces them on the table in perfect order.

"It is finished, isn't it? The play is finished?"

He stands over me.

"Yes."

"Last week you bought a large envelope. I was with you, remember? You said to me that you intended to send it then."

"Yes, I remember you were with me. You are always with me."

He sees me shudder and puts a hand on my shoulder. Beneath the glove it feels like a claw of bone.

"Write the letter."

"I can't."

"I won't release you until you write what is necessary."

I take a large sheet of paper and begin to write. I say how much I admire his work and that I have written a play that I hope to dedicate to him. All I need is an honest opinion, I add. The hand leaves my shoulder, and the stranger returns to the corner of the room. From this place, where he always sits, he says: "He will reply. I promise you."

January 4

The reply came.

First let me thank you for the flattering things you have to say about my work. Without sounding over-humble I am not altogether sure that they are justified. But I am not writing to you about my work, but your own. Being an old Roman Catholic I am out of sympathy with the extreme despair of the central character. I cannot believe in that despair. The struggle must go on until all evil is banished forever from the world. Your viewpoint, I am afraid, only appears to heighten a feeling of futility. The world is not beyond redemption and I am sure that in your heart of hearts you do not believe that it is. Yet despite the apparent negativity of your play I do appreciate that you have a certain talent - yes, a very definite talent for writing. But I am not sure that you are wisely channelling it by writing for the theatre. Have you thought of turning these scenes into poetic dialogues? I feel they would work better in book form. I am afraid I cannot see them being acted in the theatre. This of course is only a personal criticism etc, etc.

I burnt the letter and sent the play off to a fringe theatre that had advertised for new plays by unknown authors. And all the time he was there, in a corner of the room, laughing at me.

I walk for hours by the seashore to escape from him, and as I walk I imagine a child of the camps - a poor, murdered child coming to me from the waves. I have given this child the sex of a girl because every boy is a reminder and a terror to me. Only a female body can have that atrocity of detachment that I need.

What am I saying? What am I writing?

Peter has gone, and the slim, boyish figure has been burnt in the charnel house forever.

As I walk by the sea I go over and over every detail of my present play. I am gentle with its imperfections, like an animal licking its offspring's malformed limbs and wounds. I will defend to the death that which I have created. The imaginary child comes to my side. There is a look of half-serious reproach on her face as she says: "Why didn't you allow me to forgive? I wanted to forgive. You made me blame a man who did nothing to harm me."

I hold her close. I must tell her the story. She above all people must know what she suffered, and why.

"But you died."

I pronounce the last word very solemnly, and she laughs.

"Dying is a game," she says. "There was nothing to be afraid of. They did not hurt me. You exaggerate when you say they did."

"Try to understand my story."

We sit on a groyne facing the waves, and her emaciated arms cling to my neck. I do not see her face as I present her with the gift of my imagination.

"The play you are a part of takes place in Switzerland after the war. The man who is the central character used to work in the gas chambers. He was one of those ordinary people responsible for your death. He was one of thousands who simply did a job of work. He was there in the camp hospital when they put your mother to death. He watched as the doctor injected her with petrol."

"We should play, not talk."

The child's grip tightens around my throat. The pressure of the story is too much to bear, and I feel that it is the words, and not she, that is strangling me.

"And as well as the horror around him this man has to face the horror that he sees concerning himself. He is ugly, and he stutters. Every word that he speaks is a torment to him, and people laugh each time he attempts to talk. Even his victims had occasionally sneered at him. But once the war is over he isolates himself in a hotel room in Switzerland. Solitude makes it possible for him to express himself at last. He talks and he talks and he talks, and during a long night of terrible memories he remembers you."

The child loosens her grip, and before I can say another word she lets go and runs back towards the waves. As she runs she calls out to me, "Come and play. I don't want to listen any more. Come and play." But before it is possible to even make a move to go to her the stranger is by my side. He puts his hand on my shoulder and leads me back to the house. I will never believe in that story again. How can I believe it since it is not the story I have written?

"Who is Kleist?"

I turn to the stranger and ask him, but his head is turned away from me, and I know that he is pretending that he has not heard.

January 5

My play is about themes taken from the life of Heinrich von Kleist. It is about the moral and literary undermining of a writer whose work is barely recognised. My play is not about a man who worked in the camps. Why didn't I tell the child that? Why couldn't I tell the truth? And yet there was a certain truth in what I told her. The camps happened, and my guilt reminds me that I should have written about them. They were, after all, a continuation of the romantic world that let them happen.

But who is Kleist?

Who was he?

Who am I myself?

The fictitious character that I had spoken to the child about takes on a definite life of his own. He stands in front of me and he taunts me for my failure. He says, "Look at me. I am here. I can talk. Only by your listening to me can I liberate myself from my crimes."

I turn away from him, but he forces me to face him. He places his rough, murderer's hands upon my shoulders and stares into my eyes. His anguish is affecting his speech, and he has great difficulty in expressing himself. At last he cries: "Express yourself for me. Tell them what the horror means. Tell them that things, that people, are never what they seem. I had my problems. There were reasons for what I did."

He falls to his knees and begs me to tell his story.

"Forget Kleist. You are not even sure who he is, and you will never know. Only bad faith can make you pursue a romantic age that is dead and given to the dead. Write only of the camps, and the role of those responsible. Of ordinary men who let it happen; men who turned flesh into meat, men who turned man into animal. Tell how in the camps when we ran out of gas we would throw the children alive into the furnaces. I am one of those men. I demand to be heard."

I want to say to him: "My thoughts and words are your own, but how can I forget Kleist? How can I forget what I have created? Ordinary you may believe yourself to be, but it was the extraordinary, like Kleist, who made the ordinary possible." But I am tired. Tired without Peter and the prospect of a lonely death. Like the man all I can say is: "I have my problems. There are reasons for what I did. And reasons too for what I will do."

The 'extraordinary' holds out an impossible ideal. When the 'ordinary' man consciously or unconsciously realises this he rejects 'absolutes' for a 'relative' view of life. Anything then is possible. Violence and horror stem from his unconscious revolt that he cannot attain the extraordinary. He creates scapegoats for his failure. The Jews. Homosexuals. He can be 'extraordinary' in destruction. He has power after all. But to lead back to the starting point. The Romantic world view upholds the extraordinary: the impossible ideal. Kleist was a romantic, but he realised too that the 'relative' world was a definite reality. Kleist was the bridge between the 'extraordinary' and the 'ordinary'. He saw the play of opposites and it was this recognition that was too much to bear. In his everyday life he fought against the fact that he would always be 'other': that there was no total identification with a beloved or with an ideal. He wrote a play upholding nationalism. It was a way of running from the reality of a relative world where absolute values were no longer possible.

January 30

At last recognition has come. The play has been accepted, and during the coming months it will be put into production.

Peter has also returned. I say 'also' because so much sudden happiness is strange to me.

"Are you forgetting the rest?"

The voice nags at me. I say: "Be still. Be quiet. Let me go. Can't you see that I am happy?"

"You only want to be happy," the voice replies.

I read, then read again what I have just written. I tell myself that these are only words; that the voice is only a word. But I cannot fool myself. The voice is there.

"What do you mean by 'so much sudden happiness?' Peter left you. You crawled to Michael. Michael helped bring him back. You can't deny it. You can't deny the torment or what really

116

happened. That time is part of you forever."

"Can't I be allowed to forget? All I want now is a brief period of happiness."

"Do you?"

The voice sneers at me. I repeat the name "Peter." I repeat his name aloud; so loud that the name itself becomes a scream. But in the silence after the scream the voice can still be heard.

"Why did you ask Michael if he fucked him?"

The question forms itself on my lips. The structure of joy that I have built so delicately around me collapses. And it is then that doubt slips in.

"There are things that I have to forget."

"But can you forget that you asked that question?"

"No."

The two voices within me seem to be running along parallel lines. The one that I would like to believe is my own humbles itself and falters before the other's interrogation.

"Why did you ask the question?"

I know very well why, but the image is too unendurable for me to put into words. I see Peter lying on a bed face downwards, and Michael lying on top of him, and they are fucking. Peter is groaning. Groaning with pleasure. A pleasure that I am separated from.

"Do you believe what you imagine you see?"

I cannot answer. To answer in the affirmative would be to destroy everything. I was drunk when I had asked Michael the question, and now I desire to be drunk again, to forget that I ever had.

"What if you found out definitely that it was true?"

I think of my play and its eventual first performance. I think of all the years of failure that have led up to this hope of success. I concentrate on these thoughts, and in them Peter is by my side, watching the play. The audience is applauding, and he is whispering to me how proud he is of me. Yes, there is a peace and a sense of calm in that. I offer these thoughts silently to the voice almost as optimistically as I offer my play to the audiences that are to come. In that action I bring about quiet. The doubt is sealed with hope. The heart made gentle. Yet even despite this the parallel reality cannot be avoided. I am quiet, but falsely quiet, for all around me rages the storm of the impossible.

I remember how it was (how it could have been?) the night that he returned.

"I prayed," I said, "for the cruelty to end. Not your cruelty, or my own, but the blind hurt of separation itself."

I held him then, and I loved him. The ideal was swept away in the rapture of feeling his body, of receiving his unique flesh. Unique? Yes, it was true - there was no one, no thing or dream to compare with him. I accepted at last what I had avoided for so long. The faults that I still perceived in him were nothing in comparison to the joy of convincing myself that I believed in that acceptance. He was no longer monster, nor ideal, but man.

"Please don't frighten me again. I couldn't bear much more."

He said the words quietly and gently. I knew that he was referring to my demand for our death, but the desire for mutual suicide was at that moment the last thing I wanted.

"And you must understand that there are times when I don't know what I am saying or doing."

"I know," he said.

He took my hand and held it, pressing it tightly within his own. I tried to tell him why Kleist was so important to me. I mentioned his apparent failure as a playwright, his failure as a lover - yet now I no longer identified with my subject. I could love, and in loving was freed of Kleist's imagined likeness. Then I went on to tell him about the notes I was making for another play.

He asked: "But now isn't it possible for me to read the one that is written?"

"I would like you to wait until after you have seen it."

As I said the words a fear still lingered in my mind that he would shrink from what I had done. But there was time, time enough yet before the production for me to prove to him that the failure of love I had portrayed in the play had nothing to do with our lives. Kleist was dead. I was dead. The final testament

118

written. By the act of his return Peter had freed me to live.

"I want that new life you promised me. Do you remember?"

He looked at me, but said nothing. Frightened of the danger of silence I carried on talking. I told him about the child, and of the man who had appeared to me demanding to be heard.

"I feel that I have a duty to tell his story."

"A duty towards who?" he asked.

I reached out and caressed his face. I had wanted to tell him that it was partly a duty towards him; a kind of act of consecration for our future life. But saying it was unnecessary. The words were implicit in my touch. For the first time ever between us I could see and feel the sincere awareness we had of each other. We sat together on the floor, and I knew what it was to have a home.

"I feel a duty towards that unknown man," I said, "because he caused suffering and wanted to atone for it. It was somehow justice that he should come to me seeking for that atonement."

"Did he appear in a dream?"

Dream. No. Don't mention the word. Dreams. Illusions. They have done us so much harm. I never want to dream again. Aloud I said: "No, he was real. He had to be heard."

"Hadn't Kleist appeared to you? Hadn't he been real?"

I shook my head. Inside me an insistent voice reminded me of the Judas kiss. In that Gethsemane of life where Kleist and I had met, it was I who had been the betrayer. It was I who had distorted his vision, who had sold his life - and in that distortion and selling bestowed upon myself, not the silver of the priests and elders, but a corrupt, alchemical gold.

Peter was silent. He smiled at me, then reached out to draw me closer to him. We made love. Afterwards, as we lay in bed, I realised that I hadn't asked him one question about Mark or about the centre; and the guilt of that omission revived the presence of the other me that I had hoped was dead.

"Forgive me," I said.

"What for?"

The simple way he said that brought tears to my eyes.

"Peter," I whispered. "Peter, absolve me from the past."

Absolution.

The mockery of the word.

He has seen the play. His rejection of it has proved to me that there can never be absolution for the past. I know now that the years and the months that have gone by wait on for me, like an open grave ready to swallow the furtive encounters with the time to come that we call a future. But I must calm myself and relate as exactly as possible what happened.

Both the first performance and the reviews that followed were a disaster. Michael and Peter brought me the first editions of the morning papers. Failure and unhappiness had made me hostile, and I was rude and irritable with both of them. The truth of the matter was that it would have been kinder if they had left me totally alone. There is a certain pain for which there is no remedy. A pain that is caused by the deepest betrayal, and it was this that I was experiencing. I think Michael understood, but Peter seemed to have no real knowledge of what I felt. Because I had convinced myself that I loved him so much, there was hatred in my voice as I said: "Well, take a good look. Yes, this is me. On stage and off. It's what you wanted to see, isn't it?"

"Nicholas, don't..."

Michael put a hand on my arm, but I pushed him away. I asked him to leave Peter and I alone. Yet when we were alone we said nothing. I felt the revulsion he was experiencing towards me in the silence that existed between us. I was the stranger. All illusion of communication was over. When he did look at me I saw on his face an expression of sick detachment. I felt like an abomination that is avoided; a piece of excrement that is walked around in the road. Through the vision of my play I had become for him an image of total disgust.

"You despise me, don't you?"

I could no longer remain silent.

"I despise what I saw. Nicholas."

"Talk to me about the play. Tell me just how much it made you sick."

His face was pale and there were dark shadows under his eyes. The look of detachment went. I knew that I was succeeding in inflicting pain once more upon him. Inflicting pain one final time before he walked out on me; for this time I knew that it would be forever.

"There is nothing I can say."

His voice was thin, almost pleading. I hit him across the face twice, very hard, and a trickle of blood ran down from the corner of his mouth. With the back of his hand he wiped it away. I hit at the hand in a frenzy of guilt.

"Talk to me."

I screamed at him. He could hardly stand, and leant against the wall.

"I've got to leave you, Nicholas. You've got to find out what it's all about on your own."

I beat at his body as if I would kill him, then covered the places where I had inflicted blows, with kisses. He crawled away from me, and staggered to his feet. To stop him from going I stood with my back to the door.

"We were happy for a time, weren't we?"

Suddenly I wanted desperately to undo all that I had done. It couldn't be too late. I had to have him back.

"Yes," he said.

"And the play was about a dead man. About another person."

"That other person has just made my mouth bleed. That other person has just assaulted me so badly that my body aches with pain."

He stood there facing me: a mirror to the living ghost of myself. There was no escape from that confrontation.

"And me? What about me? What about the pain of seeing myself?"

"I can't help you any more."

His voice was listless. He sounded as if he no longer really cared. As if he were bored. I stepped away from the door, but he made no gesture to leave the room. I had hit at him while he could hardly stand; I had beaten him to the floor. The limit had been reached. As far as violence was concerned there was nowhere to go, and he knew that I knew it. Any physical danger that there had been in the situation was exhausted.

"I am not running away like I did last time. I am no longer afraid of you. What is the worst you can do, after all? Strangle me in my sleep?"

I closed my eyes to shut out the sight of what I had done. As if from nowhere the memory of the toad's crushed head appeared, forcing itself to the surface of my mind. I screamed and opened my eyes. Peter had his back to me, and was turning down the bed.

"I want to sleep," he said. "I am too tired to go home."

"I can't bear it..."

He turned and looked at me again.

"You'll have to bear it. The mistake I made was believing I could bear it for you."

Absolution.

I had said: "Forgive me," and he had replied: "What for?"

Absolution.

He will never return. That is certain now, and I must train myself in the art of hatred in order to survive. I see survival as a long, monotonous day leading to my own inevitable night. Alone. Yes, I must bear it. Loneliness and hatred. Yet even as I write these words the recollection of Michael's patience and understanding returns to me. All I have to do is dial his number and wait. All I have to do is call him by name and he will come.

3. The closed room.

In the darkness I hear the toad hopping across the floor towards me. Terrified, I reach out and turn on the light, but there is nothing there. I get out of bed and stand in front of the mirror. I stand there for a long time without moving, and it is only very slowly that my mind is able to bear the truth of what I see. In the mirror my body is reflected down to the last detail, but where my face should be there is nothing but a white and empty space.

PART THREE

PETER

I wish I had resisted the impulse to go and see my mother. I wish I had resisted it because it was based on guilt. She rarely saw me and because she never openly complained about it, I felt that I had to go. The meeting was a failure. We said very little. I wanted to talk about my homosexuality, about my lovers, but all the time I felt her silently willing me to be quiet. I remember particularly the second day of my visit. She was standing by the window in the living room. I was seated in my dead father's chair. Whenever I came home she wanted me to sit in that chair. It was around six in the evening.

"I suppose you will want to go out." She paused. "To meet people."

I said nothing for a moment. I knew that she was perfectly aware that I had no friends in the town.

"I'm alright here."

"You're bored. I know you're bored."

She stared at me. There was a look of terrible sadness in that stare.

"Mother, I am not bored. And anyway if we talked - "

She chose to ignore this remark about our silence, and continued to talk at me in the same ambiguous way.

"Not that there can be of much interest here. At least I've never heard that there was."

My voice was shaking as I replied: "What do you mean? Say what you mean."

"You know what I mean."

"No, I don't."

I hit the sides of the chair hard with my hands.

"Be explicit. Say it."

I could see that she was trembling. I softened the tone of my voice.

"Mother, can't we talk? It worries me that we don't. If we talked there would be some chance of us understanding one another."

"I don't want to understand. I'm alright. You don't have to worry about me."

My voice was gentle as I said: "But I do."

She came to me then, took both my hands within hers, pressed them tightly, then walked out of the room. In the hall I heard her crying.

The next morning I packed my things telling her that I had received an urgent message offering me a job in London. She knew I was lying. There had been neither telephone calls or letters for me. It would have been easy enough for her to take me up on this, but I could see that she was too exhausted to question or fight. Her eyes were puffy and her face drawn with lack of sleep. There was so much to say and yet for her it was all so dangerous. I kissed her on both cheeks.

"Mother, I am happy. I mean the way I am."

She laughed. A forced, cold laugh.

"You would say that."

"Believe it."

"Then there is no more that need be said."

As she uttered these words my heart cried out, 'But there is everything to be said. Listen to me. Talk to me. Stop imagining what my life is like. See it with me for what it really is.' But instead of saying the words I remained silent. Her closed, miserable face was only receptive to the image she already had of me.

"Goodbye, Mother."

"Goodbye, Peter."

She saw me to the door and watched me as I walked down the street. As I turned the corner I waved, but there was no wave back. In the train on my way to London I felt hopelessly depressed. It was true that I had partly lied to her. I was not happy. I was glad to be gay, but that had nothing to do with happiness. I shut my eyes and tried to get some sleep. For one minute, I said to myself, stop being homosexual. Forget what you think you should be to yourself and to others, and let your mind rest. When I at last did drift off into sleep I had a nightmare. I was still on a train, but travelling through the night, and with absolutely no idea of my destination. I got up from my seat, left my compartment and began to walk down the corridors. It didn't take me long to realise that I was the only passenger on the train. I started to run, calling for help, but the train was hurtling at a terrifying speed, and the corridors were without end. At one point I tried to open a door to throw myself out, but the speed was so great that it prevented the door from opening. I had to escape, even if it was into death. Finally, exhausted with running, I fell to my knees.

"I promise never to do wrong again."

My voice was that of a little child. I felt my mother's presence, and unseen though her presence was, I knew it to be full of sorrow and pain. I had caused that pain. I had inflicted that sorrow. I was to blame for everything, everything.

"I will never hurt you again. I promise. I promise."

A voice answered me. I was the voice, and it filled me.

"The death on this train will be my death. That crime against yourself you will have to bear to the end of your days."

I got to my feet. I looked out of the window. Night had ended, and I was travelling across a vast and desolate plain. The voice was whispering in my ear: 'See what you have done. Look at what is really there.' Then the landscape altered. The plain was now covered with burnt out houses; a whole city bombed and destroyed. Thick smoke was rising from behind blackened façades, and in what remained of the streets I saw disfigured and mutilated corpses. The train had slowed down to a normal speed. With trembling hands I opened the compartment door.

Suddenly I felt someone shaking me. I woke up.

"Are you alright? You were making a terrible noise. You were fighting for your breath. I thought for a moment I would have to stop the train."

A worried looking face stared into mine.

"I was dreaming..."

The face drew away. It belonged to a man who was sitting opposite me. We were the sole occupants of a closed compartment of the train. He picked up his newspaper and hid behind it. I felt an urgent desire to talk to him, to tell him about my dream, but the paper was an effective barricade, and I remained quiet. When we arrived at the station he got off the train first, without saying a word.

I called Mark immediately on arrival. He said that my room was ready and waiting for me.

"I had to come," I said, then decided that for the moment it was best to say no more and replaced the receiver. When I got to the house he took me in his arms and kissed me on the lips.

"I've prepared a late lunch. I thought you might be hungry."

He led me into the kitchen. He had prepared a salad, and we sat down to eat it. Half-way through the meal he said: "Is there any chance of you settling at last?"

He tried to make the question sound as casual as possible.

"I don't know."

"Why don't you know?"

I laughed.

"I don't know why I don't know."

"You can't keep running about the country. For one thing it's expensive, and you have no fixed job."

"Alright, Mark, don't start up about that."

He looked at me, sensing at once that I might get angry, and grinned. I liked his grin. I always had. It was a very American, boyish grin, and it made him appealing and attractive. I reached out with my hand and touched his arm.

"Mark?"

"Yes?"

"I want to thank you for letting me come back here."

"You can always come here. You know that. It's a real home if you want it. But then I have to be wary when I use that word with you. I always think it may sound like a demand, but it's not."

"I know that."

"Funny, it's usually us foot-loose Americans who are the

stereotypes for not wanting homes."

I got up from the table and went across to him. There was an expression close to helplessness on his face as I took him in my arms.

"Shall we go to bed?" I asked.

He broke away from me.

"I don't think that would be fair, do you?"

"It's fun. It always has been fun with you."

"Maybe I'm not the laughs I used to be."

He stared sadly at me. I had hurt him again. It seemed that I was guilty of having continually hurt him.

"So there is to be no more of that?"

He shook his head and replied: "No more of that, Peter. I've given it all a great deal of thought, as the expression goes. Sex with you would end up by meaning an involvement for me of a very special kind." He paused. "You've got a charmed, casual life Peter, and I don't mind - I can be charming and casual too, remember, but somehow both of us involved and involving one another on that sort of level won't ever work again. I love you and I'll help you, but let's keep fucking out of it."

I opened my mouth to speak, but he stopped me.

"Let me just finish. I want to make things clear. I offer you a home with no strings attached. I'm willing to look after you, and in return I hope you will be considerate towards me. I'm lonely, and I would like you around. Who knows, we may even be able to do something constructive together, like helping other people - reaching out. I would like to eventually open a centre for gays here in this house."

"That's a good idea," I said.

"Sure it's a good idea. It's such a good idea that it's been done to death, and has nearly always failed. But who knows, maybe you and I can be the exceptions and make it work. I would like that. For a start it might give you some roots. You can't trail your arse around England forever. The trouble too is that one's arse gets itself a reputation."

There were tears in my eyes as I said: "I know."

"But what you don't know, Peter, is that you have a big and

unfathomable capacity to hurt. I'm telling you this so you are aware of it. It's a deep and dark capacity that might get you into trouble, and as I love you I want in some way to protect you from yourself. So you see going to bed is not going to help, because although it might be fun for you it might just hurt me."

"I understand."

"Do you? I wonder."

He cuffed me gently under the chin.

"Well, now that that has all been said we can stop being heavy. I don't want to talk about it again."

We sat there in silence finishing our meal. It was while we were having coffee that he began to talk again.

"You know I have been presuming ever since you arrived - "

"Presuming what, Mark?"

"That you will really stay."

His face looked urgent and handsome as he said this, and I cursed whatever it was inside me that stopped me from really loving him. That word, really. Was I really capable of experiencing anything to any depth?

"It's a visit only, I'm afraid," I said.

He toyed with his coffee spoon. There was a long silence before he replied: "Well, it was an idea."

"It's good to know I can come whenever I like. It makes me feel free."

"Good."

He grinned and poured me more coffee.

"Did you know I bake my own bread now? I take care of myself. It's you who taught me to take care of myself - nature's way, you called it."

I sensed a slight bitterness returning, and to avoid any participation in subtle recriminations I went to the sink and started washing up the dishes. There was something in Mark's words; something like a demand, yet never as explicit as a demand. A frightening, unspoken need hovered over our relationship, and I felt that if it ever truly descended and found the words to express it, then it might tear Mark apart. I think he realised that too, knowing the unseen limits of just how far to go.

His next words said openly as much as he could say.

"Are you going to look after me, and cook for me while you are here? I'd like that."

"I'd like that as well."

I had my back to him, and without turning round I let him go out of the room. He was gently telling me that it was better for both of us if we had some time on our own. It was two days later when he told me about Andrew.

"I want you to meet a new friend of mine. He's coming here tonight for dinner."

I looked at him and smiled. I knew what he meant, and in a way there was no necessity for him to say more. I watched him walk across the room to the window. He stood there with his back to me, looking down into the streets below. From this window there was a view of the park in the distance. For a while he talked aimlessly about what he could see going on in the streets that led to the park. Then suddenly he said: "He's my lover, but I'm not in love with him. You know what I mean."

"I know what you mean. There was no need to tell me."

"I don't mind explaining."

He turned and faced me, then walked across to the record player and choosing a record, put it on. It was a group that I had never heard of, and by the sound of them didn't want to hear. I asked him to turn the record down or off. He did neither, but knelt on the floor and said quietly: "You can't have it all your own way all of the time."

I went to my room. I was fighting back a feeling of pain that could only be described as jealousy. But I was not jealous. Half an hour later he came to me. He took me in his arms and hugged me to him.

"I'm not serious about Andrew, if that's what you are frightened of."

"I'm not frightened."

"Then what happened?"

"You made it happen. That bloody music. There was no need."

He stopped my mouth with his fingers, then kissed me on the lips.

At around eight Andrew arrived. I found him physically attractive and wanted to go to bed with him. Both he and Mark said very little to one another all evening and towards midnight, as I was preparing coffee in the kitchen, Andrew came out to join me.

"I understand you and Mark were lovers."

"You understand right."

"Why not now?"

"Why all the questions?"

"He said you like to be free. I like to be free as well, but somewhere Mark doesn't."

"I don't think we should be talking about him."

I heard my voice and it spurned the words the instant they were spoken. Deep down inside me I had no qualms about talking about Mark at all.

"Didn't he give you what you wanted?"

I smiled at Andrew.

"I want to fuck," I said.

"I know, Mark has always been - how do you call it? - fastidious about that."

He came to me then and put his hand down the front of my trousers. He rubbed me, then undid the zip and took out my cock. While he was rubbing me Mark came into the room. Neither Andrew nor I broke away. Mark stood there, watching us, then said: "I think we should all go to bed." Andrew smiled at him, then taking me by the hand led me towards the bedroom.

It was the first time I had had sex with Mark for a long time. But the next morning I couldn't face him or Andrew, and without leaving word of any sort, I packed my bag and left the house.

I hated the town during the beginning of that summer. I hated the tourists and the packed promenade; but worst of all I hated the odd jobs that I managed to find as employment. First I found work in a gay bar, but got bored and tired with the passes that were made at me. Next I got a job as ice-cream seller along the front, but got the sack from that when they realised that I spent a lot of the time just sitting around doing nothing. So at last I decided to let the government support me, and wrote home to my mother for a little additional financial help. It was during this last period in the month of July that I met Nicholas. However much he liked to tell another version of it, this is how it really happened. I met him in a park; at a gay cruising ground at the furthest end of town, and like everyone else, he was out searching for sex. I remember having watched him for quite some time, without I think, his having noticed me. In the shadows it was hard making out any distinct features, and I was undecided whether I liked him or not. But what I did feel was a strong pull towards him. I sensed a strange power emanating from his body that seemed to draw me into his orbit. Even then, in that first hour of our not knowing one another, I was fighting it, and through it, him.

"Have you got a place where we can go?"

A blond haired boy smiled at me. He was young, probably younger than myself, and I smiled back. Slowly I shook my head. At that same moment Nicholas walked by us, but without looking at me. All the time that I had been there in the park I hadn't seen him go up to anyone. Also as far as I could tell nobody had tried to make a pass at him. I turned to the boy. I did not know it then, but he was my first weapon used to ward Nicholas off.

"If you haven't got a place, then shall we do it here?"

The blond boy asked me this, still smiling his very sure smile, and rubbing himself at the same time. The smile annoyed me. There was no doubt in his mind that I would want to do it with him; no thought of rejection. I reached out for his trousers in as bored a way as possible, looking around me all the time. I wanted to make it seem as if I was doing him a favour.

"What do you want us to do?"

It was the first thing I said to the boy.

"Anything you like."

"Sucking?"

He nodded his head, then unzipped his fly. His cock was hard and I took it in my hand. It was then that I realised Nicholas was standing a few yards away from us, watching. This excited me and I bent down and took the head of the boy's cock into my mouth. I only had it in my mouth a few seconds before the boy said: "now will you let me do it to you?"

I angrily stood up.

"Is there a hurry on?" I said.

"I like to do it as well."

He smiled the kind of smile that tells you it calls the tune. I wanted to wipe that idiotic smile off his blasted face.

"The only way we can suck together is if we lie out on the grass. I don't mind that, but we'd block the path - not to mention that horizontal in this place takes up just too much room. If you want a bedroom, boy, go cruising in a club."

With those last words the smile disappeared. Hurriedly he stuffed his cock back into his trousers, and with a mumbled, "What's it matter anyway?" he walked off. I stared after him and said, "Yes, what's it matter?" But it did matter. I was excited. The boy hadn't excited me much, but Nicholas, standing watching me sucking him, had. I knew then, and with a sudden and fierce knowledge, that I wanted him. The force of his attraction was drawing me; drawing me on, and there was no longer the slightest thought of resisting. I walked straight up to him, a thing that I rarely do. He was standing with his back to the bushes and there was light enough to clearly see his face.

"I've been watching you."

I said the words quietly, then felt suddenly foolish. I looked at him closely. He was not as handsome as I thought he might have been, and his face was marked.

"Where do you come from?" he asked.

The question took me off balance. It wasn't the question, familiar in itself, but the way he asked it. He had managed, by the tone of his voice to make a very banal and usual opening, into a serious demand. Behind the question and the deceptive simplicity of the words, I was aware of another word - relationship. Even the look on his face repelled any simple, uncomplicated grope in the dark.

"London," I replied. "And you?"

"London. Now here."

"So we are both refugees."

I laughed to ease the tension. Without a single movement of his body he was pulling me in, and for a brief, panic stricken moment I had an intimation that to stay would mean disaster. I looked away from his body and face, and the moment passed. While still looking away I put my hand out to reach for his trousers. He took my hand and held it tightly.

"No, don't."

I looked up. His voice was very nearly pleading with me. God, I thought, what am I letting myself in for? He let my hand go, then murmured, "Not here. Let's walk." We walked out of the park and down to the seashore. For a long time we were silent, and I felt the silence like a third and heavy body growing between us. I wanted to leave him, yet I couldn't.

"I feel embarrassed with you," I said.

"You mustn't feel like that."

"Were you watching me - back there in the park, with that boy?"

"No."

I knew he was lying, but I let it go. Stooping down, I picked up a pebble and threw it into the sea. He began to watch me intently, and this made me feel even more embarrassed.

"I'm glad I've met you," he said.

"I'm glad too."

This was ridiculous. I threw another pebble and wished that I had gone off with the blond boy after all. This man was intense, and whatever I did, I knew, would encourage the intensity.

"You haven't told me your name," he said.

"Peter. And yours?"

Nicholas told me his name.

"Well, what do we do now, Nicholas?"

"I would like to meet you again. Can we meet again?"

Added to the intensity was also a note of quiet, but insistent desperation. The word 'relationship' grew larger and larger, and more and more frightening. I had a last chance to break away, but instead I gave in.

"Of course."

"When?"

"Tomorrow. I'm free tomorrow."

He reached over and kissed me on the mouth, then drew back and smiled. The smile made him a different person altogether. For a start it naturally eased the tension, but more than that it broke up and softened the marks and lines on his face. It almost made him beautiful.

"You've got a good smile," I said.

Christ in heaven - what a put down that sounded. Like telling an ugly person that they have nice hair or extra white teeth. I hated myself for saying it, doubting my own motivations. He reached out for me again, and in the split second of that reaching out I was made aware of the intense need he already had of me. The need was concentrated, like a centre of pain, in the fierce longing of his dark eyes. Need and pain. The two words orchestrated in cruel counterpoint. In one brusque moment I avoided the embrace.

"I have to be going."

As much as I myself wanted him, the inner resistance was building up. But although I had said I was going I remained standing where I was.

"Stay. Please stay."

He moved towards me and took me in his arms. I kissed him on the lips, then grazed his cheek lightly with my mouth. I noticed with almost fascinated revulsion that I had nearly touched a disfiguring sore. His body tensed against mine, as if feeling what I felt, and then he drew away.

"Nicholas..."

I said his name. He smiled at me.

"Are you going to tell me now that I have a nice name? Others already have, you know."

"No, I..."

"Others have also said that it was too nice a name for me. That I didn't have the face to fit it."

There was a sharp edge of bitterness in his voice. I don't know why exactly, but it was at that precise moment that I realised he was capable of cruelty. Yet the realisation, paradoxical though it may sound, only succeeded in pulling me closer towards him. I was drawn, as if in wonder, by the promise of a pain that up until now I had never felt.

"You are your name," I said.

We stood there on the deserted beach facing one another. Looking back on the scene I have the distinct impression that from the outside we must have given the appearance of being enemies on the point of violent confrontation. I mention this because I have the feeling that we were being watched.

"We will meet tomorrow, won't we?"

There was a threat in his voice. It was not a question, more a demand.

"Yes."

"Good."

He reached out and clasped my arm. The urgent pressure of his fingers hurt. I had an erection and I wanted him, but I was not going to show him my desire.

"Peter, it has been such a long time."

That was all he said, but it was as if an invisible noose had been thrown around my neck. I was suffocating already with his need.

"Let's meet in the centre of town. At six. In the gardens - by the fountain."

My sentences were abrupt and stilted. I could hardly speak. I was entirely surrounded by the overwhelming circle of his self - yet I wanted it; yes, I truly wanted it. Releasing my arm I walked away without saying goodbye, and he made no move to follow me. As I reached the end of the beach, stepping onto the road, I paused and turned, but he was still standing where I had left him. In the moonlight he looked like an ancient, magnetic stone, and as this intuitive image reached the consciousness of my mind, I began to run.

That is how I met Nicholas. I know about the other version, because I read the section that referred to it in his diary. It was one day after we had had a violent row, and finding me reading it, he tore the book from my hands. I was never again to read anything he had written about me. Perhaps after that incident he destroyed the diary.

I wrote to Mark the following morning.

"I have met someone. His name's Nicholas. He's not at all the sort of person you'd feel attracted to, or even for that matter, approve of. He's heavy and I think he has a tendency to say too much. You, as I know, have a tendency to go to the opposite extreme and say only a quarter of what you think and feel. No, scrap what I have just said - he and I have hardly said a word to one another. I have no right to make any judgements at all."

I posted the letter, then thought about the absurdity of it. Mark would believe that I had fallen in love. I spent the rest of the day doing nothing in particular, waiting for the moment of six to arrive. It was a hot day and I watched the tourists; stared at all the milling tribes of friends and families. A couple of boys walked hand in hand down the promenade. Among the jostling and screaming thousands they were the only lovers that I noticed that day. I thought to myself that it augured well for liberation, but I was not sure whose. At six I was standing in the gardens, by the fountain, and feeling tight and constricted with expectation.

"Hello."

One moment I was looking out for him, the next he was reaching out and touching my hand. I stared hard at him and tried to smile. I looked at the marks, so much more obvious in the light of day and felt pity towards him. What in God's name am I doing here in these bloody gardens, meeting a boy that I feel nothing more than pity for?

"Peter."

He said my name and smiled. Once again the rigid, ugly lines fell away, and I wanted him. Wanted him so much that my cock ached.

But we did not go to bed that day, or the day after. We talked a lot and walked endlessly by the seashore. I told him about my restlessness, about my lack of roots - I think I even told him about my mother, but I can't be sure now, for in so many ways those two days seem out of focus, unimportant. All the time, behind every movement we made and every word that we said, I thought about us having sex. I tried to imagine what he looked like naked, and the frustration made me edgy and nervous.

On the third day he took me back to his ghastly room. The details of that black room can still make me shudder. I hated being there, yet I think it was there that we made love the best.

"Do you have a bathroom?"

He opened up a door in one of the black walls and I stepped into a white space that was mercilessly bright in comparison. A kitchen unit was in the same space as the bath. There was no toilet, and I wanted a toilet.

"Where can I pee?"

He looked embarrassed and made a vague pointing gesture with his hand.

"It's down the hall."

I made to leave the room.

"You can do it here if you want."

He looked at me out of the corner of his eye as he said this, refusing to look me in the face. His voice was slightly breathless.

"What do you mean - here?"

"There's a sink."

I understood what he meant. There was an unspoken element of perversity in the situation which excited me. He wanted to see me piss. I went up to the kitchen sink and took out my cock. He stood to one side, and although he looked as if he wasn't, I knew that he was watching me. I pissed into the sink, then stood there a minute to let my cock stiffen. The moment it got hard I thrust it back into my trousers. Then I turned round to face him.

"Alright?"

I wanted to make what I said sound like a teasing question. He looked flustered and went back into the black room.

"I'd prefer it if we didn't do anything today. I'd like to wait. It's important to me."

"Why? Have you seen enough for now?"

My voice sounded brittle and hard. The game had gone too far, and had gone on for too long. In fact I was beginning to get bored. Yet at the same time I felt the invisible noose tighten round my neck. Whether he knew it or not he had me. Had me fast. The knowledge of that invisible bondage made me angry.

"Do you want to make love or don't you? Because if you

don't, then I think I had better - ”

"Go? No, you're not going."

He stepped in front of the door. His body was shaking and I felt suddenly afraid of him.

"You can't go, Peter. I think I'm falling in love with you."

The second sentence came in a rush. All I could do was laugh, and he begged me with the one word "Please" to be quiet.

"Let's sit down," I said. I sat on a chair and he sat a little distance away from me on the floor.

"I think I am falling in love with you."

He repeated the sentence slowly.

"I know," I said.

"Don't laugh at me again."

"I'm sorry."

"Never laugh at anyone when they say they are in love."

He crawled across the floor towards me, then reached up for me. He put his head between my legs, kissing the inside of my thigh, then he began to unzip my trousers. I came very quickly into his mouth, but there was no gesture or mention of him reaching any sort of satisfaction himself. I felt sickened as I did up my clothes.

"Will I see you again?" he asked.

"Yes."

I didn't look at him. I couldn't wait to get out of the room, and as far away from him as possible. I shut the door without saying goodbye and ran down the stairs to the street.

"Mark, it's me, Peter."

The first thing I did was ring Mark. He sounded distant; much farther away than the sixty odd miles that divided us.

"I've got to talk."

"Go ahead. I'm listening."

"It's about this man that I've met - Christ, Mark, I don't understand a thing. He's older, and you know I don't like people older than myself. Younger, if anything..."

I paused. Was I hurting him?

"Go on."

"I don't understand."

"So you said."

"It's not love, Mark - not that at all. Yet I don't know."

There was a long silence. There was nothing more that I could say, and nothing really for him to add.

"I'm sorry," I said. The telephone weighed heavily in my hand. The distance was threatening. The silence was threatening.

"I'll ring you when I can," I said.

"You do that."

He was the first to replace the receiver. I stared helplessly at the dialling codes and numbers facing me on the wall, then burst into tears, wanting Nicholas with an aching longing that was more brutal than any pain. After a few minutes I re-dialled Mark's number.

"I'm sorry, it's me again."

His voice sounded quiet and patient.

"Peter, stop apologizing. Now, what is the matter?"

"I've got to get away for a bit to think. Can I come to you?"

"You don't have to ask. You know you can."

He paused before saying: "Had you thought of not running this time?"

"I'm not running."

"Well, it sounds like it to me. Are you telling him that you want to get away?"

I remembered that I had left Mark without a word.

"I'm sorry," I said.

"What about now?"

"Walking out on you the last time."

"Don't worry about me - I've come to expect it. But what about him - what's his name?"

"Nicholas."

"Nicholas?"

"Look, I can't talk about it now. Anyway I haven't got any more change to feed this bloody thing with."

"When shall I expect you?"

"Tomorrow."

"Afternoon or morning?"

"Mark, he frightens me. He's so desperate - "

"Aren't you?"

I didn't reply. A moment later the bleeping noise came, and before he or I said another word the line went dead. I left the call box and walked back to the house where I lived. As it happened it was the day my rent was due, and while paying it I told my landlady that I was going away for a while to London. At the same time I told her not to let anyone know where I had gone (I had given Nicholas my address), but as she looked suspicious about this, I told her I was trying to avoid a too persistent admirer. She had been drinking when I entered her room, and now she offered me a whisky. Seated in one of her dreadful armchairs, with an equally dreadful cat on my lap, I was told about all the gay boys she had had living in her house. During my second whisky and her fourth, she said: "I like you, you know. You're a nice boy." I smiled and said that I liked her and that I liked her house. Then she said: "And love, Peter. What do you think of love?"

I looked at her and raised my glass.

"I think it's fine. Here's to love."

"Are you in love?"

The old bitch. Did she realise that she was hitting where it hurt most?

"No," I said, with as much finality as I could put into the word.

"Quite right. Leave it for later. You shouldn't be in love at your age. You should be having fun. Are you having fun?"

I finished my drink before answering, then got to my feet. The cat leapt to the floor.

"Yes," I said.

"You know that you can bring any boy here that you like. A good-looking boy like you must feel free with his visitors. He should feel free to bring as many in as he likes. Some people would mind, but I don't. I trust you to know if they are safe. Anyway they should be with a boy of your looks and age. It's the old and ugly ones that I worry about. That's why I never let my rooms to them. They bring anything back."

She poured herself another whisky, and I backed towards the door. Her fat black cat followed me, and rubbed itself against my legs.

"He likes you."

She gave me a wink that was ridiculously and obscenely obvious. I made some feeble excuse about packing, just about kicked the cat out of the way, and left her. I went upstairs to my room, and for the first time since I had been there I bolted the door. I wanted to be well and truly alone. I think that what I dreaded most that evening was Nicholas unexpectedly calling. There is no way that I can handle him yet - not now - perhaps never. Over and over again I kept on mentally repeating the same words to myself, and behind those words I thought about his disfigured looks and the way I had accidentally brushed against the sore on his cheek. I concentrated on that sore. I visualised it. I willed myself to be revolted by it, but instead felt pity. The disfigurement made him seem isolated and lonely, and this loneliness threatened me terribly. I can't handle him yet - not now - perhaps never. Then I thought about the woman downstairs and her talk about ugly men, older men. Did Nicholas fall into that category? I shut out the thought, hating myself for it. It was not his age in years, but the ancient stone of age that I felt and feared inside of him.

The next morning I left for London. I went to Mark's house, to find a crowd of people there when I arrived.

"What's this, a welcome party?"

"It's about the centre," he said. "I forgot to tell you on the phone yesterday that there was a meeting planned. Go in and join them."

I went into the main room and sat down on the floor. Already I was missing Nicholas, and I didn't feel like joining in any discussion.

"What do you think about the idea?"

After about ten minutes there a thin young man turned to me, trying to force me as it were to express an opinion.

"I don't know," I said. "I haven't been in on the rest of the discussion."

Among the twenty odd people in the room I noticed Andrew. He came to my aid at once.

"Peter doesn't live in London. Unless Mark has told him about the plan he wouldn't know much about what's happening."

"We talked," said Mark, "the last time he came."

He didn't look at me as he said this, shuffling some papers in his lap. I remembered how he had wanted us to start the whole thing together.

"Is it going to be a counselling service?"

I turned to Andrew to ask him. The thin young man piped up, "No, not exactly. There's not so much need for that as simply a friendly centre. You know, a not too heavy place where anyone can just drop in and chat. Not a place for problems."

"Everyone has got problems," said Mark.

"Yes, but we don't want it as a place for problems. There are other places for that."

It was now the turn of a good-looking boy in the comer of the room to speak. As he spoke he looked directly at me and smiled. I smiled back, deciding that once the meeting was over I would make a pass at him.

"I think Mark is right though," added Andrew. "Everyone does have problems, and I feel that everyone who comes here should feel free to talk openly about whatever is troubling them. We must be prepared for that, and above all we must have people here who are prepared for them."

"Yes, but we don't want the place to be like so many others in London. We don't want 'problem' written all over it. We don't want to get involved in having to give out really experienced help. None of us here have the necessary qualifications for that."

The good-looking young man seemed determined on making it a no problem zone. I wondered how they would take to someone like Nicholas. I looked around the room at the other people there. I wondered how many of them had problems, but were reluctant ever to come out with them - especially here. I turned to the boy who had just spoken.

"I would have thought being a human being was a fair enough qualification." I paused. "You're fortunate in being good-looking.

I'm fortunate in being good-looking, but what about the forty year old guy who has just admitted to himself that he's gay? Imagine too that he has a wife and kids at home, and that he reads about this place and decides to come along so that he can talk about his problems. What do we say to him if he asks us for advice? He's lonely, and he's not good-looking, and he needs help."

"Yes," said Mark.

"We help him I suppose," the boy replied.

"You suppose." I said.

"And anyway you go on about looks, as if you thought we considered that important. I don't like that. You should know what Gay Liberation is about by now."

"I've read the books," I said. "I've studied the theory. So far I haven't seen much put into practice."

"I suggest you haven't been to the right places."

The boy stared hard at me. He had stopped smiling a long while back.

"This isn't the place to squabble," said Mark. "We all know what Gay Liberation should be about. Lots of people, gay and straight, consider good looks to be important - and there are cases where it prevents some people from relating and helping as they should. I agree with Peter only so far though. I don't think he had really thought out why he had brought up looks in his argument."

"But leaving aside that," I said, "How is a man like that to be helped?"

The boy replied: "By showing him that we are perfectly free and natural here. I suppose pointing out to him that we haven't got problems."

I felt exasperated with the stupid bastard.

"And you think that by showing him that we haven't got problems that that's going to help him?"

"Well, not exactly..."

He was beginning to flounder. "What, exactly? And anyway, how many of us here do have problems? It's just not true that we are free and natural, as you call it."

The boy answered more fiercely this time, clearly wanting an open fight.

"What do you want - a show of hands? Do you want a show of hands here about who has got and who has not got, problems? And if you do, what makes you think that people with difficulties want to be counted. That's just my point - a friendly place where people are not continually spilling their guts would be a welcome change. Easy and nice."

"As I said," the thin young man added, "a friendly centre. A place of peace and uncomplicated love."

I winced at this, but said nothing. I stared at the boy one last time, then turned away. I still wanted to go to bed with him. Once more my thoughts began to revolve around Nicholas. Suddenly I wanted to talk about him to them, but there was nothing I could or would say. Then Mark began talking.

"I still think the centre should be open to everyone. Problems or no problems. For heterosexuals and bisexuals too. For anyone who is sufficiently interested simply to come in and take a look."

Mark was trying to pull the whole thing together. Mark was good at rounding out situations, at making rather negative encounters meaningful. His intention was to give the end of the meeting shape and purpose, even if, as with this one, it was only an impression. Andrew joined in, adding a few things, and the boy in the comer got up to go.

"I'll see you next week," he said.

A few people said goodbye to him. I didn't look at him, and he left the room. For a moment I was tempted to follow - to hell with his opinions. After all what I wanted was to have sex. Uncomplicated, too. When the meeting was over I managed to get Mark on his own.

"You were a bit aggressive with David," he said.

"I wanted to go to bed with him."

"I would have thought there would be easier ways of showing it. So what's-his-name is out of your system?"

"If you mean Nicholas, no, he isn't."

I looked at Mark. I began to say that it would be better if I left, choked on the words and threw myself into his arms. It was a wonderful melodramatic moment, and it was good to cry.

"Come on." He stroked my hair. "Come on, you get it all out."

"I'm tired," I said.

"I lied when you arrived," he murmured. "I did remember about the meeting yesterday, but I thought if I told you it was this afternoon, you wouldn't come. Hearing from you made me realise just how much I wanted to organize this whole thing with you - "

"And Andrew?" I said.

"With Andrew as well, of course. But you come first."

"I shouldn't come first. I'm not worth it. I'm really not."

He let me go, then stood back and stared hard at me.

"Are you in love with him?" he asked.

"No."

I saw Nicholas in the park. I saw him standing alone in the moonlight on the seashore. I saw him fully clothed, while I had my trousers down and he was sucking my cock. I saw him and I wanted him, yet I knew that I had to stay away.

"I can't give, Mark. You should know that."

"I think you underestimate yourself. I don't think you give anything a chance."

"Maybe that's true - but Nicholas scares me. He wants so much already, and I know that I simply haven't got it to give. Yet at the same time I like being with him. No, like is the wrong word. He has a power that I respond to. That's the only way I can describe it."

"What's he really like?"

I looked at Mark blankly. It was a question I couldn't honestly reply to. I didn't know.

"He's not good-looking. Not by your standards, or even presumably by mine."

"Looks seem to be a particular obsession with you at the moment, don't they?"

I ignored this comment. "He's older than us. He writes, but isn't successful, and from what I can gather has earned his living where and how he can."

"But what's he like?"

"I can't tell you more."

At that moment Andrew joined us.

"Problems?" he said, and laughed.

"Peter is talking about his lover."

I glared at Mark. "He's not my lover." Mark avoided my eyes, and shrugging his shoulders, turned away. I spoke to Andrew.

"He is someone I've met - he's someone I'm vaguely involved with." I paused. "I was thinking about him during the meeting."

"What's he got to do with that?" asked Mark.

"Precisely - he has nothing to do with it. He wouldn't get on here. We wouldn't like him. He wouldn't fit in - "

"Now I think you are being unfair," said Andrew.

"No, you wouldn't like him. You wouldn't know what to do with his problems. He would be out of your depth."

For a moment I really hated them, and showed it. Andrew poured me a drink and silently handed it to me. I looked at Mark who was pale and beginning to get angry.

"Don't lecture, Peter. I don't understand what you're inferring - what you're trying to say. But I do know one thing - I think it is a mistake to project on us your own inadequacies."

He left the room. I turned to Andrew who came over to me and put his arm around my shoulder.

"I know what you want," he said.

"Yes."

"You want to fuck, don't you?"

We did it there on the floor, and all the time I imagined that I was hitting out at Nicholas.

Mark and I were out of sorts with one another for a day or two after that, then made it up. There was no repeat sexual performance with Andrew. I hated it the second time with him, and he had felt that hate and resented me for it. Despite that we remained superficially friendly, if in a rather spiky and edgy way. Mark noticed this, but made no comment. As usual he didn't show how much he felt or cared.

"How about going down to have a look at the sea?"

It was his idea.

"I'd like to see the sea," he said, then paused before saying: "It will do us all good to get out of town."

He turned to me.

"Anyway, do you think it's a good idea?"

"It would be an occasion for you to meet Nicholas," I said.

"Yes, I suppose it would."

There was a note of sadness in his voice as he said this.

We fixed the date for going, then said no more about it. Now that was decided upon I had the difficult task of writing Nicholas a letter. I had been putting it off for days, but I knew I couldn't put it off for ever and still carry on seeing him. The prospect of suddenly arriving on his doorstep without warning was out of the question. Quite simply I owed him a letter, but the thought of what I should put into that letter totally defeated me. Eventually I scraped a few non-committal words together and put it in the post. Afterwards I was full of doubts. For one thing I had signed it, 'Yours sincerely,' which was ridiculous. I had thought of 'Love', but that word was as loaded as a bomb. I had thought of 'Friend', but I wasn't and probably never would be. I thought of 'Yours as ever', but that seemed almost as loaded as love. Then I thought of 'Yours' just by itself, but it was so wrong by itself. So at last I played around with the word 'Sincerely', and after putting it back then forwards ended up with 'Yours sincerely.' It was a mistake, but then in so many other equally obvious ways, the whole thing was. My failure over handling that letter was another symptom of my complete failure in handling Nicholas. I didn't know what to do, and because I realised that far too late I never fully avoided the disasters that were to come. Anyway Mark, Andrew and myself went down as planned, and that really was the beginning of the end. Even so, in my weakness, I made the end last a very long time.

He hardly seemed at all pleased to see me when we met up in my room. I had both Mark and Andrew with me, and I could tell at a glance that they did not take to him, which obviously at the time didn't help.

"Nicholas, I have to be honest with you."

I poured him some wine that I had brought back from London. I hoped it would put him at his ease, making him less moody and more talkative now that we were alone. Above all I had to talk to him. To get through that hard, withdrawn barrier that he had thrown up - but then, when I had got through, what great change would happen then? I had said that I had to be honest with him, but then again what did the word 'honest' mean in our relationship? What was I seeking with him, if anything?

"Is Mark your lover?"

All my inner questioning suddenly drew together into one simple certainty. Jealousy. Yet at the same time as I clearly saw that, I knew that jealousy for Nicholas would be far from simple. For me that specific emotion was totally alien, and because it was so alien and frightening I saw all my other questions dissolve into its certainty. Jealousy. I had felt it concerning Andrew and Mark hadn't I? No, it was not me. Jealousy was a naked invader that had to be destroyed at all cost. I stared at Nicholas. I stared at his face, and the ugliness of its expression; the sheer possessiveness of that expression made me feel sick. Yet I had to go easy. For my own sake I had to be as gentle as I could, but a gentleness that was tempered with steel. Quietly I told him that Mark had been my lover.

"You want to hurt."

He shielded his face, as if in anticipation of a blow. My first reaction was one of intense distaste. This was familiar melodrama; a gesture from a repertory of other melodramatic gestures. But as I looked at him closely I saw that there was something else; the pallor of his cheeks and the shivering in his body. He was genuinely ill. I made him sit down and knelt beside the chair, and took both his hands within nine. The ugliness and the strain had gone, and for a brief moment I wanted desperately to hug him to me. I felt desire, and beyond that desire, a harsh, aching emotion that he would in the next few minutes put so explicitly and finally into words.

"I love you, Peter. I love you."

There. It was said. I drew away from him. He had succeeded in hitting out at me, and it was exactly there in the place of the heart; the place in fact that I dreaded most.

"Do you realise what you are saying?" I said. For the word

'love' was so completely and utterly dreadful to describe anything that could happen between us. It was a mockery, yet in that mockery it was absurdly and paradoxically the truth.

"I know what I feel."

Behind the simplicity of the surface dialogue I heard another Nicholas talking. It was a Nicholas both cruel and violent, and guarded there in the deepest recess of his self was the word 'hate.' Hatred, not love. I carried on talking, but to every sentence that I uttered I heard only one reply, and that was the clear, but unspoken affirmation of hatred. Tears came into my eyes, but I did not, could not let them fall. I was frightened of Nicholas. I was terrified of the words that were being said (in his case perhaps unheard) behind the deception of both our appearances.

"I do feel for you."

Was it me saying those words? Did I really feel, care, and if I did what did I feel? Fear, I replied to myself, nothing but fear. Yet that wasn't true either, because in the centre of that fear lurked a powerful and terrible sexual longing. I wanted Nicholas, and I wanted him now. I wanted the hatred we shared. But I had to fight him. Battle was the perversity of this love. I was disgusted by the very thing that I longed for. Then for a moment I believed I saw clearly.

"Don't you see none of this is real? I would like it to be real, but it just isn't."

Reality. The last, the little of it that had been, was going. He was sucking me in. I felt his arms around me, drawing me into the centre and circle of pain. And despite the part of me that battled against him, I knew there was to be no escape. I tightened my body against his, tensing every muscle to ward off the physical blows of his passion.

"I want to show you," he said, and I felt my body bent stiffly forward. Suddenly I had no softness left in me. Nothing that remembered flesh. He was tearing at my clothes, and as he tore at them, the refused sob began to rise inside me to the surface. I had to break free from him, but his arms held firm, and finally the battle was over; I let myself be held. He forced his cock into me and the pain was atrocious. I cried out, but he paid no attention to my cries, but kept pumping and pushing into my body. As he withdrew I had the sickening sensation that my whole inside was withdrawing with him. I fell to the floor and put my hand to my anus where it still burned with the pain. I took the hand away and looked at it, and saw that it was smeared with blood and shit. Then the tears came, almost with a kind of relief. I got to my feet and did up my clothes. I let the tears carry on flowing and all he could ask me was if I wanted to come.

"It doesn't matter," I said.

I went to the sink in the corner of the room and washed my hands. Over the sink was a mirror, and through it I watched him arrange his clothes, then go towards the door.

"Don't go," I said.

I watched him button his shirt. The last button closed. All the time that we had fucked we had had articles of clothing on our flesh. I became obsessed by that one thought - we had been choked in layers of cotton and wool. Nothing naked; nothing clean, but grubby in tangled underwear and sweat smelling shirts. Why is it then, I cried inwardly, that I want your filth?

"Don't go," I repeated.

I went towards him. I felt like the dreamer who is bound within the certainty of his nightmare.

"You know I want to stay," he replied.

He smiled. A smile that seemed to gloat.

"Nicholas, we must talk."

"I hurt you," he said. "I shouldn't have done what I did. I'm sorry."

That was not what he was thinking, and I knew it was not what he was thinking. He had wanted to do what he had done very much. And oh yes, there was no use in pretending or denying it any longer, I had wanted the pain as well. I had wanted the hatred of his pain. It was true that there was no clean flesh, but then hadn't we died within the decaying corpse of our passion? The tangled clothes had been but a symbol of the winding cloth of the grave.

"Won't you live with me?"

He took my hand as he said this. I shook my head. The mere

idea of any form of domesticity within the bond that united us was nauseating.

"Nicholas, I will run away from you. Always. I will have to run away. I can never stay with you completely, however much you may think you want it. However much I may think I want it."

I was panting for breath. The room, his presence and the invisible presence itself of our hatred/love was suffocating. His hand felt hot and sticky within mine, and I took it away, sliding the film of sweat down the side of my trousers. Then I silently counted up to ten, managed to draw breath, and began to walk up and down, up and down, in the room.

"I don't know yet if I will be able to bear being in love," I said, then added, "God, the very word."

I wanted to spit that word out at him. Love. I thought if I managed to spit it out, then he would see it for the foul thing it really was. He didn't answer. He watched me pacing up and down in silence, then after a while quietly opened the door and left.

Alone.

I was alone. He was gone.

I ran to the window. I opened it, and gasped in great lungfuls of air. During the time that he had been with me in my room I had imagined it to be black and completely shut in, the windows closed up and behind the glass, sealing out the natural night, a wall of impenetrable brick. Trembling, I turned from the window and returned to the sink. Once more I washed my hands, frantically crying to rub out the memory of his touch, the smell of my own shit and the glue of his sperm. An hour later I went and walked by the sea. When I had walked to the point of exhaustion, I sat down in a deserted shelter on the promenade and closed my eyes. But the moment I began to drift off into sleep a horrifying image leapt at me out of the dream darkness. I was going to be cut to pieces by Nicholas, who held in his hand a large carving knife. I was going to be killed by him.

"No."

I screamed the word and forced my eyes wide open. A terrible heaviness behind the eyes wanted to return me to the dream. An instinctive drive towards my own death wanted to draw me back to my slaughter. I fought against the instinct with the only weapon that I had - that of terror. At last I succeeded in staying awake.

"I must not stay with him. I must go away before it is too late."

I mumbled the words aloud, over and over, sitting there in the shelter, waiting for the dawn.

The next time we met we caught a bus and went into the countryside. My aim that day was to make the encounter as uncomplicated as possible, but things didn't quite work out like that. He put his arm around my waist as we walked.

"You haven't talked much," he said.

"I don't know what to talk about."

"Tell me about yourself."

I threw the request back at him, without in the least meaning what I asked.

"No, you tell me about yourself."

"What do you want to know?"

As he said this I realised how little facts mattered. Facts about either of us. I knew he was a writer, but I didn't care a damn what he wrote about.

"Your books," I lied. "Tell me about your work."

He told me about the play he was working on, but I shut my mind to the words and concentrated my attention on the shape of his mouth. I looked at that mouth and watched it move. I watched it tell me things that I had no interest in. And as I looked at it I remembered those same lips biting into my neck. I wanted pain from his mouth, not words.

"I suppose you wonder where I get my money from?"

He laughed as he said this. It was the laughter that made me hear the words.

"No, I don't want to know."

"Michael thinks I'm being kept. I'm sure he does."

"Who is Michael?"

The name meant nothing to me. In the field we were walking

across a man and a woman were lying in the grass kissing.

"He's someone I know. You'd like him. I'll introduce you one day. He believes in a lot of the things you believe in."

I ignored what he was saying. Out of the corner of my eye I saw the man in the field cover the woman's body with his own. I recalled the pain of having Nicholas inside me, and the recollection of that pain made me wish he would do it to me again, here.

"Would you fuck me here, now, out in this field?" I asked.

"Would you want that?"

"Could you?"

I stopped walking and made him look me in the eyes. I felt my body tremble and for a moment the desire was so uncontrollable that I felt physically ill.

"Only in a room," he replied.

I walked on, trying to repress the intense disappointment that I felt. It was rape after all that I wanted, certainly not love. One day, I promised myself, I would have to tell him exactly that.

"I'm happy you want me though," he said. "I love you so much."

"Don't keep on saying that word."

"It's what I feel."

"But don't keep on saying it."

"I mean it."

He put his hand at the back of my head, clasping my neck. Death was desire, and out here in the field couldn't he strangle me with his hatred?

"I know you mean it," I said, "and I know what you mean by it. But I've told you before, I don't know to what extent I can respond."

He took his hand away and put it to his face. No, everything inside of me rejected death. I was alive and had to escape from the very desire I felt for him. He had stopped walking. I turned to look at him. His hand still covered the upper part of his face. I could only see the lips move.

"Does my skin revolt you?"

"Nicholas, don't..."

I felt embarrassed for him. I wanted us to stop talking.

"No, it doesn't revolt me," I said.

"But you must be conscious of it." He ran his fingers across the skin. Under the harsh sunlight I saw how red and inflamed the skin was. Two marks, like boils, were especially visible. He was ugly, yet the admission of that fact did nothing to stop me desiring him.

"If anything it excites me," I added. "Imperfection can be exciting."

I reached up to touch his face, but he pushed my hand violently aside.

"Don't humour me. Don't play with me."

His voice sounded choked and I could see that he was near to tears.

"It tortures me every time I think of that boy Mark. He was your lover. He is beautiful."

"Yes, he is - but it doesn't make any difference to my response to you. There's no comparison to make. Mark is Mark and he was my lover. You are you, and you are my lover."

I said the words carefully and precisely. I knew that they would make him happy. He drew his hand away from his face and reached across to kiss me. The pity and the desire drew me to him and I held him tightly.

"Don't leave me."

He sounded like a small child. I didn't answer him, but held on.

"I wouldn't survive it," he said.

"I'm here."

It was all I could say, and in the ambiguity of that statement there was meant to be an intended comfort. I was lying, yet at the same time keeping firmly to the truth.

"Do you believe that I wouldn't survive it?"

"Yes," I replied, and let him go.

We walked on in silence for a long time. As we walked I was conscious of his scarred face, hungry, needing. I was conscious of his body that I desired, and the more conscious of it I became, the more I loathed it. The only way to ease that loathing was to obliterate myself in his flesh. And beyond that I was aware of the slavery, one to the other, that both of us were being subjected to.

Eventually we reached a village. It was laughably good to have something as commonplace as tea in a country village. Yet it was there that the pressure really began.

"Peter?"

"Yes?"

"If I wanted to die - I mean, if I -?"

He stumbled on the words, then remained silent.

"Go on."

Inside myself I began to feel fear. I felt his hands round my throat. I saw the dream knife in his hands. I tried to hide the fear and drank at my tea. It was important to do ordinary, very ordinary things. I ate a piece of cake and as I ate the cake I watched his mouth.

"I mean, would you -?"

He made a vague gesture with his hands.

"Oh, don't listen to me. Forget I ever said anything."

"But you haven't said anything - yet."

My voice was cold. I watched an elderly man get up from the table next to ours. He brushed against me as he passed my chair, and the contact of his body was an immediate and vivid reminder that there was an outside world. A world totally removed from my experience with Nicholas, and one that I would always be a part of. I watched the man pay his bill and clung on to the image as if that alone, at this moment, could save me.

"Shall we go?"

Nicholas's voice sounded thin and tired.

"I don't know what you were going to say, and I don't want to know, but there must be no more talk of your death."

I got up from the table as I said this. He grabbed at my arm. His face was very white.

"What would my suicide mean to you?"

He smiled as he said this, and I shook myself free.

"Can we stop now? Stop this death picnic you have brought me on?"

I tried to make the hatred I felt for him obvious in the tone of my voice.

"You must answer me," he said.

"Alright. It's up to you. Your death. It's your decision."

I walked up to the cashier, paid the bill and left him sitting there.

I found a letter from Mark waiting for me when I got home.

"Plans for the centre are going ahead quite rapidly. People are being a bit more constructive than at that meeting you came to. I thought I would let you know so that anytime you feel like it you can come and give a hand. I've thought if it really gets off the ground we could open up a night and day service. I'd need you then full time, and as for the money side of things, well you know you don't have to worry about that. Anyway think about coming."

I read the letter over and over again, reminding myself that this too was the outside world, and that it was waiting for me. Nicholas had been to the toilet while I had been reading the letter, and when he came back he pointed to it where I had thrown it down.

"A letter?"

"As you can see." The jealousy again. I picked it up and put it in my pocket. "From my mother. You can read it if you like."

He shook his head.

"If you had wanted me to read it, you wouldn't have put it in your pocket."

"You can read it."

"It's not important. I want to fuck. Let's fuck."

He took off my clothes, but just as he was about to enter me he lost his erection.

"I can't," he said. "I shouldn't have followed you home. We should have left things for a while. I'm frightened. I know things are going to be dreadful."

We dressed in silence, then I asked: "What things?"

He made no reply, and I went out into the kitchen I shared with the other tenants to make us some food. Once more it was important for me to attach myself to ordinary actions, for they and they alone seemed capable of keeping me sane. A minute or so passed, then Nicholas followed me out. He stood in the doorway, watching me cook. I wanted to be alone and resented him there.

"I wish you would go back to the room," I said.

"I want to watch you. I like watching you."

I turned to him, and noticed how pale he looked. When the eggs were ready I pushed past him without a word, and put them down in my room on a small table by the bed. He came in, sat down on the bed and started eating. I ate mine as rapidly as I could, then put the plate aside. The long walk back from the country had made me hungry. Suddenly Nicholas dropped his knife and fork, and started shaking violently.

"Nicholas, what's wrong?"

"I can't eat it," he said. "I can hear the eggs screaming."

He began to sob, and I went across to him, putting my arms around his body. I rocked him backwards and forwards, his terrible frailty both attracting and appalling me. Eventually the sobbing subsided.

"What's going to happen to me?" he said.

"I don't know."

"The whole world is armed. Ready to kill. I'm ready to kill, and I don't want to... I really don't want to, but I can."

His forehead was burning hot. Without replying I went to the sink and wetted a towel with water. I put it to his head, and he shuddered with the contact.

"You need help," I said. "You must see a doctor."

"You think I'm mad, don't you?"

"I think you are unwell. I'm not talking about madness."

"The whole bloody world is sickness. You included. Me. The lot of us. What can any doctor do for me, when he too is sick?"

There was no way of getting across to him, and I felt tired and drained by the continual pressure he was inflicting upon me. I put him to bed, and to escape from him I went out for a walk.

How long did that period of insanity last? Weeks, months perhaps; I can no longer exactly remember. I came and I went, leaving him and returning, always drawn back, despite any attempt on my behalf at futile reason. We had met in the summer, but we had parted by the following spring. But I am going too fast. Things happened in those weeks, those months, things that must be remembered and somehow recorded. I did love him. There, it is better said, for in saying it I can more easily accept that part of the madness that enfolded me.

One night, soon after the incident with the eggs, he tried to strangle me in my sleep. It is strange proof of how much I accepted what was happening that I can say this so calmly. I escaped from him back to London, and it seemed no sooner had I got there than I realised I would have to return.

"But why, Peter?"

Mark shaking his head in front of me. I wondered how much more Mark could take of all this.

"Why this running away, and then wanting to go back? It's not like you, and you know it's not like you."

My mouth felt furry and stale with words that could no longer explain.

"What can I say?"

I looked at him and made a helpless gesture with my hands. What words could contain the enormity of my relationship with Nicholas?

"None of us are passive - completely passive in a situation," he said. "You must do something. You must make a decision and stick to it. You know very well what I would like that decision to be. I want you here. Above all there is work to be done, and that's what you need."

He made me tired with his sure knowledge of what I needed. Didn't he have any idea that that dark, hidden part of me that was turned away from him needed Nicholas? I needed the darkness of Nicholas. I had to try and explain. I had to make a way clear.

"It's like in the old romances, Mark. Yes, don't laugh, it is. It's as if I had drunk a love potion. But a drink stronger than love. So strong that it's a physical lust for hatred."

As I said this I heard someone else speaking from my mouth. I looked around me at the clean bright colours of the house. I looked at the scrubbed wood, at the yellow and white cushions and chairs. Here I was in a world of light and order, yet casting a shadow and a darkness over it all. Nicholas's shadow as well as my own.

"I don't understand."

Mark looked at me and smiled. Behind him on the wall was a picture of black and white geometric lines. I stared beyond him at the picture. It was now my own voice that I heard.

"I wish you'd understand that although I need it, I am not a part of it. I don't belong with him. Not finally."

"Then why talk of going back?"

"Because I must. He is pulling me back."

"That's absurd."

He stood up, blocking out the picture. I closed my eyes, then opened them again and looked at him. He was pacing the room in the same way that I so often paced.

"It's over ten days now since you came back. We have made plans for the centre. Good plans. We have people interested - and Christ knows that that's hard enough to do. We have done it. We're ready to start. And now you want to go back to that - that death again."

Suddenly he stopped pacing and shouted at me: "What do I have to do to make you stop?"

I waited a moment before answering, then said: Let me go, Mark."

"Alright, go - but you know what final end is in store, don't you? One or the other of you is going to slip over the edge, and then it will be plain bloody murder. You wait and see. It will happen like that."

I laughed at this.

"Don't be ridiculous."

"Am I? You're digging your own grave. Yes, just like in the old romances." He paused. When he next spoke the anger had gone out of his voice. "Tell it to me again. What did he do to you to make you come here? Tell me, because I want you to hear it. I want you to keep on repeating what he did to you, so that you will understand."

"Mark, I'm tired."

"How do you think I feel?"

He put his hands to his face.

"I know he tried to throttle me," I said, "but he didn't mean to. He was dreaming. He's sick. That's all."

"That's all? Peter, listen. I don't know if you fully realise this, but throttling kills. He could have killed you. Power he may have over you, but surely the prospect of your own death still means something. It must be able to shock, to frighten you - doesn't it?"

At that moment there was a knock on the door. The boy David with whom I had got angry at the meeting, came into the room. Mark turned to him at once.

"David, talk some sense to him."

I smiled and shook my head. David looked embarrassed, obviously not knowing what was happening or what to do. I looked at him, but this time without desire. It was as if over the distance that separated us, Nicholas was drawing all possible sexual energy from me.

"He needs talking to, David. Better still he needs going to bed with."

I stared at Mark and laughed. David said nothing and looked down at the floor. I felt sorry for the boy and decided to treat the whole thing as a joke.

"I think there are other ways of telling David that I find him attractive," I said. I grinned sarcastically at Mark. "But then you have always had your own way of doing things, haven't you?" I turned to the boy who was now looking at me. He too was grinning; a wide and empty grin. He was so much without shadow that he appeared totally one-dimensional.

"Do you want to go to bed with me, Peter?" he said.

I got up without another word and left the room. As I closed the door behind me I caught a last glimpse of Mark putting his hands once more to his face.

I sat in a chair and watched him as he slept. I had returned that morning to find him locked up, by his own will, in his room. The state of the place was disgusting, the air fetid with the smell of stale food and urine. He looked old and tired, his skin only too clearly revealing the weeks of self-imposed incarceration. I took him back, feelings alternating with emotions of pity and longing. Even in the state that I had found him in I longed for the sexual contact of his body.

We had talked; we had argued, afterwards grazing each other physically with our separate identities, but not for one moment meeting on any real common ground. I sat in a chair and I watched him. His face looked young in sleep, the marks and lines less distinguished. I stared at him for a long while, but the more I stared the more I realised that there was nothing there I wanted to see. Perhaps, I had thought, in sleep I would discover something approximating his true self. Eventually, bored with the useless search and my own ambiguous motives I got up to switch off the light, but as I was about to do so, I noticed an old photograph album lying on a side table. He had turned over in his sleep, and having his face to the wall, there seemed no possibility of his seeing my gesture as I approached to pick it up. Album in hand I returned to the chair, and found to my surprise that my fingers were trembling. I knew intuitively that to open this book would be to enter his world, to trespass on a frightening and private universe that I was, in my own way, struggling so desperately to escape from. I held the album for a long time, not looking at it, but staring at his back and watching him breathe. Then I looked away from him, and began to turn the pages of the book.

Images. No words, but images. The first that I saw was the most frightening. My eye looked at a pen and ink drawing of a large toad. It was a toad except for the head - and the head I recognised to be an exact memory drawing of my own. I shut the book loudly, and thought for a moment that the sound had woken him up, for he murmured in his sleep and then turned over onto his back. I remained very still and quiet, waiting for what seemed hours for his regular breathing to begin again. When it did so I re-opened the book. There were other drawings and photographs. Most of them were of concentration camps, and the rest consisted of detailed copies of more personal physical atrocities. Some were sexual, and usually of a sexuality involving brutality, but despite the horror of these varied images I could not forget the image of my own face. I turned to the page again and there was the fat toad staring up at me, but with features that would not have been dissimilar if I had been looking in a mirror. I got up and put the book back in the place where I had found it. I stared at Nicholas lying in the bed and saw that he had woken up, and was watching me.

"You saw," he said.

I looked down at him, and for the first time in my life I too experienced the desire to kill.

"Yes, I saw."

"You could call it a scrapbook. Even I don't realise that I'm keeping it. It's a secret, even to me."

He lay there looking up at the black ceiling. I fought at the desire to pick up his bedside lamp and smash it down on to his head.

"Why," I asked?

"Why what?"

"Why me? There in the book? The toad?"

"Oh, the toad."

He sighed, then stared hard at me.

"I don't know," he replied.

"You must know, otherwise it would not be there."

"Peter, why didn't you come to bed?"

"I'm asking you - why the toad? It had my face. My face, there in that pantheon of horrors."

There was a long pause before he said: "I never want you to become ugly. I could bear anything but that. For years now I have seen it happen to other people, but it should never happen to you. It would be the worst thing of all if you should become hideous and decay. The toad is ugly, but the head is beautiful."

My hands reached out for the lamp. I picked it up and held it. All it would need would be to raise it, and then - yet he was staring at me, fixing me with his dark eyes that knew precisely what I was tempted to do. Slowly I put the lamp down. It had a heavy bronze base and would have so easily smashed into him.

"I will grow old," I said, "eventually."

"Not you, Peter."

I walked away from him and sat down in the chair. He got out of bed and came naked to me. His body looked dreadfully white against the dark of the room.

"Keep away, Nicholas. You frighten me. You will always frighten me."

"I know what I am saying," he whispered. "Not you." Then, as if in a delirium, he murmured, "but the toad I can never explain."

He reached out and began to undo the buttons on my shirt. In a moment he was tugging the shirt from my trousers.

"Usually that album is hidden away. But while you were gone and I was shut up here, I kept it out."

He carried on talking as he undressed me. He went down on his knees and pulled my trousers from my body. I felt paralysed with a fear that even now I am incapable of describing. All I know is that he was manipulating me with his fingers, and that I was bound.

"It's a book of memories," he said. "The worst memories. That is more proof if you need it why I cannot take your centre seriously. Whatever they do to people like us will never be as terrible as the atrocities recorded in those pages."

I said weakly: "It's not true, Nicholas. It's just not true."

He was sapping all strength from me. Soon I was naked, and once I was naked he sat back on his heels and looked at me.

"You are beautiful," he said.

He said it as if he himself needed convincing of the fact. The fact that he had created.

"I am nothing," I replied.

"Will you be faithful to me?"

He reached out and began to stroke my legs with his hand. His hand felt like ice and I shrank under his touch. But even as I sat there, trapped, rebellion managed to return. I had to fight him - had to if I was ever to escape.

"You could perhaps persuade me to say yes to your fidelity," I said, "but it would only be a word. It has no meaning in my relationship with you."

My voice felt like an echo coming from very far away. He

stopped stroking me and getting up, returned to bed.

"It all has meaning," he replied. "The image is in the book, but the image is here."

I crossed the room and stood by the bed. "It's true what I said earlier today, Nicholas. We can never become one another. We can never become one person, and because of that you will always suffer."

He stared, up at me, and the stare was horrible in its utter desolation.

"I know you must never change, Peter. There is nothing else that I can say."

He reached out and switched off the light. Now that the lamp was out the darkness in the room was total. I got into bed and his flesh felt cold and clammy against mine. Then he crawled on top of me and covered me completely. I gasped and suffocated under his weight.

"I can't," I said.

"I want comfort."

Almost as soon as he had said this he fell away from me, and a minute or two later I heard him begin to snore. I thought, this is the ancient child that I came back to find.

The summer passed. Autumn came. Most of the time we spent in tense silence; a silence punctuated by the cries of our increasingly desperate orgasms. I shared the time between my room and his, and in neither place did I ever get the feeling that I was at home. Occasionally I would go to the place where we had met, and there I would have a brief sexual encounter. Nearly always I would return to him after the act, if anything the encounter serving to increase the desire I felt for his body.

One night I decided upon a particular action. I sucked a boy off, and instead of swallowing all of the sperm I kept as much of it as I could in my mouth. I returned immediately to Nicholas. The first thing I did on entering the room was to take him in my arms and kiss him. I passed what was left of the stuff from my mouth to his. He knew at once what had happened, and pushing me violently from him, went into the bathroom. I listened to the sound of running water and heard him gagging. Inside me a triumphant voice kept on saying - you've shown him. You've shown him at last how you can be. After this he will never expect fidelity from you. When he returned to the room he sat down on the bed and watched me. Every so often he would put his hand to his mouth and rub it, as if to wipe away the taste of the sperm.

"There was no need," he said.

"Wasn't there?"

The sound of my own voice was harsh and shrill. I was afraid, and the fear excited me.

"I could - "

He didn't finish the sentence. I went and sat beside him, and gently I took both of his hands in mine.

"What could you do?" I asked.

"I love you."

Tears were pouring down his cheeks. His body began to shake, and with the same gentleness that I had taken his hands, I brought one of them up to my face. I held it firmly and patted it against my cheek. He looked at me and his face was distorted with pain.

"Could you do that?" I paused. "You know what I want," I said.

His body went rigid, and then I had the impression that he was shrinking from me. I caught at his hand harder and made him hit me with it across the mouth.

"No," he murmured.

"But this is what I want."

My own body felt weaker and more and more frightened, but at the same time a frantic sexual excitement forced me to continue. Tonight he would hurt me. He would fuck me and he would hurt me, and then perhaps after that I would finally be delivered from him. I had to sicken myself in an excess of passion for him. My bowels ached and contracted, longing for him to split me open, to spill blood. I too had the taste of the stranger's sperm in my mouth, and with that taste I was ready for the catharsis of nausea. But he drew his hand away and shook his head from side to side.

"Am I entering your territory?" I asked.

"I don't understand."

"This is your territory, isn't it? Aren't you master here? I trespassed with the scrapbook - aren't I trespassing now?"

"Stop it, please."

"I'm bored, Nicholas."

"Stop it."

The tears had ceased. His face looked pinched and white. Slowly, very slowly he was becoming angry. I could see that anger in the rigid whiteness of his expression. I fed that anger as I would have fed a fire.

"I'm tired of our bodies scraping together. Routine scraping. Remember the violence? But then, there is no violence anymore, is there?"

I was pushing him further and further towards the brink. There had to be an end. I had to be saved from him. He got up and stood over me. I raised my face, longing for him to strike me.

"Go on, Nicholas," I said. I smiled at him, then added: "Don't you want to kill me?"

For a few minutes there was the terrible vertigo of silence. I felt the violence and power concentrate and become taut in his body. I felt that power boil up within him, and for a while after the explosion I hardly felt the pain. He was hitting at my face and body with his hands and as I began to feel the pain, I rejected it. No, no, this was not what I wanted.

"Please, Nicholas - "

My skin was sore with the blows. I threw myself face downwards on the bed, and he stopped beating me, covering my body with his own. His hands were burning as he put them inside my clothes, touching my flesh.

"No more," I whispered. "That's enough."

"I love you," he said again.

He kissed me then on the back of the neck, and I felt his cock push between my legs. I turned round to face him and bit at his tongue as he embraced me. I bit it so hard that he cried out.

"Have I hurt you?" I said. "I want to."

The words excited him. We rubbed our bodies fiercely and brutally together until we both reached a climax. Afterwards I lay back on the bed, all excitement gone, but feeling a sensation of satisfaction that I had never felt with him before. He sat up, and with his hands touched at two places on the bed.

"Blood," he said. "There is blood."

I looked at the red marks on the sheets, then I looked at him. He was crying, and large, gasping sobs tore at his body.

"Why?"

He pulled at his clothes as he said this, then began to dress.

"Don't always ask," I replied. "And anyway you know."

"This is not how I wanted it to be," he said.

I lay back on the bed, remaining in the same position as when I had climaxed. Oh what voice was it inside me that kept on urging and talking and talking? I had no power to stop it, and because I had no power I realised that it was I who was ultimately in control.

"Get dressed," he cried.

"No, I want to stay as I am. I want you to look at me. See me."

"I've seen enough."

I knew he wanted to leave the room, but as much as he wanted to go, I knew that he was trapped. My voice would not stop. Endlessly there seemed so much to finish, so much to say.

"What about death?" I asked. "You want to die, don't you? That's what you told me - remember?"

"I want to live here with you."

"If I really believed you wanted life, then I would stay with you, but afterwards I would regret my decision and go away again. I will always go away, and you will never be able to stop me."

He crossed the room and opened his wardrobe door. He got out the album, flicked through the pages, then stopped. He brought the book over to the bed, thrusting it into my hands at the page he wanted me to see.

"Look," he said.

My head that had been drawn on the toad was rubbed out. In its place was a smudged and dirty grey emptiness.

"I don't need to see it in that way anymore," he added. "You will become yourself, but you will no longer be the toad. Ever."

He closed the book and took it away from me.

"You are real," he said.

"No, not that. Rubbing out a drawing doesn't make much difference. Not that I understand it. I have never understood the drawing."

I got off the bed, and as I did so I had the impression that I was about to return to myself; to return to the person I had been before I had carried the unknown boy's sperm in my mouth. The madness of the night appeared to be over, and I felt suddenly like the victim of a fever who is made abruptly well. I went into the bathroom and washed my body. I would leave him now and go back to my room. But he followed me, and standing in the doorway said: "Do you remember the conversation we had a while back? I said then there was only one hope that you could fulfil."

"About me dying with you?"

"Yes."

"Well?"

"You said then that if it would help you would live with me. I replied that it wouldn't help, but now - "

"Now is too late. Now makes it impossible."

I rinsed my face with water and carried on talking to him as I dried my skin with a towel.

"You see," I said, "you have given me a taste for violence, Nicholas. For the rough stuff. Maybe it's always been there, but the only love I feel for you is certainly not one that we could live with. Let me explain more clearly. I am on a visit. I don't know for how long, but it's a visit. I am not a part of your world. I am passing through. During this stay I have learnt a great deal from you. You have taught me how to enjoy pain."

He hit at the door savagely, roughly with his hand.

"I want you."

He screamed the words at me.

"I want you, and if you go I will die."

"That's your decision. But then, I have told you that before."

I felt bored. It was as if I was looking down on him from a great height. Whatever love I had imagined I had felt seemed completely and utterly gone. At that moment in time he just appeared pathetic.

"We are not saying anything new, Nicholas."

"And the book? I changed the head. You are you, and I want to know you."

I laughed.

"Don't laugh at me."

"But the head on the toad is a blank now, isn't it? The picture of me has gone. I've gone. There's nothing there. I was more real to you in that picture as I was than as I am now."

"I don't know what I meant," he said.

I walked past him and put on my coat.

"Precisely. Now I'm tired and I'm going home to bed. I'll meet you tomorrow."

"Have you had your fun then? Have you had your kicks?"

He grabbed at my arm and squeezed it till it hurt.

"Leave me alone."

I tried to pull free, but he had me fast.

"So I have given you a taste for the rough stuff? How badly you put it. How wrong of you to put it like that - and anyway it's not true. On the bed you soon cried, enough." He paused. "Don't you see the true pain is deeper? The bond of pain that keeps us together is not a weekend exercise in sadomasochism. It's not a holiday thrill. It's us. It's our love."

The words cut into me and I knew that what he said was true. He was right, but I could not admit to him the truth. I wrenched my arm free and rubbed at it in silence.

"But I don't want it," I said at last. "And it is that part of me that you will never hold."

I went out into the night and left him alone. So many nights to record, but it was that one that burnt itself upon me. I stood looking out over the darkened waves, and the sea seemed to converge into one black dot, all the waves rushing and converging together into a black dot and then disappearing. The sea was sucked into its own invisible centre as I had been sucked into mine. Yet the love, I said, the love is there where everything has gone. It cannot but one day return. But what return? What was the paradox of love itself? All relationships exist in doubt. If one should say or even know what one thinks or feels for his/her partner, then both would be destroyed. We say what we do not feel, we say what we do not believe, to save ourselves and others from destruction. To know the truth of a relationship would be to accept that destruction where all opposites unite, and by uniting - as expressed in the language of the world - die. I murmured the words (nonsense words?) until the light of day broke up the darkness of the sky. Looking out I saw the sea, and hopelessly enough I knew that that too would return.

But I must go on. I must continue the story. More happened. Other days. I could describe different variations of our violence; I could tell about his continual drinking, and the drugs that he added to the drink. I could describe more of the airless, bound prison that I had made for myself, but I want air - I need light. I cannot constantly plunge into the depths of that ghastly relationship and still survive. Even the memory of all that happened has the capacity to kill me. But then I tell myself that I am free now that he is dead. He is the one that died, not I. Air. Light. That day, walking across the fields with him, telling him that I was going away.

"When will you come back?"

His face in the afternoon light, the marks on his skin making him look ugly and old.

"I will ring you from London. Perhaps you could come up to stay."

Why had I said that? I didn't mean it. I avoided his look.

"With Mark there?"

"With lots of people there. He's not the only person I know."

He stopped walking, and stooping down, tore at the grass, grabbing handfuls of it into his fists. I watched the small child in his endless despair.

"You don't really want me to come," he said.

"Then why would I have said it?"

He looked up at me sharply. Could he tell that I had been lying? I touched his face with my hands and for a moment it was all alright for him. He smiled. I realised how absurdly easy it was, after all, to make him happy.

"It will be Christmas in a few days time."

Even my voice was adapted to the child. He straightened up and we carried on walking. I felt the death of the countryside around us and shivered. In the distance I could see bare trees, and scattered on the ground dead leaves, mixed in with fern. He put his arms around me and drew me to him.

"We have got through," he said. "I must trust you. I know you will call me."

I wanted to say, but don't you see that this is to be the final escape? Instead I remained quiet, looking out at the darkness that was already descending over the fields. Air and light. How soon it was fading and going.

"I will call you to make the final arrangement. Or I will write."

Yes, this was to be the end. I was running one last time, I told myself, and I would never return. To think I had believed it then, avoiding the issue, avoiding the basic fact that my need for Nicholas, however much I wanted it to be, was not yet destroyed. All the same I went to London, and it was after a visit from his friend Michael that I came back to the town again.

Michael rang me at Mark's place one afternoon.

"Peter?"

"Yes?"

"This is Michael. Nicholas's friend. We met one evening last October."

I remembered. More than anything else I recalled his look; the way he had of staring at me. The boring desire that was so obviously there.

"Yes," I kept on repeating, "yes," then the invitation, God knows why, for him to come over to the house. Mark came into the room as I replaced the receiver.

"A friend of Nicholas," I said.

He shrugged his shoulders, but I could see that he was surprised. Threatened?

"He's coming over."

"Do you want that?"

"I don't know."

"Won't he want to talk about Nicholas?"

"I suppose he will."

I went into the kitchen and sat down at the table. I picked up the book I had been reading when Michael rang, and without much enthusiasm finished the page. All I wanted at that moment in time was to be quiet; to just sit and do nothing. Empty my mind of all the decisions made, and all the decisions that were to come. I didn't want to think about Michael's visit, about what it would mean. After a while Mark followed me into the kitchen.

"It's not good enough, Peter," he said.

I pushed my book aside.

"What's not good enough?"

"The way you're behaving. You shouldn't have agreed to that man coming here."

I looked at Mark. He was showing signs of strain and tiredness. For the past week there had been intense discussions about the centre, and I realised that I hadn't been of much use to him. I had been withdrawn and unresponsive when he needed me; immersed in my own emotional indecisions when I should have been helping him.

"I'm sorry, I haven't been much of a help," I said.

He made a vague, almost despairing gesture with his hands, then sat down opposite me.

"I know that it's going to take time," he said, "but I don't think having this man here for a talk is going to do much good. It seems to me that you are still compromising with your emotions."

"You don't know what I did, Mark. I didn't tell you everything."

"Then tell me everything now."

He reached out and took my hand. I responded to his touch by entwining my fingers with his. It felt good and it felt warm, and I realised then how much I needed his presence and his love.

"I hurt him in a way that is unforgivable."

"Like doing what?"

"I went out one night to the bushes. It's a park at the end of town. I had sex with a boy."

"So?"

"I sucked him off, and I - I kept as much of the sperm in my mouth as I could. I went straight back to Nicholas and took him in my arms and kissed him. I passed what was left of the stuff from my mouth to his."

I hadn't looked at Mark while I had been recounting this. His hand had remained within mine, and was it my imagination alone that made it suddenly seem lifeless and cold?

"It's like the taste will never go away."

I stopped talking. Quickly I looked into Mark's face. It was pinched and pale. He avoided my eyes, and said very slowly: "We all of us do things - sometimes - that we later regret. I know why you did it, and you know why you did it. It doesn't alter what happened, but you must be precise in your own mind about the mechanics of what happened. The only way to live with the memory of an action like that is to understand the reason."

I took my hand away from his, and getting up from the table went over to the window. It was a bitterly cold day, but the fierce cold that I felt was more within than without. I stood there by the window with my back to Mark, hugging myself with my arms.

"There was no reason," I said. "It was a mad act, a panic act. I was in a state of panic because I had to get away from his possession of me."

"Wasn't that reason?"

"No - it was cruelty. Blind, panic cruelty. I could pretend it was rational. I did. I tried to." I paused. "Oh God, Mark, I can't feel, you know. Not really feel. I tried with him. I tried to be what he wanted me to be - and in the trying I got a taste for the pain that was the only binding emotion between us. I needed the pain that he could inflict, and that I could return. People often lie when they talk about pain. It can have very little to do with either suffering or sensation. Sometimes I believe it can be the strongest emotion of all."

"So you can feel something, Peter. And because you felt what you felt wasn't it reason to take revenge?"

"But there was no thought to it. No reason."

I turned round and faced Mark.

"It was a completely spontaneous action."

Mark picked up the book I had been reading and turned it over in his hands. I watched him, fascinated. This small, almost insignificant gesture suddenly appeared to be all that there was in life to carry on for. The simple gesture of picking up a book without so much as looking at it, and turning it over, contained more of the essence of duration than any other action that I could think of. The terrible incident of the sperm was trivial in comparison to the emotion, the enormity of the emotion I felt watching this apparently superficial act. I knew at that moment that it was to the simplicity of things that I had to return. Mark put the book down.

"There's not much point in going over again what took place between you," he said. "I want you to think of the future, Peter. I love you, and I want you here. I have no desire to possess you, so you need never have to be afraid of that. Anyway, as far as I'm concerned, I've got Andrew for sex. But you - "; he got up from the table, and crossing the room, put his hands on my shoulders and squeezing gently, murmured, " - you need someone as well."

"You mean a casual relationship? Like yours with Andrew?"

He nodded his head.

"I wouldn't say casual exactly - I would say a necessary outlet. Something that's there, but that's undemanding."

I didn't look at Mark, but continued looking at the table. I wanted to go and pick up the book, but remained where I was.

"David would like to be your lover," he said.

The name bounced off me like a ball. I laughed.

"Oh, him."

"Why not? He's good-looking. He's your type. I know that. He's got money, and although you don't have to worry about that here, a little extra is always useful. To say the least, it's an advantage."

I broke away from Mark and sat down again at the table. I stared at the book, but there was still no way of touching it.

"Does he really want me?" I said. The words were meant to be, and sounded mechanical.

"In his simple way he thinks he's in love with you. But it's not the sort of love you would have to worry about. All I know is that he would be generous - he has already gone a long way in helping the centre. His father has a lot of money and supports him well. He has brought his father here."

At that moment I began to cry. For the first time in a very long time I experienced the simplicity of tears.

"Peter, I'm sorry, maybe I shouldn't have approached it in that way."

He came to me and took my face in his hands. Gently I pushed his hands away.

"No, it has nothing to do with that."

"What is it then?"

"It's Nicholas."

"What about him?"

"It's finished - but it's not, Mark. It's not finished at all."

I touched the book. Mark turned away from me.

"Give David a try," he said.

"I will if I can."

"You can," and his voice was firmly cold as he said this. "You can because at friendship level alone you owe it to me. I count in this for something, you know." Then he smiled and asked, "Now what time is this man coming?"

"Four."

"Are you sure you want to go through with seeing him?"

"It won't be dangerous in any way, Mark. I can promise you that."

Soon after four Michael arrived, and Mark left us alone together. I was tired, above all tired of talking and it took a while to make the smallest effort to respond to him. He reminded me of a big dog; the kind of dog that is perfectly contented with the occasional pat and word of kindness. In a way I rather liked him.

"I don't think I will be going back to Nicholas ever again," I said.

As I said the words the whole of me cried out suddenly - no, no, that is not what you mean. Both Mark and this man will make you say things that you don't, and that you will never mean. Once more I saw Nicholas's marked and suffering face in front of me, and I wanted to go to him with the same simplicity of action as I had responded to things. I wanted to reach out and touch him with the same directness as I had contemplated in picking up the book. I wanted -, but then the thoughts stopped, and I listened to my other self, and its own voice as it was speaking.

"I don't like self-destruction. Nicholas is destructive."

And so the voices continued. Three voices, weaving round each other, saying words, contradicting, making statements. Michael stating facts. Peter stating facts (truths?) and then only to have another fact affirmed by the second Peter. I followed the patterns of sound of my other self until abruptly, without warning, in the middle of a sentence, my two selves met, and for the first time since Michael had arrived, joined as one. It was fairly late into the night when it happened, and we had had a lot to drink.

"Shall I tell you about the first time I thought I had fallen in love?"

What was his name now? Philip, David, Peter? Yes, that was his name - Peter. The same as my own. The purgatory of love. The purgatory of the similar. Facts, yes; truths, maybe. So here at last I had reached a memory that had the absolute clarity of beginning. In that recall I rediscovered my very first pain, and it had the sweet sharpness of the cleanest of wounds.

"We used to meet late at night," I said. "We met in a park when our parents were asleep. I got involved with him. We weren't any more than children, yet the involvement had a freshness, a simplicity, that now I realise only too well will never come again. It went on for months our secret meeting, and our kissing - because, improbable though it may sound, that is all we did. Then one night he didn't turn up. I waited nearly all of that night, and returned the next, and the next after that. Eventually it sunk in that he would not return. And with that knowledge the park itself even changed. I knew that the park would never be innocent again."

For a moment, while I was talking about the boy Peter, I remembered another boy in a similar park, and I was on my knees sucking his cock, and Nicholas was standing by, watching. Then the image went, and I concentrated my attention on the memory of the more distant, yet for all that, clearer past.

"One morning though we met again in the street where I lived. I thought that he had at last come to see me. I think I must have been shaking when I went up to him. He was so handsome and smiling, and said he had just come back from a holiday. I asked him then if he had come to see me. He looked surprised and said that he had friends of his parents living a few doors away from me. He had come to see them. That was enough for me. The innocence was gone forever. I walked away. It was then, I think, that I learnt my first and most important lesson. I learnt that only life could improvise such a corny, heart-breaking encounter. Then the next lesson was Nicholas. What I learnt from that was that if you let life in then it must - must break your heart. Only when the heart is broken can it remain forever cold."

As I finished my story I felt my two selves part once more. The other self was speaking as I touched Michael; the other self was saying, no, as I mechanically allowed him to caress me and take me to bed. But all the time that he fucked me I let the whole of me, the real me, wander back to the park that I had left such a long time ago. I left my other self as I would have left a corpse.

The following morning, after Michael had gone, I decided what I should do.

"You will go back to Nicholas," I said aloud, "and you will take each day as it comes."

"Did he fuck you?"
"No, Nicholas, he did not fuck me."
Standing together in the square of the black room. I feel suffocated in the square of piled books and darkness. I long to go out, to go anywhere that is other than this room. But since I have been back, there has been no escape from the total absorption of Nicholas's world. At first there had been the illusion of relating; we had talked, actually talked and listened to one another, and the illusion had been good. Yet now the ritual of mental and emotional slaughter had begun again.

"Did he?"

"I have told you, no. What do you want?"

Standing together in the enclosed space, waiting in the narrow, tight-fitting night of our world for battle and pain.

"I want the truth."

"I have told you the truth."

"But he stayed the night with you?"

"Not with me - at the house. There is a difference."

My body trembling, standing on the brink of the truth, wanting to say, yet drawn back into the lies that he had woven around me. But at the same time thinking that if he continues, I will have no alternative but to plunge.

"Did you want to go with him though?"

I laugh at this. The dull, ridiculous absurdity of the words.

"Tell me."

His face is white. He clenches his hands into fists. I see the child tugging at the grass in the fields. In the same way he is tugging at me, and in a moment, yes, in a moment, I must give way.

"I want to know what happened. Did he try to get you into bed?"

I look at him, feeling nothing. If this is the price that he wants to pay, then he must be allowed to pay it.

"Yes," I say.

"Yes, what?"

"We did it. We fucked. But you knew, didn't you? What truth is there in hearing me say it when you knew all the time?"

He closes his eyes. I can see him falling within the abyss of his own body, falling backwards and down into the hell of jealousy he has created. I have fallen too, but outside, not within. I have fallen once more, and perhaps decisively this time - away from him.

"Give me the details."

The eyes open. He is looking at me from the centre of the pit.

"Do you mean who fucked who?"

"I know," he says.

"Then if you know, what other details can you want?"

"Did you enjoy it?"

I laugh again - straight in his face. He winces as if I had hit him, but I know that there will be no actual physical blows in this confrontation.

"So there we are," I say, "at the heart of it."

I am jeering and I cannot stop. He is small in his hell like a guttering candle about to be extinguished. And I am going to blow, blow upon him until the destruction and obliteration is finally achieved.

"Did I enjoy it? You can't conceive of that can you? Have you ever really enjoyed it, Nicholas? No, wait, I don't mean with me. I mean with anybody? Have you ever known the simplicity of it, the going into it for the pleasure alone?" I paused. "No, you haven't, have you? It has always had to be to the accompaniment of your own wretched mental pain."

"The pain is real."

He is whimpering like an animal that has been thrashed. I blow and I blow, the air-whip of words curling round his exhausted body.

"What do you know of any reality? Is it there in your books?"

I move away from him, and going to the cupboard, take out the scrapbook. I open it at random and thrust the image at him.

"Tell me what you see, Nicholas. What is the first thing you see when I open your most private of books for you?"

He looks at the page and shakes his head.

"Take it away, Peter."

"What is the image? Do you want me to tell you what you see?"

I look at the page. It is a still from a film. A man is walking through a forest with hands outstretched, feeling his way. His face is disfigured by blood and pain.

"Shall I tell you what the image is?"

"I know."

"It is of a man with both eyes gouged out. A man who cannot see."

I shut the book.

"And now, Nicholas, tell me if that has any meaning for you?

And if it doesn't have any meaning for you now, tell me what it had then - the day when you chose it from all other images."

"None."

His voice is very low, beaten, wanting me to put an end to what I am saying. But I am the torturer. It is my turn to hurt, and I continue.

"Did you choose it - in an arbitrary way? Was it taken out from any number of other possible terrible images - without relevance? Could it have been just that, irrelevant?"

I am cold, and my words are cold.

"I want to know," I repeat. "Was it irrelevant?"

I am surprised at the harshness of my own voice. I am shouting at him.

"It could have been another image," he says.

"And Michael could have been another man. Almost any other man. It was just as arbitrary. Just as irrelevant."

"I don't understand."

"I think you do."

He takes the book out of my hands and slowly, very slowly, begins to tear out the pages one by one. Soon the book is torn into many fragments, and he falls to his knees and buries his hands in the pile of paper.

"No, it is not true," he cries. "I chose them. I chose them all."

"But they could have been any other image. They weren't real then, and they're certainly not real now." I pause before continuing. "You have never ever experienced any of these images. They are fiction. Perhaps somebody's truth, but fiction for you. An arbitrary fiction that appealed to your desire for pain, not to the pain itself. And because they were never experienced, any other image would have done as well."

I get on my knees beside him, and take his hands away from the paper. I raise his hands to my lips, and he shrinks from me, and I realise that perhaps he thinks I want him to hit me again.

"I didn't want to destroy this," I say.

"Didn't you?"

There are tears in his eyes. He takes his hands away and covers his face with them. I stand up.

"Don't leave me."

The sound of his words is barely audible from behind his hands. I want to leave the room now and he senses this. I tell him quietly that I have no intention of leaving.

"When you came back," he takes his hands from his face, "when you came back I told you that I prayed for the cruelty to end. I did pray for it, Peter."

"But it hasn't, has it? It doesn't seem to be able to ever end. I hoped too that it would be changed, different. I hoped that we could be understanding, that we could be kind."

I look down at him. The intense coldness has gone.

"Get up, Nicholas," I say, and he gets up.

"You're wrong," he murmurs, "about it being arbitrary. I have chosen everything - even when there was so much to choose from, and any sincere choice seemed impossible. I know who the blind man is - "

"And I know who Michael is."

He stares at me, waiting again for the pain.

"He is nothing. Nothing that anyone else couldn't quite as easily be for me."

"When you say that, I think of us. Is it like that? Is it like that for us?"

He bends down and begins to pick up the pieces of the book. As he waits for me to answer, he puts down the pieces, then sweeps at the carpet with his hand. I watch him as I reply.

"I don't know what it's like, or if it's like anything. I thought it was something; not love as you imagined you wanted it, but something. Now I no longer even care to know."

He cries quietly as I leave the room.

Where did I go when I left him? How clearly certain times and places stand out when others, which seemed important, fade and are forgotten. When I left him that night I went to a club and danced. It was the only freedom that seemed possible, to dance. I went from one partner to another, not caring who they were or what they looked like. I danced between them, and in front of them. I danced around their bodies, and I both laughed and cried at the simple joy of having escaped from that dreadful room. But when dawn came I re-entered the black room, and closed the door once more behind me.

When I first started recounting this story it was wide like a circle - and like the circle contained; imprisoned in its roundness; where the only journey possible was inwards to the point, the centre. Now I am at this point. I am there in the whirlpool of darkness, where all light from the space of the circle has concentrated, and become tight as the arse of hell. I use this image because it is the last image that I want to hold of Nicholas. It is the pivotal image of the final experience between us; an experience that I can only just bear to tell.

"Don't turn on the light."

The voice of Nicholas, harsh, commanding. I stand in the doorway of his room trying to make out where the voice comes from in the shadows of the black square.

"Don't turn on the light."

He repeats the command. I hesitate for a moment, then I flick the switch. There is immediate brightness. A shattering brightness that illuminates the naked figure of Nicholas facing me in a corner of the room. For a second I think he is praying, for he is on his knees and has his hands joined together in front of him; then I see that they are joined together lower down, not praying, but pulling at his cock.

"Nicholas."

I say his name, more in shock than for any specific reason. This is the first time that I have ever seen him masturbating. He looks at me. The face is blank, expressionless. He carries on pulling at himself, a little faster now. I stare at his hands and I find that I am both fascinated and repelled by what he is doing.

"You look as if you have never seen anyone do this before."

My voice is shaking as I answer him: "I have never seen you do it before."

"We've done it often enough together." He laughs. I look again at the expressionless face. A line of a smile divides the emptiness of the space into two parts. Yet on either side of that line there is nothing, nothing at all. I am afraid, but my fear prevents me from running. And all the while the draw of fascination impels me to look down, to look at the hands and the erect penis between the hands.

"Stop it, Nicholas."

He does not stop. He continues to pull at his cock and I cannot bear it.

"You disgust me."

I say the words, and they, if nothing else must make him stop.

"I know," he replies. "I know I have always disgusted you. Not only my touch, but even the look of me. You have never been able to look at me."

I stare at the face once more. The line has contracted to a point. The point of the mouth talks and talks, but there is nothing around it, nothing that I can see.

"Hasn't my face always disgusted you?"

The point opens wide into a scream.

"Answer me."

I feel a sudden, tight pain across my chest. I cannot bear it - I cannot.

"I cannot see anything."

I tell him the truth. But it is only half of the truth, for I see very well the hands in their terrible motion, pulling upwards, then down.

"Shall I tell you what my face looks like? Shall I describe it to you? It has lumps on it. Like the lumps on the back of a toad."

I close my eyes. I murmur to myself that this is the worst. This is the worst that can happen. I say to myself that if I wish hard enough he will disappear. It will be as if he had never existed. If I keep my eyes closed for a while longer, then open them, he will be finally and forever gone. I open my eyes. The face in front of me that had been empty before is now covered with marks and lines. His words, the revulsion of his description has jolted me back into seeing. The smile on the face is no longer an abstract line, but a pitiful human mass of flesh made up of many inter-connecting, criss-crossing lines. Nicholas, I say to myself, almost with horrified wonder, is a human being.

He begins to gasp. The hands move faster. He is nearly there, and I throw myself at his body and knock the hands away. He lies back on the floor and looks up at me.

"Don't you want to see it - now that you have turned on the light?"

"Get up, Nicholas."

"I will not get up. I will change position. That will make it easier or at least make it less visible for you."

He kneels, then turns on his knees, and remains very still with his back to me.

"Now you no longer have to look at my face."

I move away. I step towards the door. Suddenly the voice begins again, but the tone is different. It is no longer harsh and commanding, but filled with a yearning, pleading sadness.

"Do what you want - please."

I stand there looking at him, watching the back of his head, listening to the sound of his words coming from a mouth that I can no longer see. Then my eyes concentrate on the neck. I want to bite that neck. Then I look at the scarred back, and the base of the spine.

He reaches out with his hands and touches the wall. He parts his legs a little wider, still remaining in the kneeling position. Between the tangled hair I see the pink opening of the anus. He is open for me. Waiting for me.

"Do what you want," he whispers.

I move towards him and place my hands on his back. I reach down and caress his arse, then touch with a finger the entrance that leads into his body. He presses backward at the same time that I push, and says, "Yes. Yes, do what you want with me. Do what I have always wanted."

I stare at the back of his head as I move my finger in and out; stare at the thick, curly hair, and I imagine that he too is all that I have ever wanted. At that moment I am drawing towards the black centre of desire; I am on the brink about to fall into the loss of self. Yet as I am about to dissolve, my ego gathers together, fortifying me against that very loss I had momentarily yearned for. My body separates itself from his.

"I can't," I say.

"Do it," he murmurs, "enter me. I am nothing. Nothing."

"No." I stand up. "I can't."

"Tell yourself that I am nothing. You have never seen me - remember? You have never known or looked at me. I will be totally yours because I will be nothing."

The suffocating madness of the room makes my head spin. I feel giddy with shock and frustration. I want the body that is offering itself to me; I want it with a burning fierceness, yet I know that if I touch I am lost.

"Do it, Peter. I will whisper to you as you fuck me. I will tell you how you have succeeded in making me realise that I no longer need to exist. Oh, Peter, it's true. This is the truth at last. I am nothing. I no longer have a face. I no longer have eyes. I am in the dark and I cannot see, and you are entering that night with me. I will take you in. I will hold you and cradle you, and ease you into the heart where nothing need matter again."

I am going to faint. I steady my body against a chair. I look across the room at the white flesh; I look and I open my mouth and I scream. I have the impression that his anus, his bowels, are forcing excrement and blood into my mouth to stifle my screams and cries.

I don't know how long the screaming lasted. When it stopped it was as if I had regained consciousness after a long, excruciating nightmare. Nicholas was still on his knees, completely motionless, with his back to me. But within me there was no longer the slightest recollection of sexual want or need.

"Love me."

The voice was pleading. I felt free, detached from it. I was beginning to feel strong.

"Aren't you tired of love," I asked?

It was then that he turned round. The pitiful body turned and faced me, the drawn face accusing in its ugliness. We were confronting one another for the last time. He gasped out the insult as if it was the climax of all possible desire. He gasped out this final word and afterwards there was nothing left between us. It came from the entrails of possession. It came, dragging with it all that we had endured together, all that we remembered. It debased the feminine as it debased the masculine, and in the fury of the word I found the opening door of my prison and the means for my escape.

"You cunt," he said.

I heard it as one would hear a parting endearment. I think it was the only true word of love he had ever spoken.

"Yes," I replied, and smiled.

Of course I could go on from there, but there is no need. The rest of that incident and all the other incidents that followed would be nothing but useless description. Nicholas had given me my name, and in the naming had released me from the point in the circle. I moved into another dimension now, another world.

The last scene of my story could be described as a postscript.

I am in Mark's house. We are four at table eating our evening meal. Andrew is with Mark, I am with David. The telephone rings. Mark answers it.

"It's for you, Peter."

He holds out the receiver. I look at him in alarm. My look says, is it Nicholas? If it is Nicholas I don't want to speak to him. I say aloud, "Is it him?" He shakes his head.

"It might be about him," he says.

I sigh impatiently and cross the room. I turn round and smile at David as I reach for the receiver.

"Yes," I say.

"Peter?"

"Yes."

My voice is deliberately cold, unquestioning. I recognise the voice at once. Of course, Michael. How remote it all seems. I watch David who looks bored. He is fidgeting in his chair. I feel nothing for him, but then I have at last totally accepted the fact that I will probably never feel anything for anybody.

"What do you want?" I say.

"Have you heard?"

"Have I heard what?"

"Nicholas is dead."

I ask him to repeat what he has just said. I don't believe it, but then I always knew that it had to come. I don't believe it, but it was always true. My voice is trembling as I ask for details. Mark, Andrew and David have drawn close to me. They form a circle around me.

"How?" I ask.

"It was suicide. He threw himself from a train."

I put down the receiver without answering.

"He's dead," I say. The circle draws closer. I tell them exactly what Michael has told me. A voice speaks from the circle. Is it David's voice? I do not look at the faces. The voice is simple in its sudden cruelty.

"What a romantic way to die."

I hit out with my hands in anger, but the circle doesn't seem to withdraw. If anything it crushes in on me more strongly. I hit out at them, but as my hands beat at their bodies I realise that it was I, and not one of them who had said those words.

"What a romantic way to die."

I let David take me in his arms, and I close my eyes.

PART FOUR

THE STRANGER

Nicholas is alone, walking through a park that is both familiar, yet utterly strange. It is at that hour of night that hovers between light and darkness, and he feels afraid. Suddenly he notices movement in the bushes at the side of the path, and a moment later sees a large brown crab appear. It is followed by another crab, then another, and he stands there petrified with fright as more and more crawl into view. Among the many that have crawled into view are a group that are different from the others in this respect; that their shells are deep red, not brown. He knows that they are all moving down the path towards the beach at the bottom of the park, and he also knows that there is no way for him to reach the sea before them. His will urges him to turn around and escape, but the fear is so strong that he is unable to move. All that he can do is stand and watch. The red crabs emit a foul odour as if the meat inside their shells had already gone bad, while the brown remain odourless. At one point a red and a brown separate themselves from the rest, and their claws clasp together in a battle embrace on the path. The red wins, and the shell of the brown crab splits open, revealing nothing inside. Nicholas realises that the brown crabs are nothing more than their shells. He also sees that in their instinctive desire to reach their destination they do not hesitate to crawl over each other to be the first to arrive. He knows that the battle he has just witnessed is more the exception than the rule. To all appearances the crabs have no other motivation than to reach the sea as quickly as possible, and without any regard for each other in the process. Brown back climbs over red, red over brown. In his despair Nicholas remains motionless, observing their journey to the sea.

Monday.

He woke up and lay for a long while in the darkness. At last, to his surprise, he found that he could move his limbs. He got out of bed and turned on the light. He stood in the centre of the room and put both hands to his mouth. The light was on in the black room, yet the darkness in his mind was total.

I am going to die.

He sat on the edge of the bed and longed for the burning tears to flow, but they would not flow. He stayed motionless for a couple of hours, and in his despair his body became cold, almost as cold as if he had actually died. I am going to die. The same words echoed in the room and in his head, revolving and turning on themselves until they became meaningless. He would go on living.

Towards dawn he stood up again and slowly began to dress. He fumbled a long time with his shirt, and broke a button. When he had finished dressing he looked at himself very quickly in the mirror and combed his hair. Now I am ready, he said, but he was not quite sure what for. He stood for a while longer staring vacantly round the room, then confusedly decided that this was to be the last day that he would spend there. Rapidly and methodically he sorted out his clothes, then put them into the only two suitcases that he possessed. This is all that I will take, he thought, then remembered the pile of his manuscripts in the corner of his wardrobe. He opened the wardrobe door, and took them out, one by one. The top manuscript was the play he was working on, and with the same determination with which he had collected his clothes he tore the manuscript into many small pieces. Picking up the pieces he took them into the bathroom and threw them into the sink. The sink was dry and he set a match to them. He watched until the last piece was burnt away, then turned on the tap to wash down the ashes. Returning to the black room he avoided looking through the other manuscripts, leaving them as they were piled up on the floor. At a quarter to seven he was standing on the landing locking the door of his room. Then he descended the stairs to the street.

In the street his steps were at first uncertain. He had to

control a momentary impulse to return to the room, which appeared for an instant in his mind to be the only possible place of safety. Having controlled the impulse to retreat his steps became surer, his mind now totally accepting the fact that he was walking in the direction of the station. The morning was bright and the day, even at this hour, extremely hot. He found that he was sweating profusely, and his hands were sticky and wet as they clutched at the suitcases.

"I want a single ticket to London."

He handed his money over for the ticket, at the same time asking the man behind the counter at what time the next train left. He was told that he had half an hour to wait. He took his suitcases to the station buffet, then went back out again to re-check the departure time of his train. Satisfied he retraced his steps to the buffet and bought himself some tea. He closed his eyes as he drank the tea, then opened them abruptly as he felt a tap on his shoulder. He turned round, only to find that there was no one there. A few paces away from him a black woman was on her knees washing down the floor, and as he looked down, she stared up and smiled at him. He got up from the table and literally ran from the place. It was only after he had got on the train that he remembered his suitcases, but he was by now far too frightened to go back and fetch them. It doesn't matter, he kept on saying to himself, it doesn't matter. Then the train lurched forward, and he was on his way.

Gradually, as the journey progressed, the fear subsided, and he began to worry more over the practical loss of his clothes. Mentally he recalled each item of clothing, and as he remembered them another more pressing and urgent thought pushed its way into his mind. The thought said, don't worry, you will not have time to need more than the clothes you are in. The thought resonated in the echo chamber of his mind, and for a while he felt that his head would completely burst apart. Burst apart, thrown open under the pressure of doom that these words implied.

"I will go on living."

He said this aloud, and the passenger next to him, startled by what he had said, asked him if he was alright. He laughed at the question, and the force of laughter, releasing him from the mental pressure, made him feel better. Looking out of the window he saw that he had reached the London suburbs.

"I am going to live here," he said.

The woman next to him smiled.

"Which part?" she asked.

"I don't know," he replied.

She turned away from him.

When he arrived at the station he jumped from the train, running and pushing his way along the platform, absurdly convinced that he would only arrive at his destination if he was the first to reach and pass the ticket barrier. Once outside the station he stopped running. He joined the taxi queue only to realise that he had no address to give, nor any destination in mind. By this time the day had become unbearably hot, and the suit he was wearing felt itchy and uncomfortable. The perspiration was trickling down his arms to his hands. He smelt the heavy odour of his body, and he remembered that lethargy had prevented him from taking a bath for several days.

"Are you waiting for a taxi?"

A bald headed man who was standing behind him smiled. He looked at the man and did not return the smile. He shook his head, and the man said, "Excuse me," brushed past him and got into the taxi. It was at that moment that Nicholas realised he was holding up the queue.

"Can I give you a lift?"

The man was looking at him from the open taxi window. He was still smiling, and when Nicholas made no reply to the question, the man opened the door so that he could get in. After a moment of brief hesitation he got in, without so much as looking at the man as he did so.

"I don't know where I am going," he said.

The man bent forward, giving the taxi driver an address, then shut the connecting window. Nicholas leant back and closed his eyes. He no longer even remotely cared about a destination. Quite simply he would travel where the taxi took him.

"I was watching you," the man said.

"Oh," Nicholas replied. He kept his eyes firmly closed.

"I was watching you, and I thought you looked lost."

"I am lost," Nicholas said.

That sounded too much like a confession, and he turned his head and stared at the man. At this point in time, he thought, it is best to smile, and he smiled. The man reached out and touched him gently on the arm.

"So you have nowhere to live."

Was that a question or a statement? Nicholas looked out of the taxi window to avoid having to look at the man again. He remembered and felt the protecting darkness of the black room that he had left, and wanted to return to it.

"I have a home," he said.

The man took away his hand. The taxi came to a stop outside a house in a cul-de-sac. Nicholas got out of the taxi first.

"It's a nice place," he said to the man as he followed him into the house.

"It's my home," the man replied, then turned to him in the hall and kissed him on the mouth. Nicholas raised his arm and would have hit the man only he too raised his hand and caught at Nicholas's wrist in time.

"Don't," Nicholas said. "I don't like being kissed."

As he said this he felt a fool growling at the bald headed man. He realised how foolish this pretence at being tough was, when all he really wanted to do was cry tears.

"Do you want to go?"

The man stood by the door, looking uncertain and afraid. Nicholas smiled for the second time.

"I am tired and I am hungry," he said.

The man relaxed at these words and told him to follow him to the kitchen. Once he had eaten Nicholas felt better and stretched out in his chair. All he needed now was a wash or a hot bath, and the feeling of physical contentment would be complete.

"Where is your home?"

The man got up from the table as he said this. He began to prepare some coffee.

"It's not here," Nicholas replied.

He didn't want to be mysterious or evasive; he didn't want to be a mystery at all to the man, but at the same time he had absolutely no desire to explain.

"I am not going back," he added.

The man stopped what he was doing and looked at him.

"Run away?" he asked.

"You could say that."

"Why?"

"I don't want to talk about it."

The man looked at him for a while longer, then continued preparing the coffee. Nicholas could see that he was ill at ease and the silence that ensued between them was a terrible pressure. Nicholas wanted silence, yet at that moment he felt that it was a wrong silence.

"Do you want to have sex with me?"

The man nodded his head. Nicholas asked if they could go and do it now. Once in bed he whispered the word, fuck, fuck, fuck over and over again, using it as a means to break the silent barrier. But when the man wanted to fuck him or be fucked by him he refused, and lying back in the bed he searched his tormented mind for another adequate word to say. Then he thought of Peter. Not only thought of him, but felt him there, pressing down on top of his body. Peter had taken on the form, the features and the ugliness of the man.

"Why do you hide," Nicholas cried out, "when I know and can see the toad beneath the mask? I know it is there."

The man's face stared down at him with a terrible fixity. Nicholas reached up with his hands to pull the mask away. The man caught at his arms and pinned them back against the bed.

"You won't escape," Nicholas said. "You are ugly; ugly as you have always been."

The mask fell of its own accord, and he saw that the toad was no longer there. Instead he looked up at a stranger.

"Forgive me," he murmured.

The man released the hold he had on his arms, and sat on the edge of the bed. The man was far from him and the isolation total. At the window thick curtains had been drawn, and the room was dark.

"Forgive me," he said again. "Peter is the toad." And then, "I am Peter."

He paused. The nightmare, and the knowledge of the nightmare was endless. He began to tremble and wanted comfort; any comfort from the vision of his fears.

"I am tired," he said.

The man moved on the edge of the bed, and got up to turn on the light. The brightness startled Nicholas and he buried his face between the pillows.

"I will run you a bath. You do want a bath, don't you?"

He heard the voice coming from the other side of the room. He said, "Yes," into the darkness of the pillows, and when he at last lifted his head he saw that he was alone. He lay there without thinking or moving for what seemed a very long time, and then at last the man was there again, and standing by the bed. He stared up at the man who had his face turned away from him.

"Why don't you look at me," he said?

The man looked down at him.

"I hurt you, didn't I," Nicholas said?

There was no reply. Nicholas got off the bed and went across the room to the door. He went out into the hall, wondered where the bathroom was, and as if in reply to his unanswered question, heard the man's voice behind him.

"It's upstairs. On the right."

He went upstairs, and turned as he reached the landing, looking down to the hall below where he saw that the man was standing, watching him.

"I shouldn't have said what I said."

As Nicholas uttered them he knew that they were useless words. The man shrugged his shoulders in silence, and then went back into the bedroom. For a moment Nicholas felt tenderness, or was it pity towards him? Then he felt intense shame towards himself for how he had behaved. He went into the bathroom, and the first thing that he saw was a long mirror, but as hard and as long as he looked he saw no image of himself reflected there. He shuddered and cried out, in the heat and steam of the bathroom feeling suddenly cold. He wrapped a towel around his body and stood by the bath, afraid of the room, afraid of the water. The man appeared in the doorway and stood there watching him.

"I don't feel well," Nicholas said.

"Get into the bath. It will do you good."

The voice was firm, yet gentle and he obeyed it. Once in the water warmth returned, and slowly he felt the tension fall away and his body relax. The man came into the room and sat on a stool by the bath and carried on talking, as if intuitively realising that the sound of his voice had the power to soothe.

"I know you are not well," he said. "I know this and I do understand. What you said in the bedroom does not matter."

Nicholas moved in the water, and raised his body so that he could see himself more clearly.

"I don't exist in the mirror," he said.

The man reached out and touched him on the shoulder. He flinched at the touch.

"Are you so afraid of being touched?"

Without replying Nicholas reached up and placed his own fingers on the exact area of flesh where the man's hand had been. He flinched again as he felt the sore mound of a boil.

"Did you touch this boil?" he asked.

"I touched you."

"Did you touch it?"

His voice was shaking with anger and humiliation. The words came out with the fierce urgency of a scream.

"Can't you see what is on my body? How can you see it and not recognise? They burn on me."

"I touched you. That is all."

Nicholas sank back into the water. He closed his eyes and asked the man quietly to go away, but when he reopened them he was still there.

"The water is cold."

"Let me wash you."

Once again he heard authority in the voice and obeyed. He stood up and handed him the soap. Gently the man reached out and covered Nicholas's body slowly with the soap, rubbing it into the skin and avoiding as delicately as possible the scars and boils. After it was finished Nicholas lay back in the water, and as he lay there he no longer felt anger or shame in the presence of the man.

"It felt good," he said.

"I want you to feel good."

He looked sharply at the man. Had he really meant that? He stood up and the man wrapped a large towel around him. They said no more to one another that day and half an hour later he was falling asleep in a single bed in the spare room.

Tuesday.

When he awoke he thought at first that he was at home in his black room, but then he realised with a terrible ache of empty pain that he no longer had a home. He was somewhere else. He looked round the strange room that he was in. He looked at the door (which led where?) then remembered the man. Slowly he got out of bed and dressed. He did not want to have to think about the man or his surroundings. If it was true (and it obviously was true) that he had no real place to live, then it did not matter where he was. After a while there was a knock on the door, and without opening it, the man told him that breakfast was ready. He made no reply. Then he washed his hands and face, combed his hair, all the time avoiding the mirror, and made his way to the kitchen.

"Did you sleep well?"

Nicholas smiled politely.

"I didn't dream," he said, then thought that was not perhaps the answer that was expected. For a moment he felt awkward, but the man touched him on the arm, and with that briefest of touches he knew that it was all alright.

"I have cooked you breakfast. I hope you like a cooked breakfast."

The windows were open and it was a hot day; far too hot a

day for a cooked meal, but he sat down at the table and obediently began eating. The man was very hungry and finished before Nicholas, pushing his plate to one side with a loud sigh. Nicholas stopped eating and looked at him.

"Do you have to work?" he asked.

"Yes."

"Am I preventing you from going?"

The man shook his head, then sighed again, this time less loudly.

"I mean if I am, tell me, and I'll hurry. We'll leave together."

"There's no need for that. I work here."

Nicholas felt better after having heard this. He felt safe. It all was alright. He didn't have to go. He finished what was left on his plate, then asked: "What do you do?"

"I am a writer."

Nicholas stared hard at him, inside his stomach feeling a sudden and overwhelming nausea. He wanted to get up and run, but then the nausea decreased, and he was once more in control.

"What do you write?"

The man lit a cigarette before answering. He appeared reluctant to talk about his work. Nicholas recalled the day before, and his reluctance to talk about himself. He respected the man's desire for privacy, regretting that he had asked. He said aloud that he was sorry. The man made the slightest of gestures with his hands and murmured, "No, not at all. There's nothing for you to be sorry about. I write 'things' that people see. 'Things' that appear on television. If one was being kind one would call them plays. They make a lot of money and they keep me in a comfort that I am accustomed to, but don't deserve."

He leant back in his chair. He looked across at Nicholas. He saw immediately that something was wrong.

"You look unwell," he said.

Nicholas had begun to tremble.

"I'm sorry, I'll be alright in a minute."

"Don't you think you had better go back to bed?"

"No, I will be better - in just a while."

Nicholas looked at the figure facing him. He looked at the round, well-fed, flabby face and felt the return of an emotion that he remembered once having: it was hatred. He got up from the table, but felt too weak to really make a move.

"Doesn't it disgust you?" he said.

The man stubbed out his cigarette, got up and went to where Nicholas was standing. He placed a hand on his shoulder.

"Often," he replied.

"Then why don't you do something about it?"

Nicholas had the sickening sensation of battling with a force, in the dark, that he was both afraid of, yet afraid to see. Hatred had obscured any possible light and there was only the blind will to destroy. Above all, in this slaughter, it was the writer who had to be annihilated and destroyed.

"I don't want to write," the man added, "but I do it well and it's what others want."

He sat down again at the table. He smiled at Nicholas awkwardly.

"I have nothing to apologize for," he said.

"Have you ever thought of killing yourself?"

Once the question had been asked Nicholas felt an excitement that was almost sexual in its urgency.

"Yes."

"Why don't you do it?"

"No one has asked me to," the man replied.

"What if I asked you to?"

"Why should I die for you?"

"You need not die for me, but you could die with me."

The man shifted uneasily in his chair, then stood up. He kept his back to Nicholas. His voice shook slightly as he said: "I have an extra key. I want you to have this key. You can stay here with me for as long as you like. I will make no demands."

"Are you sure?"

"I am sure."

By the time he turned to face Nicholas his voice was completely composed. He reached down into a trouser pocket, took out a key ring with three keys on it, and handed one to

Nicholas.

"I will make no demands," he added. "Now I have work to do."

"Are you sure you can bear it?"

"Bear what?"

"The demands I will make."

The man said nothing.

Ten minutes later Nicholas was out of the house and walking away from it as fast as he could. The excitement of having asked the man to die with him had gone. He walked quickly, without thinking for a long time, then knew that because he had not paid attention to where he was going, that he was lost. The sun was beating down directly overhead, and there was no shade on either side of the street. His steps slackened in their pace, and very soon he felt so tired and light-headed that he wondered if he would be able to carry on walking at all. Than, abruptly and apparently out of nowhere he saw a familiar figure walking ahead of him in the distance. He recognised the walk, recognised Peter. For a moment he felt that he would faint. The outer world had grown dark, yet within it was white with pain and shock. "I can't meet him," he said aloud, yet continued to follow. The distance between them was growing, for feeling so exhausted he found it hard to keep up. He brushed away the sweat that was trickling into his eyes and started to run. Then the figure turned a corner and was gone. Immediately he felt panic-stricken. "God, this is worse," he said. "To have seen him and to have lost him." He continued running and turned the corner to find the figure still there in the distance.

"Peter."

He called. He wanted his call to be a plea, a scream, but the hot air of midday overwhelmed him and the name came out as the smallest of cries. Then the figure stopped walking, paused for a moment outside the front of a church, then went into it.

"No, you are not Peter. You only remind me of him."

He reached the church. He hesitated, then went in. Inside he told himself that to meet Peter face to face was the last thing he could bear to do, even to consider. Yet the words contradicted the movement of his eyes. Despite himself he was searching for him. He stared ahead, then looked behind. It seemed there was no one there in the building except himself, but that was impossible. He looked harder. He peered into every corner, behind every monument and statue, but it was true, there was no one there but himself. The horror of total loss forced him to his knees, and he buried his face in his hands. After a while he raised his head and stared ahead of him; stared directly at the gaudy statue of Christ to the right of the altar. In front of the statue was a tiered row of candles. He got up from his kneeling position and walked slowly up to the statue. Without a moment's hesitation he reached out for one of the candles and wrenched it out of its bracket. He held it up to the face of Christ; held it so that the flame burnt at the plaster features and made the paint run. When all possible resemblance to a face had been destroyed he replaced the candle, retracing his steps to find the door. He remembered having pushed a curtain aside to enter the church, but on returning to the curtain, found that it no longer concealed a door. Behind the material was the stone of a wall.

"Peter."

He called, or thought he called, and turned around. Although the name had been spoken it did not seem to have come from his mouth. The name echoed all around him, and it was there, a tangible presence, holding him within the prison of the church. The name was a form that his eyes were imprisoned from seeing. He pulled at the material of the curtain, his fingers tearing and ripping in their panic to find the opening. Then, out of the corner of his eye, he saw. He saw a figure move with the speed of light down the central aisle towards the altar. He turned to face it, but in that one second of full seeing it was both there and then it was gone. He had, he thought, recognised himself. Grasping desperately at the curtain his hand hit at the hard iron latch of the door, and within a moment he was outside, suffering the harsh glare of the day.

He walked, not conscious, or caring about the direction he was taking. The thought that he was being followed made him feverish with fear. A cold sweat poured from his face and hands.

"I am going to die," he said. Then, "They are going to kill me."

Someone caught at his arm and asked him if he needed help. The figure seemed to be standing in shadow, although the street was in full sunlight, and Nicholas screamed until the hand let go. He heard people running, and he began to run as well. To escape them he rushed into the entrance of a cinema, hurriedly pulled out some money, paid for his ticket and entered the darkness. He sat down near an exit sign and closed his eyes. He had to collect himself. He had to think. Slowly the panic went from him and he decided to stay where he was, feeling like a hunted animal that has temporarily found safety.

It was eleven-thirty when he turned the key in the lock and opened the door of the man's house. He had left the cinema at about eight in the evening and had spent the rest of the time drinking in a nearby pub. But he had no recollection how he had spent the evening or how he had found his way to the man's house. When the man came out of his bedroom Nicholas was silent. His mind felt confused, and he had no idea what to say.

"It's late. I waited for you for dinner."

Nicholas stared at him. As he stared he began to focus more, and although remembering nothing of the evening, he was aware enough of the man to be (or so he thought) sober.

"I'm sorry," he said, and reached out to steady himself against the wall.

"You had better go to bed."

The voice was cold. He looked at the man, and perhaps because of the drink, perhaps because of the horrifying experience in the church, felt a feeling of affection and pity towards the figure before him.

"I'm sorry," he repeated.

"You're drunk."

"I would like some coffee."

The man walked ahead into the kitchen. Nicholas observed with wry amusement that he was wearing baggy and very bright pyjamas. He tried to recall when he had last seen pyjamas on anyone, and failed. He started to giggle, then the giggle became a laugh. The man ignored it.

"If you're hungry there's still some food left."

He pointed to the fridge as Nicholas sat down.

"I had an awful lot to drink, you see."

Nicholas giggled again.

"I can see."

"It was silly of me, but I felt depressed."

"Do you feel any better for drinking?"

The man filled the kettle, and went about making the coffee without once looking at Nicholas.

"Are you always so emotionally polite?"

Since leaving the house that morning Nicholas had spent the day in almost total, frightened silence. Now he wanted to talk, for if he talked, then maybe he would be able to escape further from the phantoms that pursued him. The man waited until the kettle had boiled, made the coffee, then at last turned and faced him.

"What do you mean, am I so emotionally polite? I would like you to explain that."

"You know what I mean."

"No, I don't know."

"Instead of making coffee and offering me food you should kick me out."

Nicholas was aware of the man's pain as an extension of himself. He realised with sudden, brutal clarity that he was responsible.

"You are hurt," he said. "I could have come back earlier. You've been kind and this is how I repay you."

"I said there would be no demands."

"I made a demand this morning. Do you remember what I asked you?"

"It seemed more of a request than a demand."

"I know what agony it is to wait, even though you want to wait. But today I wasn't aware of time passing. If I had been I would've come to you. Sincerely."

He was no longer Nicholas, but Peter as he wanted Peter to be. He was Peter talking to a crushed and disappointed Nicholas. In the cold artificial light of the kitchen he was in the centre of a past that he could no longer think about, but only refer to obliquely. The way to survive was to be removed from reality, and to remove himself he had to be the boy who was his past, yet ever present tormentor. I am Peter, he whispered to himself, but as the words were inwardly spoken he looked and through the eyes of Nicholas saw that the man existed too. He was one of three in the room and continuing a conversation. For a while the shadow of Peter stood aside.

"There's a poem," he said, "that I discovered one day - 'Insomnia of swallows. The calmness of the friend who waits at the station.' "

"I don't know the poem. I'm tired."

"Don't go," Nicholas cried. "Please. I never wanted to hurt you."

The man came and sat down opposite him. Nicholas reached out across the table and murmured: "Then give me your hands. As a sign of trust that you believed what I said."

Their hands joined, and when they were joined the man began to speak.

"There is no south left for the swallows. It's all finished. They will sleep: sleep deeply, for there is no journey now. I know about the quiet friend too, but I can assure you that he never arrived at the station. Oh, of course there were reasons. There had to be reasons. He made his excuses, and then perhaps the desire was not as strong as he had thought."

"Tell me more," Nicholas said, and pressed the man's hands tightly within his own. The door of the kitchen was open, facing where he was sitting, and for a moment he believed he saw a figure pass in the hall.

"Could it be that there is another here with us" he asked. "I was so sure that I saw him."

The man looked at him without understanding, then carried on with what he was saying.

"No, the desire was never strong enough. Shall I tell you

why? It was long ago, back there in a past when I was not so emotionally polite. I showed my needs, and I fell in love. The boy was my own age and we were devoted to each other. The romantic story promised a romantic ending, but we had not counted on the loss of love and the weakness of desire. Time too. Yes, the loss of that. He was the love of my life and I said no to him. I said it without saying the word, and let time itself do the silent turning away."

He began to cry. Nicholas watched the tears.

"We had our alternatives though, even then. We had our choice, and that choice consisted of going to a big city or making a life in the small town where we were. The first choice was the city, and the promise of the company of people living the same lives as ourselves. We talked about it and knew that there would be a semblance of acceptance there. We would be able to be, we thought, ourselves. The second choice was the making of a quiet and almost exclusively solitary life in a town where all open acknowledgement of our love would be forbidden. We considered our choices carefully."

"What did you choose?"

"We chose not to choose. Neither alternative was valid. The town was claustrophobic; the claustrophobia that stifles love, and the city was unknown. And in its vast unknown far too frightening to plunge into. We were so romantic that neither of us were strong enough for reality. We failed because we lived for the romantic ideal. We wanted it all to be perfect from the start. The perfection that doesn't ask for decisions. Both of us wanted to fly south. Both of us failed to choose a destination. Yet we had our reasons. Life was tough in those days. It was hard to be in either city or town - to be truly what we would know and now call 'liberated'."

"And do you think that now we are any more liberated? Do you think that it has changed?"

Nicholas took away his hands. A weight was pressing on his eyes. He felt tired and he wanted to sleep.

"I would like to make a last attempt," the man said. "It cannot be the friend at the station, but it can be something else."

"What?" Nicholas asked.

"A compromise."

Nicholas looked at the man. The tears had dried and the face was expressionless.

"All living together becomes a travesty, a mediocre impossibility," Nicholas said. "Neither the city or the town can hold the dream."

As he voiced these words he wondered if it was Peter finally telling him this. Peter or himself - but then who were they, if not one and the same? He stared at the face in front of him and said; "But we can die."

"Yes," the man replied.

"Then you will die with me?"

The man looked down at his outstretched hands that no longer held on to Nicholas.

"Yes," he said.

"When?"

He got up and slowly backed towards the door.

"It's so final," he said. "And real."

He turned and left the room. Nicholas watched him go, then got up from the table and stood for a long while in the centre of the room. He put both hands to his mouth to suppress a scream. The thing that he found most difficult to comprehend was that the three who had been in the room had now been reduced to one, and that he, Nicholas, was alone. Then, with a shudder, he remembered the figure of the stranger that he had seen pass in the hall.

Vision 1. The Park.

We will meet in the park. Michael will come towards me, and as he passes by me his hand will brush against my thigh. I will stare at him and be the first to smile. He will look wonderingly at the white suit that I will be wearing.

"It's a beautiful night."

The opening introduction. His introduction. Standing on the edge of the park gazing towards the sea. It will be a warm night in late spring. Michael will point towards the shore.

"Shall we go down to the beach?"

He will ask, and I will reply: "Yes, for a swim. Can you swim?"

He will laugh and touch at my suit with the tips of his fingers.

"But are you dressed for it?"

"Clothes can be discarded." Then I will ask again: "Can you swim? I don't remember."

There will be a warning in my voice; an ambiguous warning that he will not dare to understand. It is I who will realise that the naked and the water are there to be feared.

"I will if you will."

He will begin to walk away as he says this, walking down towards the shingle that leads to the sea. I will follow, and when we near the still line of the water I will reach out and touch him on the arm. He will turn, and thinking that I want to make love will attempt to take me in his arms.

"Not yet."

I try to make my words sound firm, yet at the same time, gentle. I will undress, and lay my clothes on a patch of sand.

"Are you going to do the same?"

He will stare at my nakedness, then look around him, uncertain for a moment, perhaps afraid that we are being followed or somehow observed.

"Why not?"

He will shrug his shoulders, then undress slowly.

"I have an erection," he will say.

A statement. Nothing more. Nothing that I will hear, or that will arouse me. The night bright beneath a full moon. I will step away from him and into the water. Small waves will lap at my groin and I will be as far removed from desire as I have always been. He will follow a little heavily, even more unsure as to what to expect, unsure of what has happened already. His thick body will plunge first taking the lead. I call after him as his legs begin to swim out.

"Do you remember him?"

He will not hear properly, his arms making tougher waves.

"What did you say?" he will call back.

"Nicholas. Do you remember him?"

For a moment there will be stillness in the very movement of the water, then he will return and stand up next to me in the draw of the wave. He will be silent. Amazed. He will not want to hear.

"You were his friend while the rest were lovers."

I say the words slowly. In his confusion he will caress my skin and I will let him, watching his hand as it curves down my side.

"Have you nothing to say?"

He will shake his head, and I will stop his hand.

"I never really knew him. Did you know him - well?"

He will pause before using that last word, and how obvious it will be the disappointment that I have pushed his hand away.

"I came to hear about him from you. I was told that you knew him better than anyone."

"Then the person who told you that lied."

"Yourself?" I will ask.

He will avoid looking into my eyes.

"The water is cold," he will say. "I am not used to the water at night."

Although he starts to move I will not follow, but stand where I am in the water. When he sees that I do not follow he will grudgingly return.

"Do you know nothing? He died. You remember? Do you remember how he died?"

"Yes."

There will be long minutes during which neither of us will move or speak. The waves will respond to the change in the sea. The tide will begin to turn. I could, but will not react to the fear that I feel emanating from him.

"You are beautiful."

He will be the first to break the silence. His voice will have that curious note of timidity so out of place in a person normally brave with words.

"You have kept your beard," I will say. "Does it protect you well?"

Not understanding that I know, that I have always and will always know, he will avoid the admission of remembrance. I will be solely the sex; the cock and the anus that he desires. He will not recall this future past in his present of need.

"You are very young."

I will smile at this absurdity, not unkindly, but sad at the screen of his blindness.

"I am what you see."

"Will you let me touch you? Here in the water? Or shall we go back to the beach?"

"Have you really heard nothing that I have said? Is he gone so far from you?"

There will be blank indifference, and my words will have no meaning. The swell of the tide pushes us towards the shore.

"Then let us go back to the beach."

I will try to make my voice sound as resigned as possible. I will feel his fear. He will wade before me, eager to reach the stones, eager to leave the water. Once on ground not covered by the sea he will be less timid, less afraid, more sure of himself sexually. He will point to the stretch of sand; to the place where I have left my clothes.

"Let us lie there."

I will walk with him, but will not lie down. He will look up from where he has positioned himself, touching at his own body, trying to attract me with an exhibition of his own private intimacy. I will remember a death that I have felt and that I have seen; relive the crushing and splattering of flesh against stone. I will long to speak, yet know the fatal silence that is to be preserved towards those who have forgotten.

"Hand me my clothes."

He will reach out and lay a hand over my white suit.

"Please do as I say."

The hand will not move. Then slowly, surely, he will press the clothes down, further, deeper into the sand.

"I want you. You are the most beautiful boy that I have ever seen."

"I did not come to hear that."

"Then why did you undress?"

Endless reproach in his voice that I cannot answer for.

"I had to be naked. I had to come to you in simplicity."

"To arouse me?"

"No. So that you would know me." Having come so far and been gone so long I will bend down over his outspread body, and touch at the hair on his chest. I will pause in my caress hoping to reduce the sensation of touch, yet in touching reach perhaps the heart. I long to reach the heart. For this will be the final gift of time for him to remember in.

"Nicholas," I will say. "He was your friend. Remember that."

"I never knew - "

Then his voice will hush into silence. He will sit up, repelling my touch, burying his face in his hands. "I never knew."

In silence I will slowly put on my clothes. Dressed, I will tell him that it is time for me to leave.

"It is late," I will add.

The emptiness of a separation that never had a joining. The endless emptiness. He will not look at me.

"It is late. Too late."

I repeat the words and begin to walk away. It is then that he will leap up and run naked after me.

"I want to know who you are."

He catches at my arm with his hand and I will continue walking. All that I will be able to think is that he should have known.

"He was a stranger," he will say, "to us all."

When he says these words I will stop, and then stooping down will take at random three stones and place them in the palm of my hand. I will put both palms together, forming a hollow and shake the stones once and let them fall. In the future I will already see a future. The stones fall in the moonlit darkness, and although lost amongst other similar pebbles I will have followed their course.

"If you do not see me, and do not see him, then see at least this - that when the longing is great there is suffering; that when

214

the suffering is accepted, passion dries to stone."

"I want to know who you are."

There is nothing more for either of us to say. I will leave him there and retrace my steps to the first bushes that lead up, back into the park.

Wednesday.

He dreamt that he was a snake gliding down the sands to the water's edge, but when he reached the sea he found that the uplifted wave had been transformed into a concrete wall, and when he tried blindly to break through it his head was crushed against the stone. He cried out and awoke, to see the man standing at the foot of the bed.

"It's alright," the man said.

Nicholas dressed and followed him downstairs. He drank a glass of water, refusing the food that had been prepared for him.

"Could you let me have a clean shirt and some underwear?" he asked.

"We're not exactly the same size."

"It doesn't matter. Lend me what you can. I can go out and buy the rest."

When the man had brought the clothes and Nicholas had changed, they sat in silence at the kitchen table. It was the man who was the first to speak.

"It's the third day," he said.

"Yes."

"What are we going to do?"

Nicholas looked briefly at him, then transferred his attention to the window, and the clouds outside. He saw that during the night the weather had changed; that the intense heat had at last cooled down. Then he began to scratch. He felt uncomfortable in the shirt that had been given him. It made his skin itch, and although too large for him, felt tight around his neck and across his shoulders.

"What are we going to do?" the man repeated.

Nicholas turned his head from the direction of the window and stared at him.

"You mean surely what am I going to do?"

"Yes, you. Both of us." The man paused. There was a tremor, almost of fear in his voice as he said: "I know what I would like."

"What would you like?"

Nicholas smiled, feeling removed from him; detached from all emotion, no longer even recollecting the affection or the hatred that had possessed him during the previous days. All he dreaded now was that the man would use the word love.

"I would like us to live together."

"Yes, I know," Nicholas said, "but that's not what I want."

There was another long silence, broken by the steady pattering of rain against the window. Nicholas got up from the table and began to pace the room, his hands in his pockets, his head lowered as if deep in thought. But as he paced he knew that there was nothing left in him, nothing whatever to be filled or taken. Nothing to think about. He was the emptiness of death, without mind or soul. The man watched him.

"Could you eventually feel for me?" he asked.

Nicholas stopped pacing. He had been asked to think. He spoke slowly, unsure of the very words he used, even as they were spoken.

"I don't know. Yes. No. Not in the way you would want me to, but it never is, is it? I suppose I could - I mean feel something in time, but there isn't much time." Nicholas paused. "I want death, but it isn't your death; yet at that moment of death, if we went together, perhaps we could attain a mutual love. In peace."

The man had not understood. Nicholas realised that he had understood nothing. The words had come so slowly, and it was only in the speaking of them that he realised that he had meant what he had said. A feeling had been born, however ambiguous, towards the person in front of him.

"I am not sure that I am ready," the man replied.

"But you have nothing to live for. I know that."

The man glanced at him sharply, almost in terror.

"What do you know?"

"I know that you are ugly and that you are finished. It would be good to die with me. I would love you - as much and more as you have ever been loved - in death."

"Even though I want life?"

"Even though you think you want life."

The man got up and stood in front of Nicholas. His face was white, and his voice trembled with anger.

"How can you say I am ugly when you haven't really looked at yourself? It will be over for you too, soon. How long do you think you have? How long do you imagine the chances last? The world is closing in on you. The world will be the killer, not yourself."

He began to sob, then reached out for Nicholas who held him tightly in his arms. The rain fell harder against the window. Inside the room the heat that was left was turning to cold.

"It is an unending hell to die alone," Nicholas murmured. "It is amazing how many people thinly manage to squeeze through that door, persisting in their own condemnation of solitude. Yet it is an emptiness even greater than emptiness. They squeeze through, but the self is annihilated. Those who know do not go on that journey alone. Those who know that the only salvation possible is together. I realise, of course, that if we went together it would not be ideal. Neither of us resembles the person we would have chosen. It would not be what either of us have wanted or hoped for, but at least it could be something. Something bearable. You are right, I am ugly, and will be uglier, but I am better than nobody."

The man broke away from him, stumbling slightly. He steadied himself against the table. He drew his hand hesitantly across the surface of the wood.

"But there are things left," he said. "I believe that things at the last can help sometimes more than people. Touching what is not alive is perhaps better than the living contact of ugliness in another person."

"This table will not comfort you as your body falls away. It will not be there as you topple into yourself."

"And will you be there?"

The man turned to Nicholas, his eyes red with weeping, his voice harsh in its fear.

"I cannot promise. In the same way that I could not promise to feel for you - yet already I am feeling. You will only know when the time comes. To die with a lover means to die in security, but to die as we would die - I don't know."

"If I could be sure that you would be there; be there to take me into death, and not desert me, then I would gladly go."

"I cannot promise, but the risk is better than nothing at all."

The man walked towards the door. As he put his hand to the door he said quietly: "But you are still a stranger to me."

Nicholas laughed, and it was in that second of laughter that he felt love for the man. He felt a certainty that bound him to him; a certainty that whatever happened between them would happen, however inadequately, for them.

"We are all we have," he said.

The man shrugged his shoulders, both as a sign of acceptance and of denial. He left the room without another word. Nicholas followed him, but only as far as the hall.

"I will go out for a while," he said.

There was no reply. Nicholas opened the door and stepped out into the rain. His mind emptied immediately of all the complex thoughts and emotions that he had tried to express. He walked rapidly, taking the direction that led to the centre of the city. The rain increased, and in the distance he heard the low growl of thunder. When he reached Piccadilly Circus he decided to take shelter in the Underground. As he descended the steps he thought, I am the snake. I feel the scales of my skin, and with my mouth I will turn and swallow my tail. He walked round the circular space time and time again, occasionally glancing at the various signs leading to the street. He wanted to escape, yet was imprisoned in the circle. Then a young man appeared, stared at him, and without any real desire Nicholas followed him into the tunnel that led to the men's toilet. He walked up to the stall next to where the young man had positioned himself, and stood there without making any gesture of encouragement. The young man looked at him for a moment, pissed, shook himself, then walked away. Nicholas was standing alone in a row of empty stalls. He had neither the inclination to move or to stay. He began to think about the man, and wondered if he was waiting for him to return. Then he felt a presence behind him and a tap on his shoulder. He turned round in surprise. 'Who can this be?' he thought. 'I don't know this man.' There were in fact two of them. They were showing him a card. Was it one of them, or was it both of them showing him a card? He was confused. He smiled.

"We're police officers. Could you step to one side."

He felt the shock of a reality that he couldn't even begin to imagine. He stepped to one side, and the man who had spoken first cautioned him and told him that he was under arrest.

"I don't understand," Nicholas said. "What was I doing?"

"You know what you were doing."

He began to walk out of the toilet with the men on either side of him. Up the steps and out into the street. He felt the irony of a terrible, claustrophobic protection. I am being looked after, he thought as he walked between them.

Once at the station he was questioned and charged. He signed the document that he was asked to sign, too shocked to realise that it could harm him. They wanted his fingerprints, and he had to be shown how it was done. Then for no apparent reason he was thrust into a cell. The walls were disfigured with graffiti, and on the plank bed a single brown blanket had been thrown down. In a corner of the room he saw there was a toilet. Wanting to relieve himself he went up to it, but when he reached the rim was sickened by a piece of shit floating in yellow water. At that moment the man who had arrested him came into the cell.

"Take down your trousers," he said.

Nicholas took down his trousers.

"Bend over."

As he bent over he was cruelly conscious of his penis dangling between his legs. He felt the man's hands roughly part the cheeks of his arse. A moment later he was told to stand up, and the man said: "We want to know what that cream is for. The cream we found in your pocket."

He stared at the man, at first not believing the question.

"Well? What is it? What's it for? Do you use it for your arse?"

He found that he was powerless to answer. The words that could have been spoken remained trapped in his mouth. He looked at the blind face of the man and thought how ugly it was, and the man stared back at him.

"I haven't got all day."

The man began beating his hands together as though he were clapping. There was a threat in the voice. There was a threat in the gestures. Nicholas wondered if he remained silent whether the man would hit him. If he hits me, he thought, then I will be kept here. I couldn't bear being kept here, so I must answer.

"I use it for my face," he said. "I have bad skin."

He was polite, ridiculously polite, almost smiling. The man left him alone in the cell. For a while the feeling of panic was total. All that he had refused to feel since he had left the house rose to the surface and overwhelmed him. He began to cry out, then rushed to the door and hit at it with his hands. A voice from outside shouted at him to be quiet. He moved away from the door and went and sat down on the bed. He stared at the opaque glass that passed for a window in the cell. I cannot kill myself in here, he thought. They have left me with nothing.

"Peter."

The name came involuntarily to his lips. He crushed his fist into his mouth. Then he heard the door being opened.

"Alright, you can come out now."

They were nice to him, offering him a cup of tea and something to eat if he was hungry. He realised then that he had been there for hours. He refused the tea and the food, and he was told to present himself at court the following day. He was given the paper on which was written the summons. As he stepped out into the rain he felt a burning sensation on his shoulder where the hand had reached out and tapped him. He closed his eyes, opened them, then began to walk. As he walked fragments of his immediate experience were recalled. He remembered the completely fictitious address he had given. He saw himself bending down, and the man peering up his anus.

"I can't. I can't," he said.

The cry was like a nudge to those who passed by him. He saw people staring, and ran.

"They will be after me now," he said. He was not sure if the "they" were the people around him or the police from the station. He heard the cell door clang shut, and the piece of shit bobbed obscenely up and down in the rank and yellow water. Then the panic passed, and he felt suddenly calm. After all, he thought, this is going to end. He looked around him at the streets, brightly conscious of where he was and the direction he had to take. Within a very short time he had reached the man's house. He found the man in his study, sitting in front of his typewriter.

"I was arrested," he said.

The man turned and faced him. For a moment his face went white, then his hands began to tremble.

"Have they got this address? Did you give them this address?"

Nicholas shook his head.

"I gave a false one."

"Do you realise what that means?"

The man got up from his desk and came slowly towards him. Nicholas backed towards the door, wanting now to get out, to run, to escape, (but where?) - there was nowhere left to go, but only the here of this place; these walls and this man. He put his hands to his head and cried out. Yet even the sound of the cry was no real release. He felt it return, felt it violently follow its passage backwards, through his mouth, to explode inside him.

"Stop it," the man said. "Stop it. We must think. We must do something now that the damage has been done. I have a lawyer who - "

Nicholas dropped his hands to his sides. He felt drained and exhausted, and stared about him at the room without comprehending, without really listening.

"I have a very good lawyer."

As he said this the man made a helpless gesture with his

hands. Then he looked at Nicholas and asked: "Were you guilty?"

The words had no meaning for him. Nicholas heard them, but they made no impact on him. He managed to say very quietly: "I was standing there and I was thinking of you. Yes, I was arrested in a toilet. I suppose I was making up my mind to come back here when I felt this tap on my shoulder. The police, of course. If I was doing anything, I can't remember what."

"Was there anyone beside you?"

"No."

"You mean you were alone standing there?"

"Yes."

"Had there been anyone beside you?"

"Yes, but - no."

"What does that mean?"

In the confusion of his present state of mind all Nicholas realised was that he was being interrogated. Would they never stop? Would the voices themselves never stop? Behind the voice of the man he heard the cries of the torturer in the concentration camp, demanding, pleading and even at times howling to be heard. The voice cried, 'Listen to me. Tell my story, for I must atone.' But inside Nicholas, muffled though the voice came his returning cry - 'I cannot. I cannot do it. No one can do it for us. No one can pay for another's crime. No lawyer, no witnesses; above all no second hand witnesses to atrocity. Do not ask for expiation from others.'

"Nicholas, answer me. I must know."

"Why must you know? Does it matter?"

He heard his reply to the man's question, the inflexion of his own voice spiky and edgy. He was being pulled through a net of barbed wire, and inwardly the frustrated scream was growing. "I am hollow with all their cries," he said, but the man did not hear. The man was questioning, asking, and the absurdity of the questions made him long even more for the death that was his right, for the dying that had to come.

"It matters if I am to help you."

Nicholas spun round and seized the man by the throat.

"Be quiet," he said.

The man gasped and tried to push the hand away. Nicholas grabbed and twisted the man's arm with his free hand, and the man squealed with pain.

"I could kill you."

He let go of the man who fell back against his desk. As he fell he hit against the typewriter, knocking it to the floor.

"I have always wanted to kill. Listen to me, not to yourself. Not to those questions of what I was doing and why. I was in a toilet doing nothing. Nothing at all, and they came. There was no crime committed, no obscenity. I was doing nothing but thinking, thinking about returning here to you. Yet it is the thoughts - "

Nicholas tapped again and again at his head.

"Here it's all wrong. Here is the crime, but they didn't, couldn't arrest me for that. They couldn't arrest me for wanting to kill you. I could kill you because I have always wanted to kill. Listen to me and forget your questions. There is no lawyer who can atone for my guilt. Why should I want any man's atonement when I have my own?"

He panted out these last words, then went towards the cowering figure of the man and hugged him to him. He held on to him tightly and said: "I don't know what I'm saying. I don't know what I'm doing. Help me, help me. Don't you see?"

The man struggled away from him and picked up the typewriter. He was shaking with fear. When he had tidied the desk he put his hand to his neck.

"I hurt," he said.

He sounded like a child, crying after an accident. The pain of the words whipped at Nicholas's sense of guilt. He ran out of the room; ran down the stairs to the bathroom, and returned after a few minutes with a piece of cotton wool soaked in water. In his other hand he clutched at a tube of antiseptic cream. The man reluctantly bared his neck so that Nicholas could dab at it. There was only a small mark there, but to Nicholas's feverish imagination it was the mark of all the tortures that the world had caused or ever inflicted. He dabbed again and again, not heeding the man's words that it was enough, that he could stop. At last the man broke away.

"It's alright. I don't need it."

He stared at Nicholas, perhaps more afraid of him now than he had ever been.

"I am in no pain."

"But I want to put on the cream."

There was a pathetic, pleading whine in his voice. He came towards the man. He opened the tube, spreading the cream onto his fingers, then reached out to touch the man's neck. The man backed away. He raised his arm as if to protect himself from Nicholas, and it was at that moment that Nicholas saw the far larger mark on the arm.

"I did that?"

"It doesn't matter," the man replied, and with a sudden action that seemed ridiculously fearful hid the arm behind his back.

"I couldn't have done that to you. You didn't deserve it. I swear to you that you didn't deserve it."

Nicholas's voice was hysterical. Slowly it was coming to the surface, the scream that he was withholding, the scream that he had repressed.

"Peter deserved it. I could have killed him. I could have killed him and watched the pain, but you - "

Then the man cried out.

"Stop it. Enough."

Nicholas bowed his head, not daring to look at him. The man had screamed for him.

"Now, can we go back to the beginning?"

"Yes," said Nicholas.

"Tell me, were you guilty?"

"I was not guilty."

"Then we must do something."

Nicholas raised his head and watched as the man went towards the telephone, watched as he lifted the receiver and began to dial.

"No," he said.

The man replaced the receiver and turned to him.

"I don't want you to do anything. I will not go to court."

"It will only make matters worse. It will make it all the more difficult for me to help."

Nicholas shrugged his shoulders and said that he was tired. The man led him by the arm out of the study and into the spare room. He felt the man gently undo the buttons on his shirt, felt as the shirt slipped from his shoulders, falling to the floor.

"Sit on the bed," the man said.

Once more he was obedient and sat down. The man knelt on the floor and untied the knots in his shoelaces. In a minute his feet were free of shoes, then he felt his socks being pulled off. The man asked him to raise his body a little, and he watched as his trousers were pulled down. With a voice that was almost near to wonder he questioned: "But you must love me?"

The man looked up at him, but made no reply. After he had finished undressing Nicholas he put him into bed, and turning out the light went out on to the landing and from there to his own room.

Vision 2. Hell.

I was there, had been there, cradling him for many nights against fear, suffocation and the terror of his dreams. I watched over him, I who had no need of sleep.

"I have to die."

He opened his eyes and pushed me from him. He sat on the edge of the bed, then slid to his knees, and on his knees began to cry out his desperate prayer.

"I have to die," he said. "I have to submit my life to death, for only in dying will he love me. When he is told of my death he will realise I could have lived. Then, in the truer fidelity of the imagination he will see me alive and hold me in his arms. He who had dreaded fidelity will no longer need to fear its threat. I could have lived, but died to secure his love. I could have existed, but better that he regrets the loss of me. To become reality is to die. The reality of a myth, no longer threatening to destroy life with life. Sure at last that there is nothing to be feared he will say the words I have died to hear. He will speak to me, and I will be loved."

The voice stopped. He got up from his kneeling position on the floor and stood in the centre of the faint light that encircled the bed. He stood without shadow in the circle, staring at me, but not seeing me. I was watched from within, yet unrecognised. I reached out for him and he pushed my hands away. It seemed that in the very lack of shadow of his nakedness that he was holding off the night. Holding it back as he held me back; held us both from him, both of us being one and the same, and to be feared. I was, in the white of my waking sleep, the simple death.

"Come," I said, "you are surely ready. It is time to extinguish the light."

"I have to die," he repeated. "Then why am I afraid?"

I left the bed, and crossing the room opened the wardrobe door. I knew exactly where he kept the bottle of pills. Spilling them into the palm of my hand I held them out to him.

"Here," I said. "The right number. Come, you are surely ready. Enough to be sure. Enough to not make a mistake."

He took them out of my hand and held them in the hollow of his own. I went into the bathroom to get water to help him ease them down. When I returned he had already swallowed most of the pills.

"Oh, it is almost finished," he whispered.

"Not quite."

I held out the glass of water. He took it and drank.

"Now the rest of the pills."

He obeyed me, swallowing them quickly, then returned to bed. For a while neither of us moved or spoke. Then suddenly he screamed: "I cannot bear it."

"What do you see?"

I lay beside him, cradling his feverish head against my neck. I felt his breath against my flesh, burning me with its pain, reminding me that in his death I would have to follow.

"Tell me," I said, "is it great what you see?"

He shuddered against me.

"No, it is small. So small."

His cry twisted through me with aching urgency. I placed a hand over his mouth, and he bit me in his agony, drawing blood.

"There is nothing there but my self, and the self is a dot - a black dot circling and revolving upon a hard, square surface like a table. I am giddy with the pull of it, with the attraction of the surface that wants to pull me down and crush me."

He wrenched himself out of my arms, and sat upright in the bed, his hands frantically clasping and tearing at the blankets and sheets.

"Is this the death?" he cried. "Is this all it is? It is a flat world that is drawing me down. Once there I will topple. I will fall off the surface and drown. Beneath the table is the sea"

He turned, clutching at me. I felt my body harden against the impact of our twin fear. I caught at his hair and pulled his head violently back so that I could stare at him.

"What is there? Tell me what is there."

"You. Nothing but you," he whimpered. Then he opened his mouth wide, making a gagging sound, and I said, "No, no, you must keep them down. Beside yourself what else is this surface made of?"

I held on to his head, and he stared at me for a long time in terror before answering.

"A park leads down to the sea. We are there. I am there. The trees in the park remember us, call us by name. The smell of those trees is so terrible that I hold my nose. I am afraid that because this death is so small, so thin, that I will never get away from it."

"Be clear," I said. "Tell me what you see."

I tightened my grip on his hair, adding pain to pain. His mouth opened wider, saliva trickling down his chin. With my other hand I wiped his chin dry. As well as concentrating on his words I had to be sure he kept the pills down. In my stomach I felt the nausea rising like a great sick wave.

"Peter," he said. "He is there. He is us, and he is there. We are following, but at the same time we are leading the dance. Between the trees they have built bonfires, and on the wood of our flesh they are burning desire. But I am so small that I cannot burn. No flame will burn me. And the suffocation. How can I get beyond the suffocation? It is smoke and it smells, and the black dot continues to revolve above the table."

I let go of him, and he fell back on the bed.

His body lay there, fully stretched out, pinned to its furthest extremity of suffering. Yet in that suffering I realised that he had found a momentary centre of quiet. He was, as I felt he was, balanced for a moment in the certitude of agony.

"I have to die."

"Yes" I said, "but before tell me what you see. Be a witness."

"They are killing us, and I too am killing. Peter bends over. The slit that leads to the hole in his arse is made for the knife. I hold the knife to the slit; I slide it down towards the hole - and plunge. It is icy in the hot depths. I am suffocating. No, not yet. He is not ready yet. It is the ultimate act to receive such a precious death, and neither of us are worthy. I withdraw the knife. The sacrifice can come to nothing in the world we have made. He stands up. He turns and faces me and takes the knife out of my hands. There is a mask across his face, and the mask lips are speaking. The mask looks like you, but it is me. It is my own unrecognisable face."

"What does the mask say?"

I bent over him. He was lying there on the bed with eyes closed. I touched at his body and scraped with my fingers at the surface hardness of his flesh.

" 'The world is in its nature corrupt. We must torture one another to remind ourselves constantly that it is corrupt. Gentleness, love, they are nothing, they will only create illusion. Truth is torture. Torture is real. Our love for each other must be torture. To live in torture is to accept the guilt of corruption. To inflict suffering is our only revolt against what we cannot change.' Oh, yes the mouth speaks. The mask knows. I am there with Peter, with you. I am there with myself; with all of our selves in the words that everlastingly fail."

(Who said these words? I am with him, by his side, in his dying, a part of his dying, yet I do not know who said these words)

I held him to me. He reached out, lurching away from me towards the edge of the bed. He lay there, as if on the edge of a precipice, his head flung down towards the floor. I pulled him back, and slapped him across the face.

"It is time," I cried savagely. "It is time you were dead."

He raised himself up, looking at me.

"He is not ready yet," he said. "Nicholas is not ready. It is too thin for him."

I hit him again, but still he continued to shake his head.

"You made Nicholas write the letter to the man," he said. "The man is a writer. He will reply. Is that not worth living for?"

As he uttered these words I felt his death escaping from me. In my failure to make him see me for the death that I had always been, I had given him a reason for life. Yes, I had made him write the letter. I had made him send the play. Life was once more positive assertion; the cycle of illusion was about to commence again. I started to laugh, and in that laughter was dispelled my desire to see him dead. I too, after all, wanted to live.

"You love too much the embrace of death to lose yourself in it. You have made it live too much to want to die into it."

Yet even as I said these words I could see that the physical process of dying was taking its course. I imagined the atrocity of a physical death while the inner body still remained alive. I saw both he and I in the cold region, unable to return, yet bound to all that we were.

"Help," he said, "I am going. You are taking me into death without ever having told me whose story this is. The men who died in the park, in the vast burning of the park, told the story - but then so did the assassins. I cannot go without knowing. I want to know who the author is. I may be yourself, or I may be nothing. I cannot tell you what you must know."

At the sound of these last words I forced my fingers down his throat. With my other hand I held his head firmly so that it would not move. He coughed, then gagged, coughed again, and I felt the hot torrent of vomit pour between my fingers, felt it run down my arm. When he had finished I drew away from him.

"There is something more," he gasped. He opened his mouth wide, so wide that I thought his jaws would crack. In the faint light I saw a movement other than the self that united us.

"Don't you see?" he said. "It is in the vomit. Don't you see the toad? It has escaped, and now I am lost forever."

I reached out with my arm to grasp and trap whatever was there.

"It is too late."

I echoed my own words. The room stank of the life that had returned to us.

Thursday.

When Nicholas awoke to his fourth day in London he realised he would have to make it his last. The first matter to be considered was money, and he was almost out of it. The second, that he had been charged with a criminal act, and as he had no intention of appearing in court, that he would be wanted by the police. This last thought terrified him. He could not bear it. He knew that in reality all he had to do was ask the man to pay the fine, but he had gone too far in the dark for that to be possible. It was time to create the ending.

"You have to be there at ten."

The man had come into the room.

"I'm not going."

Nicholas got out of bed. He was pleased about the expression conveyed in his voice when he had said that he was not going. It made the decision final, and he knew that the man had understood. After he had dressed he took the man in his arms.

"I can't," he said. "I mean it."

The man broke away from him and sat down on the bed. He stared at his hands as he murmured: "I love you. I don't know why I love you, but I do. I want you to go to court, and then I want you to come back here - to me."

When he had finished talking he looked up quickly, briefly searching Nicholas's face for an answer. But Nicholas felt nothing for the man; felt nothing for what he had said, but realised that despite the lack of feeling that the man was his only means to salvation. He could not, would not go alone into death. He forced a sort of tenderness into his voice, a tenderness that in his desperation was both artificial and real, as he replied: "I know you love me. I accept that. I am bound to it - "

As he said this the man looked at him and smiled. Nicholas saw the smile of hope on the face and shuddered.

"Do you think you could feel for me?"

"You asked me that yesterday. I told you then that it was possible. Already there is feeling."

"Could you love me?"

Nicholas knew that in giving him hope he had increased his expectancy. Now there would be no end to the demands.

"I don't have to tell you again what could make me love you."

"Not death," the man said.

Nicholas watched the hope go from his expression and in the space that was left the features were once more ugly in their emptiness. He crossed the room and placed his hand on the man's shoulder.

"It will be easy," he added. "I will make it easy. And at the final moment I promise there will be love."

The man began to caress Nicholas, and Nicholas closed his eyes. He had not had sex with him since the first day, and he knew that he would not be able to go through with it again unless he was drunk.

"I want some whisky," he said.

"After."

The man's voice was hoarse with desire.

"No, please. I need it. Then we can."

The man got up from the bed and walked towards the door. The dressing gown he was wearing opened, and Nicholas saw the folds of fat on his stomach and the short, thick penis. It was in that second of seeing that feeling returned. Hatred returned. Inside he cried out, why aren't you Peter? Why aren't you beautiful? I must be drunk when I die to pretend that I am dying in Peter's arms. As if hearing the unspoken words, as if sensing the disgust, the man drew the dressing gown tightly round him. He stopped at the door and said: "If I bring you what you want will you let me fuck you? I've got poppers too. Amyl nitrate."

The words hit at Nicholas. He had not expected this from the man. The drink yes, the drug, no. In any case that drug would only accelerate life, not decrease it.

"Yes," he replied.

"And will you fuck me? I want that."

Nicholas nodded his head.

While the man was gone he paced the room. He could not think. All that was left to him was to get drunk and then, finally and forever, to act. It was in the action; in the illusion of the action that he would be saved. He held on to the word, saved, creating, moulding it to the shape of the eternity that awaited him. He made it into something more than it could ever be. He made it into the invisible, redeeming force of Peter.

"Peter is my saving," he said aloud. "I will die with him."

The word was big with Peter's name. And because it was so big it had nothing of the reality of Peter in it. It was a talisman. A glorious illusion of a talisman that would lead him to the lasting deception of his death.

"Peter."

He said the name louder than before. The man was standing in front of him. In his hands was a tray, and on the tray a bottle and two glasses. Beside the bottle the cylindrical shape of the inhaler.

"So you still love him."

A statement. The tray was put down.

"No," replied Nicholas, "I do not love him."

The man poured out the whisky. Nicholas drank it down and asked for another. It was important that he should lose all practical sense of what was happening. With enough grace the drink would get him behind the mask of what he saw; behind the façade of seeing itself, until the deeper illusion became revealed. While he was drinking his fourth whisky the man knocked the glass out of his hand. Nicholas smiled, picked up the glass, then heard the man say: "That is no way. No way for either of us." He looked at the face in front of him and saw that it was weeping. Although the drink was beginning to take effect he could still feel the power of pain in the man's words.

"I do love you," the man cried. "All I want is for you to stay with me. I've got enough money. I'm famous. The money alone from one of my plays would be sufficient for you for a long time - just let me try. You are all I have."

Nicholas reached for the bottle and drank from it. He had to shut out the insistent sound of pain. He hoped, as he drank, that the burning in his throat would suffocate him.

"I don't want to hear," he said. "I don't care. I'm a playwright too, but I don't impress you with it. How could I even begin to impress you with it when there's nothing there that you could recognise?"

There was no anger in his words. He watched as the man silently turned away. Then he realised that the drink had taken effect, and that he was ready.

"Now," he whispered.

Nicholas undid his trousers.

"Now."

The man turned round.

"You do it to me first," Nicholas said.

There was a smile on the man's face. His mouth, transformed suddenly from the experience of pain, was open wide for pleasure. Beneath the anaesthetic of the drink Nicholas felt a longing to inflict violence on that mouth, on that face. The man came up to him and threw off the dressing gown. Impatiently - perhaps not impatiently, but simply afraid that Nicholas would change his mind, he pushed him down onto the bed. Nicholas felt the first stab of pain as the man's short little cock pumped into him. It was like an obscenity that short penis. It was abject. It was humiliation. The man grunted and gasped. He dug his nails into Nicholas's shoulder, then bent heavily down upon his back and bit him in the neck. A moment later Nicholas felt the liquid come inside him.

"Is it finished?"

He whispered the words very quietly. The man fell away from him. He had not heard the words. Nicholas repeated them.

"Is it finished?"

"What?"

"Is it over? Or do you want me to do it to you?"

There was no reply.

"Then I assume we can wait."

"Yes, we can wait."

Nicholas stood up. After taking another drink from the bottle he said: "I know what we will do. I have it planned. I will take the pills, and what with that and the drink they will not take long to work. You will give the pills to me. You will watch me take them just to be sure. I know the number. The exact number. There is no fear of it failing."

The euphoria, the satisfaction of gratified desire was gone. The man was watching Nicholas, his face white with fear.

"I won't take them," he said.

"You won't have to," Nicholas replied. "As I fuck you, as I come inside you, I will close my hands round your throat. It will be all over even before the pleasure ends."

The man was trembling. Stronger than the fear that he actually felt was the fear of showing that he was afraid. He sat up. He put his legs unsteadily to the floor. He stood up, wrapping the dressing gown round his body.

"In a while," he said. "I want to wait."

Nicholas watched him, but the drink had blinded him to the man's fear. He was inspired by the ending he was creating. He was now in the world of the word, and the word was Peter.

"We have time," he said. "We will write letters. I want everything to be clear about our death. You will bring me pen and paper and envelopes. I will write to those outside, even though they do not especially care. But clarity is necessary. We must leave a reason that is evident to them. We must tell them a story."

The man said nothing.

"Have you a key to your bedroom?" Nicholas asked.

The man nodded his head, but still said nothing.

"Then you must lock yourself in while you write your letters. You must not be disturbed. I will knock on your door when I am ready, but if you have not finished then there is no need to reply. Then, when you are, you must come to me. Is there a key to this room?"

The man said, yes, there was a key.

"Don't forget to leave it with me."

Nicholas paused. His head was on fire. The sensation of vertigo was returning. He could no longer make out any expression on the man's face. The man had simply become the means to his dying, and as such it was no longer important to see him.

"Shall I get what you need?"

"I will come with you."

The man left the room, and Nicholas followed him to the entrance of the study door. Oh, how big the word was; how surely it contained him. He was conscious of following in the steps of myth. He was no longer himself, but Kleist and Peter. He was beyond the real at last, and even the writing of the letters would only have to be simulated. All that was needed was to follow the action of the pattern that the myth had set down. He was Kleist, more precisely, more totally in a pretence of being Kleist than in any meagre reality. He, Nicholas, would kill his lover by the waters of a fictitious sea. For already he was on that river that leads to the sea; in his exaltation nearing that mark, that invisible point where river and larger wave meet. And in all this the man was the mere instrument, and nothing more.

"I have to die," he said.

The man handed him notepaper, envelopes and a pen. But at the same time that he was being handed the materials something else was happening, something that would destroy the myth. He looked, and through the distance of his imagination he saw a white and petrified face. The voice was saying: 'Get out. Get out. If you don't get out I will call the police.' He made a gesture to throw off the hand that was pushing at him, but as he did so the voice screamed. He heard the word 'police' again, and it was like a hammer blow upon his head. It was the intrusion of reality; it was all that was other to the dream. He hit at the hand. He hit at the face, at the terrible lips that were saying the words, and when he had stopped hitting he began to run. He opened the front door and began running down the street. And as he ran he thought he heard footsteps following.

Vision 3. The Return.

I know what he will do. I follow him, but I do not follow him. I am in his place, in his footsteps, in his fear, in the heart of the aching pain, and yet I am other. I have a visit to make. I have words to say. From the future I will speak for a moment of the past that is now.

I am the only one who can tell what really happened, because I was there all of the time. I was both his hope and his invisible madness, his continuation and his death. In the pattern of his life I directed what had to be. To him I was the stranger, and so it is only right that in this last version I should keep that name. My real identity is irrelevant; irrelevant precisely because it is so obvious. There is no real mystery in it, but neither can there be absolute clarity. I do not know myself when I return from death. Quite simply I was the one who was there, and there within.

Now for the present past.

Peter and David.

I am their unwelcome visitor. An attic flat in a quiet street away from the centre of the city. In a corner of the living room a cat plays with its tail, turning round and round upon itself - then suddenly stops, and stretches out on the carpet. Peter is seated cross-legged in the centre of the room rolling a cigarette filled with hash. David enters the room when Peter has finished preparing the cigarette and smiles. I pass between them, but they do not want to see me. I choose a record and place it into David's hands who then places it on the turn-table. Music loudly adds to the silence. David sits down next to Peter, and I sit down next to them. I begin.

"Nicholas," I say.

Peter looks up as if listening for an echo. He draws on the cigarette, closes his eyes, then hands it to David.

"Nicholas," I repeat.

Peter looks at David.

"I heard his name," he says. "Someone said his name."

"In your mind," David replies.

He draws on the cigarette, and looks at me as he says this, willing me not to be there. I stare back at him and smile. I wonder how long it will take before they begin to openly acknowledge my presence. I laugh a little, calling myself the clearest, most open ghost they know. I reach out and place a hand on Peter's arm, but he draws away. I know that it is not because I have touched him, but because quite simply he has been touched.

"What did he give you?"

My voice persists. I will haunt them. I will continue to haunt them. I have to be quick, for they are retreating so fast behind their mask of drugs. It is of crucial importance that I make them recognise me now.

"What did Nicholas give you?"

No answer.

"What did you give him?"

Peter looks down at the floor. David has closed his eyes. He is far away; far away from himself and from Peter. It will be impossible for me to reach him now, but in a way it is unimportant. Peter is the one who must see me. I reach out and touch him again.

"I am not in your mind. I am real. Look up. Look at me."

Peter shakes his head. He continues to stare at the floor. I watch him sink ever further into himself.

"Nicholas." I repeat the name. Then I say the words: "I am his death."

In that simple statement I have come the nearest to revealing myself. The statement has shocked him. He looks at me. He smiles an awkward, frightened smile. He hands me the cigarette. I refuse it.

"No, I would rather live to die in his death than ease myself in your forgetting."

David rocks himself backwards and forwards as he sits on the floor. His eyes are still firmly shut. The cat comes up to him and rubs itself against his body. Peter watches what is happening, and it seems to me that he is aware for the first time of what is happening.

"I don't want to speak to Nicholas," he says. "You know I don't want to ever speak to him again."

"But you see him," I answer. "You see him very clearly. He is walking towards your door; he has already walked towards your door, asking to be taken in."

"I won't see him," he says.

I reach out with my hand and grip his arm. The touch of his flesh reminds me of his passion. I feel the blackness of it, the endless night of it. I hate him for the world of our death; for the world that he has helped create.

"You won't see him alive. Dead, yes," I say. "Dead is safe. It is the realm of no demands. The domain where manners are everything. What a way to die, you will say. What a romantic way to die - but you will not know. You will not feel the impact, nor even hear the tearing sound. The gulf of his dying will be a safe separation. No more responsibility, no more realising. In fact the cancellation, the pure, hard cancellation of everything that counts."

Peter hears me all too clearly. He shakes off my hand. He stands up, looking in panic around the room.

"Are you looking for a way out?" I ask. "The doors are closed."

David mutters something under his breath. The words are inaudible. Peter goes up to him and shakes him by the shoulders. Reluctantly David opens his eyes. There is no recognition, no acknowledgement in them.

"I need you," Peter says.

I laugh at his words. He stares at me.

"Don't laugh at me," he screams.

David reaches for the cigarette, drawing on it, inhaling deeply. I can feel the panic growing in Peter. He rushes to the door, but bangs against it in his blind attempt to get out. Already for him, the door is no longer there. He knocks and knocks on the wooden surface. Without moving from where he is sitting David yells at him to be quiet. Peter's arms fall to his sides. He stares at where the door could be, cries a little, then begins to whimper like a trapped animal. Knowing that I have him at last,

I say: "What do you really think of him?"

He turns away from the door and faces me. His face is neutral, but not expressionless. The expression says that he has accepted me, and by that I know that the acceptance also includes his own death.

"David?" he asks.

"No, not him. He is not important. He's not even there. Nicholas. What do you think of him?"

Peter is like a dying man struggling with his words.

"His skin revolts me," he murmurs. "His teeth. The imperfection of him. The decay of his body. His teeth that bite into me are rotten. And then there is his love. His hunger. His need that took no account of my revulsion. Yet I pity his love - and in a way must love him for it."

"Must?"

I question the word. I get up. I move towards him. Gently I push him out of the way, and open the door.

"The end is ending," I say. "I must be there to meet it."

He does not look at me, but walks like a somnambulist towards David. I leave the room and hurry down the stairs to the street. But although I am going now, although I have to hurry away, I will return. I will haunt and torment him. I will be in every drug he takes, in every sleep that he hopes to sleep, in every moment of sanity and madness. Nicholas can die happy, for I promise that Peter will never be alone again.

Thursday continued.

The final moments were telescoped into a second of accidental panic.

Nicholas ran from the man's house. Ran and ran until his mind boiled with confusion and fear. Instinctively he headed for the station he had arrived from. All the time he was running he heard the footsteps behind him, and the word 'police' echoed in his brain. He did not dare turn round. He looked in front. When he reached the station he pushed his way through the crowd. He bought his ticket and made his way to the platform. He believed that once through the barrier he would be safe; that he would be able to make his way home. His ticket was clipped in the same mechanical way that all the others had been clipped, and he passed through. No one looked at him. No one gave him any special attention. Once on the platform he felt calmer. His limbs ached from running, and he was utterly exhausted. All he wanted to do was to get inside the train, close his eyes and get some sleep. He wanted only to have to wake up when he had reached his destination. A fellow passenger jostled him as he got onto the train. Nicholas started, jumping away from the man in fear. The man said he was sorry and Nicholas smiled at him, but that accidental contact had reactivated the terror. Nicholas hurried down the corridors, running towards the front. If I reach the front of the train, he thought, I will be safe. But his running only accelerated the fear. The train began to move, and at first Nicholas was moving faster than the train. But as it picked up speed their movements coincided. And then suddenly he had reached the front. He had reached the door that by being locked said he could go no further.

"Help me," he cried.

He began to move backwards, away from the door, back down the corridor. His eyes never left the door that was locked. The train was leaving the station, moving very fast now, out into the space of the rails. The terror began to subside.

"I'll be alright," he whispered.

A hand tapped him on the shoulder just as he was about to turn round. He heard the words: "Will you please step to one side," and the next moment he had opened the carriage door and jumped. His head struck concrete. He had no time to realise what he had done.

I pulled the alarm cord and stopped the train.

Vision 4. Purgatory.

Soon I found myself walking. Finding a call box I rang Michael's number. I heard his brisk, but lazy voice. He did not want to be disturbed so early in the day. It was six in the morning and I was already in the streets. He mumbled a few complaining words to me about how early it was, and then I asked to meet him later in the day. He paused for a long time. I asked him again, and then there was a long silence. It was as if he had gone, but I could hear him breathing down the phone. He no longer wanted to talk. I said that I would ring him later and hung up.

It was now hot in the streets, the sun blazing white in the sky. I saw many people I recognised, and there was no one else in the town but them, walking in the streets without shadows. There were no strangers. No one I did not know. I looked at them and some I knew to have been long since dead. Others were alive, but all ignored me, and then I realised I was in a town of purgatory: that interim state of place where the living and the dead walk. Turning a corner I saw Peter and hurried up to him, but he had a mask over his face, a second Peter imposed upon the first one. He was both himself and not himself. He was neither living nor dead and the sun beat mercilessly down upon the mask of his face, making it glint and shine, and in parts of it I saw signs of the beginning of a melting. He was silent and stared, not at me, but away in the distance, and all the while his mask melted. I ran from him. Ran and ran in that town of the living and the dead, but ultimately I had nowhere to go. I knew that I would never again be able to tell the living from the dead or find my way out from the purgatory of never knowing. I was alone. Alone in this indeterminate world, dismissed from either eternal bliss or everlasting horror.